Other Books by Kathi Harper Hill:

Falling, A Christian Romance Novel
The Crow and the Wind: A little book about a BIG GOD
Out on a Limb of the Family Tree
The Christmas Closet and Other Works

Adele

Signs From God

Kathi Harper Hill

Book Cover and
other illustrations by:
David L. Hill

Copyright 2012 by Kathi Harper Hill

Signs From God
Published by Yawn's Publishing
210 East Main Street
Canton, GA 30114
www.yawnsbooks.com

This book is a work of fiction. Names, characters, incidents, places, businesses, organizations, and events are either the product of the author's imagination or are used fictitiously. Any similarity to locales, incidents, or actual persons, living or dead, is entirely coincidental.

All rights reserved. No part of this book may be reproduced or transmitted in any form, electronic or mechanical, including photocopying, recording, or data storage systems without the express written permission of the publisher, except for brief quotations in reviews and articles.

Library of Congress Control Number: 2012951857

ISBN: 978-1-936815-67-8

Printed in the United States

Luke 2:12 and this shall be a sign unto you; you shall find the baby wrapped in swaddling clothes...

To Molly: Who always stops and smells the roses

Acknowledgements:

To David: *for making Clancy look like Clancy should,*

To Anna Kate: *who read through the first draft and graciously pointed out errors,*

To Marsha: *who read the second draft and made helpful suggestions while doing the second "weeding",*

To Bobbie: *for editing, one more time, and catching what none of us caught previously (your nickname is "Hawkeye" from now on!),*

And,

To My God: *who inspires me to write – may I always obey!*

CHAPTER ONE

A SMALL TOWN IN THE NORTH GEORGIA MOUNTAINS

Cooper McGuire squinted in pain as the rising sun poked at his pupils. The bright morning light winked between the peaks of the neighbor's roof. He moaned softly and attempted to turn over, forgetting his six foot four inch frame had been precariously perched, asleep, upon his great Aunt Cynthia's considerably shorter wicker loveseat. He crashed to the porch floor, emitting a startled yelp as he felt the planks shudder under his weight.

Rising up to all fours, he raised his head to find himself nose to nose with Aunt Cynthia's English bulldog, who was growling softly. "Hey, Ernest, it's me, Coop." The dog sniffed at him, then growled again. "Come on, buddy, give me a break. I know I'm not supposed to be here…"

"Cooper! What on earth?" Aunt Cynthia appeared in the doorway, coming from the kitchen to her screened in porch. "How did you get back here?"

He stood. Sheepishly, he explained. "I slid my credit card through the crack in the screen door and flipped the latch."

"For goodness sakes! I can't imagine what's happened to make you think you have to sneak around instead of coming to the front door to knock! And I surely don't know why you'd need to do either this early!"

"I got here about three and didn't want to wake you up. I, uh, needed a place to sleep."

His Aunt Cynthia looked at him with wide eyes. "Why would you need a place to sleep?"

"It's Cayden. She threw me out."

"She threw you out of your own house?" Cynthia asked incredulously.

Cooper sighed heavily and sat down on the wicker loveseat he'd just fallen out of. It made a groaning noise as it once again accepted his weight. "Yeah. We had this ridiculous fight over Stu Holmes, this guy she's dating. I guess she didn't appreciate my opinion."

Cynthia came and sat down beside Cooper. "Honey, Cayden is old enough to date whomever she chooses. You're her brother, not her daddy."

"I know, I know. But she's just eighteen! I've been responsible for her for seven years and I can't turn her loose. She isn't ready."

"Really? How do you know?"

He jumped up and raked his hands through his reddish blond hair. "Because she's only eighteen! What other information do I need?"

Cynthia laughed. "Well, just seven years ago, that's how old you were, and you were making financial decisions and raising Cayden."

Even in the midst of being upset, Cooper couldn't help but smile fondly down at his great aunt, pink curlers sticking out every which way from her grey hair. "With twenty-four/seven help from you, that is. I was scared to death and you know it. I couldn't have done it without you being there." He shook his head. "This is different, anyway. I had no choice but to grow up quickly after Mama and Daddy were killed in that wreck. Cayden, on the other hand, has been pampered by yours truly till I think I've ruined her."

"You've done a fine job, Cooper. Cayden's not ruined. She's simply trying those wings, like most of us do. You never got a shot at trying yours. You had to be a man instantly and missed the experimental stage." Cynthia stood up and patted him on the arm. "Come on in and let's fix coffee and breakfast. I can't wait to hear how in the world Cayden threw you out of the house." At the word breakfast, Ernest jumped up and waddled into the kitchen ahead of them. Cynthia's eyes twinkled as she grinned up at Cooper. "Did she bodily throw you out?"

Cooper followed Aunt Cynthia into the kitchen. "Very funny. We were fussing, and I took her car keys away. She started crying and ran to her bedroom and slammed the door. In a few minutes the phone rang and it was Kate. You know me; I walk around when I talk, so I wandered out of the house to the back patio. After I hung up, I went to the back door and it was locked. At first I thought I'd accidentally locked myself out, so I went to the front door but it was locked too. I tried the side French doors. Locked also. Then I knocked. And knocked." Cynthia snickered as she fed Ernest a dog biscuit. Cooper gave her a stern look and continued. "Since I had the phone in my hand, I called Cayden's cell phone. I told her I'd locked myself out of the house and to come down and let me in. She informed me she had locked me out, and I could stay out until I came to my senses. I said I was at my senses, and to let me in the house. She hung up on me. I tried to call back, she wouldn't answer. It started raining, so I got in my car. After several more attempts to call Cayden, I crawled under the car and got my spare key, drove over here, jimmied your screen door and slept on your settee – which by the way is extremely uncomfortable, not to mention short." He arched his back and tried to crack his spine, but felt pretty sure he was crippled for life.

Cynthia was trying to hide her amusement, but they both knew it was hopeless. Laughing out loud, she plugged in the coffee pot. "So now what? Are you going to apologize to Cayden?"

"Absolutely not! I have nothing to apologize for!" Cooper crossed his arms over his chest. "She doesn't have car keys, can barely put two pieces of bread together to make a sandwich, and was probably scared to death staying there the rest of the night alone." Smugly, he finished. "She'll call soon enough to make amends."

"Oh, for heaven sakes, Cooper!" Cynthia slapped the counter top, startling Ernest, who sprayed slobber and dog biscuit crumbs all over the floor. "She's got a boyfriend who can drive and buy her breakfast. Let's hope she wasn't *too* afraid to be alone, or he may have helped her out there too."

Cooper paled. Then he stiffened, and his six foot four inch frame grew to look like seven. "I'll kill the little twerp if he so much as lays a finger on Cayden Alexandria McGuire." He turned to leave, but Cynthia stopped him.

She reached for the phone and dialed. Cooper heard a sleepy voice answer. "Hey honey, this is your Auntie Cynthia. How are you this morning?" Cynthia's heavy southern accent got heavier with sympathy. She nodded to the news she was hearing, the pink curlers bobbing and weaving in the air. "Um hmm. Oh, that's too bad. Well, you know Cooper just loves you to death and cain't help himself." Nodding again. Bob and weave. "I know it's hard, honey. It's been hard on both you and Coop. I thank God you have each other though." Cynthia smiled into the phone and winked at Cooper. "I'm sure he's fine. He probably found a warm bed at a buddy's house." Her voice became tinged with sadness. "Or maybe he slept in his car somewhere." He could hear Cayden's voice rise. "Well, if you're worried about him, why don't you call him on his cell? Okay, darlin'. I'll talk to you later. I love you."

Within seconds, Cooper's cell phone rang. "Yes?" He snapped. "Oh, hey Cayden. Yeah, I'm fine, I guess. A little stiff. Hard to sleep in a place that's way too small for me." He rolled his eyes. "Sure, I'll come home if you'll let me in. But I think I'll get something to eat first," he said, eyeing the bacon Aunt Cynthia was lying out in the iron skillet. "You go ahead and fix yourself something and I'll see you in a little while." As Cynthia pressed her lips and arched a brow, he sighed. "And Cayden, we'll work this out. I know you're growing up and I over react sometimes. Let's just do this together, okay?" He nodded his head. "Okay. Great. See you in a little while. Bye, Sis."

CHAPTER TWO

Bailey Crawford was stacking storage boxes on top of one another in his garage when his cell rang. Before plopping himself down on one of the bigger boxes, he scooped the phone out of his front pocket. "Yeah?" He leaned back against a wall stud and briefly closed his eyes at the luxurious feel of sitting down for a moment. "Hey Coop, what's up?" He listened intently, grinning at his friend's agitated voice hammering over the line. "You know she's eighteen. Lighten up, it's not like she robbed a bank. In fact, I think it's hilarious that she locked you out." Bailey stood, stretching and considered all the work still to be done. "I've got an idea. Why don't you come on over, and you can complain all you want. I'm workin' in the garage."

After getting an affirmative from Cooper, he slid the phone back in his pocket. He took a complete look at the garage and sighed. Running his hand through his black curly hair, he figured he'd be thirty before he got this mess cleaned up. He and his new bride, Anna, had moved into the old home place his grandparents had left him. The six month honeymoon period of their marriage had allowed them both to turn a blind eye to all the chaos that his grandparent's stuff, his stuff, and Anna's stuff colliding had created. They decided Anna's two week summer vacation from work at the bank would be spent right here, he beginning in the garage, and she in the basement.

It looked like it was going to be a long two weeks. However; knowing Cooper the way he did, with the frustration level he heard coming through the phone, Bailey figured he ought to get a half day's work out of Cooper anyway, before his friend even knew what hit him.

With an ever widening smile, Bailey turned back to the waiting boxes, keeping one ear out for the sound of Cooper's car.

🐾 🐾 🐾 🐾

"If I hear one more person say 'She's eighteen, Cooper, she's all grown up, Cooper, blah, blah, blah, Cooper', I think I'll deck 'em." Cooper muttered as he backed his car out of the driveway.

He and Cayden had made up, she tearful for locking him out of the house. He'd readily forgiven her and sort of apologized for being so protective. They'd reached an uneasy truce and had agreed to talk tonight before bedtime about some ways they could compromise regarding Cayden's entry into adulthood and demand for freedom.

He suddenly remembered he'd promised Kate he'd be at her place for supper. Well, they'd just have to call it an early night.

Kate Roe was the first real girlfriend he'd had since high school. They found they had a lot in common, as Kate had lost both her parents at a fairly young age, too. Her father had been killed in an explosion at the plant where he was employed when Kate was ten, and her mother had passed away from complications with an aneurysm when Kate had just turned nineteen.

Before meeting Kate, he had hardly dated since his senior prom, the last real night of his childhood. His parents had been killed that same night in a terrible wreck, leaving Cayden and himself orphans. Because he was already eighteen and because Aunt Cynthia and her husband Bob, (who had since passed away) lived in the same town and were willing to oversee them, Cooper and Cayden had been awarded the privilege of remaining in their home and living a fairly independent life. With Social Security income, a large life insurance policy his father had left them, and a tidy sum following settlement from the wreck, there had never been a fear of financial straits.

He had been able to attend college full time and was employed at the local Middle School as a history teacher and little league coach. He loved it. The kids took an immediate shine to him, and he to them. He was able to stay at the same church he'd grown up in, keeping the support of older people in his life. He kept his same best friends. Life was great.

Which is why he wanted Cayden to do the same thing – go to college full time – that is. He knew Social Security would continue to pay her if she was a full time student, which was a plus; but more importantly, he didn't want her to lose steam by letting high school get too far behind her. Their argument last night had started out about college, morphed into Stu the new boyfriend, and in Cooper's opinion, Stu's bad influence on Cayden.

Since their parents had died, Cooper didn't think he and Cayden had missed church more than two Sundays in a row. And those absences had never been due to laziness or disinterest, but illness or the rare vacation out of town. He had become a Christian at age nine, and at age eighteen, when he became a 'parent'; he felt more than a duty to show Cayden what Jesus was all about. She, too, had given her life to Christ when she was twelve. Christ and His way had always come first in their lives.

At least, until now.

Cooper observed Stu's behavior and lifestyle, none of which he was overly fond. He didn't like Stu's occasional, casual swear word, his disrespect for adults in authority, and his apparent lack of ambition. He was a year older than Cayden, but had yet to find any kind of substantial employment. And Stu had made it abundantly clear he was uninterested in higher education of any kind. Cooper had overheard a few conversations between Stu and Cayden that indicated he was encouraging Cayden to 'take some time off from school' instead of starting college in the fall.

Cooper's grip on the steering wheel became increasingly white knuckled as these thoughts swirled through his head. He didn't realize his jaw was clenched until he rounded the corner and saw Bailey in front of the garage, waving at him. When Cooper saw the massive amount of junk strewn all over the yard, apparently dragged from the garage, he groaned. But he also found himself relaxing and waving back. Maybe a few hours of mindless, back breaking labor was what he needed to get his mind off Cayden.

🐾 🐾 🐾 🐾

Cayden McGuire sat listlessly on the patio, twirling a strand of curly red hair around her finger, staring at the small pond's water fountain spraying the air. Over the guilt of locking her big brother out of the house, she felt anger returning toward him for treating her like a child. She began to nervously jiggle her leg as she thought about Stu's imminent arrival due to the absence of Cooper. This dance was getting old fast, but she didn't know what else to do.

She'd be danged if Cooper was going to push her around any longer! But the truth was, Stu was getting pretty old too. The more she saw him, the more she, well, saw him. Arrogant, shallow, self-serving. And lost. In the beginning, she thought she could change him, soften him, and maybe trick him into going to church. He was having none of that, and even made fun of her, in a sly way. She felt cornered. She wanted to ditch him, but that would make her look like she was being obedient to Cooper, which would just facilitate his belief that she should be obedient. Lord! She stood up in frustration and stomped her foot. What was she going to do? Well, for sure, she wasn't going to let Cooper McGuire boss her around!

CHAPTER THREE

Cooper opened sleepy eyes and found himself face to face with an extremely wrinkled, jowl mugged creature, whose head was bigger than Cooper's own. Cooper groaned. "Why is it I keep waking up with guys like you right in my face?"

The dog responded by grinning and coming closer. "No - doggie – no!" But it was too late. He'd been slimed.

"Clancy! Come here!" He heard a whispered hiss. "Don't wake up Cooper, he's sleeping!"

Cooper carefully took the edge of his rumpled t-shirt and wiped saliva off his face. "No, Kate," he said slowly, "No, I'm not sleeping anymore. I'm drowning in dog drool." He sat up. "And I am probably doomed to chronic pain, trying to sleep on your loveseat."

Clancy sat on his rear and plopped both enormous paws on Cooper's lap. "And ain't this dog a 'Dogue de Bordeaux' ? French, right?"

Kate smiled. "Yep. He's a beaut, too. Perfect specimen and fine example of the mastiff breed. Except he's extra big. One hundred and sixty-eight pounds, to be exact."

"May I ask why you named him Clancy instead of Pierre or something?"

"Cause he's a red head. Irish, you know?"

Cooper rolled his eyes, scratching Clancy between his cinnamon colored ears. The dog closed his eyes in blissful contentment. Attempting to digest this bit of illogic, then giving up, Cooper said, "Remind me again why I'm dating you, blondie."

She made a face at him. "Because I'm the only female around here that will put up with you. Including your immediate family, or so it appears." She widened her eyes to look innocent. "I mean, isn't that why you're sleeping on my loveseat and being kissed by my dog?" She asked sweetly.

Cooper sighed. "Yeah. Thanks for reminding me. With friends like you …" He stood up and Kate flinched when his back popped like a cork.

"Oh, Cooper! I am sorry I didn't have anything better for you to sleep on. It's just I'm having to buy one piece of furniture at a time, and the couch is still on lay away."

He walked over and bear hugged her. "Ah, lovey, it's okay. I'm just grateful you were willing to risk your reputation by letting me sleep over."

"You were so upset last night I didn't ask much. What happened this time?" Kate asked as they walked into the kitchen.

'Déjà vu all over again' Cooper thought when Kate handed Clancy a dog biscuit. "When I left here after supper, I went back to Bailey's house. I got home late after helping him finish up in the garage. I found my baby sister and Mr. Stud Muffin making out on the couch. We had words. Lots of words. He called me names and I helped him to his car. When I started back in the house, I was locked out. Again." He shook his head in frustration and closed his eyes. "Unfortunately, I had laid my wallet on the hall table when I came in, so I was ousted."

Kate looked at him carefully. "What do you mean you

'helped him' to his car?"

Sheepishly, Cooper looked down at her. "I mean I pretty much trapped his arms to his sides and carried him out. I even offered to put him inside his junk car and push it to the street."

Kate looked alarmed. "You didn't hurt him, did you?"

"Nah. Well, I hurt his pride." Cooper's hands were fists at his side. "He is such a jerk, Kate! He was screaming obscenities and burned rubber as he tore off down our street. I thought about calling the cops, but I want Cayden to speak to me again someday."

"Lord, Cooper. Do you even see what you're doing? Cayden is eighteen-"

"DON'T tell me how old my sister is! I KNOW how old my sister is! Everyone keeps telling ME how old my sister is!"

Kate arched her brow. "Sore spot much?" She softened and put her arms around his middle, laying her head on his chest. His heart was pounding. "Cooper, I know you love her beyond reason. I even understand why you're doing what you're doing. But I don't think Cayden understands. She may be eighteen, but she's still a kid in some ways too. This may push her to stick it out with him, even when she begins to see his true colors." Kate looked up at Cooper. "And you know she will. You've raised her right and the Holy Spirit won't allow her to be blinded to this guy's spiritual void."

Cooper dropped a kiss on Kate's forehead. "You're right. I'm an idiot. When I went by Aunt Cynthia's house last night and told her what happened, she about blew a gasket. She read me the riot act and wouldn't let me stay at her house." He grinned. "She would have carried *me* out to the car if she could have."

"So now what?"

Cooper rested his chin on top of Kate's head. "Try to get Cayden to talk to me, I guess. I don't know what I'll do if she won't talk to me."

"Maybe Pastor Mike can intervene. Sounds like ya'll need someone to."

"That's not a bad idea. Somewhat embarrassing, but maybe I ought to be embarrassed."

"Speaking of, you best get out of here. If Mrs. Peabody sees you leaving my house at this time of day, I'll have an S tattooed on me before sundown."

He turned her loose and gave a last pat to Clancy. "Right again. I'm outta here."

Kate walked him to the door. "Oh, no. She's already outside." Kate's toes curled on the rug in fear.

Cooper saw Mrs. Peabody standing at her paper box. She glanced up when Kate's door opened. He bravely stepped out and headed straight for her. She dropped the newspaper on her fuzzy slippers as she gaped at him.

"Good morning, Mrs. Peabody!" Cooper said cheerfully. "I'm sure a good Christian woman like yourself is wondering what the Sam Hill I'm doing coming out of Kate Roe's house at six o'clock in the morning. Well, let me tell you: I had a big old fight with my baby sister and she locked me out of my own house!" He boomed, a big smile on his face.

Mrs. Peabody's hand went to her heart. "Well, my goodness!"

"Yes, ma'am. It's awful. Aunt Cynthia – you know my

Signs From God

Aunt Cynthia, don't you?"

Mrs. Peabody nodded slowly. Her hand twiddled with the button on her housecoat.

"Well, she sided with Cayden and wouldn't let me stay at her house either! I didn't know Sis was going to lock me out while I was throwing her boyfriend down the driveway, so I left my wallet in the house. Poor Kate here has risked her valuable reputation by letting me sleep on her living room loveseat. Wasn't that sweet of her?"

"Well, I-"

Cooper stepped closer. He looked deeply into Mrs. Peabody's eyes. She swallowed hard as if half afraid and half mesmerized. "I want you to know, Mrs. Peabody, without a shadow of a doubt, this was not sexual."

Mrs. Peabody gasped and clutched her robe around her throat. "Well, of all things! I - "

He reached out and hugged her to his chest, her head barely above his belly button. "I knew you'd understand. Thank you, Mrs. Peabody, thank you!" He let her go, and waving wildly to her, he crossed the lawn and got into his car. He gave a sideways glance toward Kate's door, and saw her shaking from laughter. She wiped her eyes and closed her door.

Mrs. Peabody stood there; robe askew, the newspaper still lying neatly upon her fuzzy bedroom slippers. She never moved as Cooper sailed smoothly out of sight.

Cooper walked up to his own front door, squared his shoulders and knocked. Cayden opened the door a crack. When she saw Cooper, she hesitated a moment, then opened the door the rest of the way.

Eyes swollen and red, she glared at him. With a

pleading look on his face, Cooper opened his arms to her. When she didn't move, he stepped up to her and embraced her. It was like hugging a telephone pole, only stiffer.

"Mrs. Peabody caught me coming out of Kate's house this morning. I went over and told her it wasn't sexual." He felt the telephone pole giggle. Ah, progress. "She dropped the newspaper on her blue fuzzy bedroom shoes, and it was still there when I drove off. I don't think she even blinked. She's scarred for life emotionally, and if you keep locking me out of the house, I'm gonna be scarred for life physically, sleeping on everybody's teeny tiny loveseats." He felt her soften a bit more. "I'm ready to listen now, Cayden. I won't yell, I won't order you around. I just need to understand. Will you talk to me?"

He felt a slight nod. He let her go and they walked into the living room. Cayden curled up on the end of the couch, and Cooper sat himself in the recliner. He longed to stretch his poor aching body out, but didn't want Cayden to think he was in any way casual about this whole thing, so he sat with his elbows on his knees, hands clasped between them. "I know I've been overbearing. I know I've been bossy. But Cayden, I want to protect you. I don't know how to stop doing that."

Cayden sniffed and reached for a tissue. "You embarrass me to no end, Coop. I'm humiliated and don't know how I'm going to face my friends, or even the neighbors, for that matter."

"Yeah, well, I'm sorry about that. They probably were all hanging out their windows yesterday. Can't say as I blame 'em, either. But tell me this. Weren't you even more than a little embarrassed by Stu's mouth and stunt driving?"

She gave a bitter laugh. "Well, you don't have to worry about that anymore. He called and said he won't be back. He said you should consider yourself lucky that he didn't beat your a-uh, rear."

Cooper snorted. "Yeah, I only outweigh him by a hundred pounds. I'm terrified."

Cayden's blue eyes filled with tears. "Couldn't you at least be sorry that I've been dumped?"

Cooper lowered his head. "I'm sorry he hurt you. But don't you see his whole life is so selfish and prideful? It's always all about him. He's never considered your feelings, not once, Cayden. Didn't that hurt too?"

Her eyes flashed and her head snapped up so fast her copper hair swung around her face. "Of course it did. But it's none of your business. If you'd stay out of my business, this whole thing would have blown over a lot faster." Her hand flew to her mouth, but it was too late, she'd said it.

Cooper scratched his head. "Yeah, well, I understand that with my mind, but my emotions can't seem to quite grasp the fact that the line has moved when it comes to what my business is and what it isn't regarding you. I promise I'll do better." His voice softened. "I don't want to lose you Cayden. Not in any way. I need your help. Talk to me, tell me what was good about Stu so I can shut up about it."

She dabbed her eyes, then her nose with the tissue and balled it up on her hand. "It seemed like there was a lot of potential good in Stu, at first, anyway. He's popular and made me feel pretty."

"You are pretty, Cayden."

She narrowed her eyes. "Shut up, Cooper."

"Right." He nodded. "Sorry."

"In the beginning he seemed interested in my life, and how it was different from his. We talked about church, and I thought I could get him to start attending. But then he began to get irritated when I brought it up, so I quit mentioning it. Then he began to sort of cut me down about it. We had a couple of arguments over it. He started pushing me about other stuff too, you know, to take a drink or go further sexually than I was willing to go."

Cooper found himself coming out of the recliner, fists clenched. Cayden shook her head.

"This is why I've kept my mouth shut. Are you going to hunt him down now and kill him?"

Cooper rubbed the back of his neck. "Yes. No, I mean. Give me a minute." He took a deep breath and closed his eyes. Oh, yeah, he wanted to beat that little twerp into a pulp that his own mother wouldn't recognize. "Look, Cayden, it's hard for me to hear this. But I won't do anything. I'll listen. I will have to occasionally calm myself down, is all." He turned and looked at her. "Imagine someone trying to cause me harm. Wouldn't you have protective feelings?"

"Sure. I didn't say I don't understand your reaction. It's such an incredible pain in the butt that I don't want to deal with it, though."

"Okay, I get it." He sat back down.

"Anyway, my friends have been trying to get me to break up with Stu, and I knew that's what I wanted too, but dang it, Cooper! You kept me from it."

He jumped back up. "What! How can you say that! I've done everything I know to make you stop seeing him. Oh... That's why you wouldn't? Pride?"

"Call it that if you want to. But how am I ever going to grow up if all I ever do is what you say? Don't I need a little room to make my own decisions, even if they're wrong?"

"Absolutely. I need to cut you some slack, and you need to do the same for me. This is all a first for me too. I'm trying to do right by you. I hope I've learned from this. I hope you've learned too. Don't close me out, okay? And if I start pushing too hard, talk to me so I know to back off."

Cayden nodded. "Sounds fair. Make sure you listen when I do talk."

"Sounds fair." He agreed. They sat for a few minutes, mulling over everything. Cooper's stomach rumbled loudly, making Cayden laugh.

"Let's fix breakfast. Then I'm going over to Paul and Samantha's to swim. Why don't you go to bed for a few hours and stretch out. Appreciate your bed, Cooper. You've been neglecting it lately."

"My sister, the comedienne. I'll go upstairs and wash up while you get the food started." He stood and headed for the stairs. "And Cayden? If Mrs. Peabody calls, I'm not here."

CHAPTER FOUR

Standing in line at the back of the church to speak to the pastor after services on Sunday, Cooper felt himself becoming more uncomfortable the closer he got to the preacher. He'd never had to ask for any kind of 'counseling', although he vaguely remembered someone talking to them on a regular basis after their parents died. He guessed that was counseling. As the line snaked forward, a few people scattered, finding others to speak with, taking children to the bathroom, giving up and going to find lunch. Cooper found himself directly behind Mrs. Peabody. He grinned and tapped her on the shoulder. She turned and stared upward just as the line moved and she was in front of the pastor. She clutched her pearls and made a startled "Oh!" sound and scurried out the door.

Pastor Matthew stared at his empty hand, hanging in mid-air for lack of Mrs. Peabody's hand to grasp. He arched an eyebrow and looked expectantly at Cooper.

"Um, long story, preacher."

"I see. It's not often I witness a member act like they've seen a ghost at the sanctuary door."

"Well, I may have alarmed her a little bit the other morning when I was coming out of Kate's house."

"I'm feeling a little alarmed myself."

"No, I mean, well, that's probably what Mrs. Peabody was thinking too, and I wanted to set her straight, and uh, I may have been a little too assertive in my explanation of our innocence. Mine and Kate's that is." Cooper finished lamely.

"Cooper, if you're trying to confuse me, you have succeeded. Where's Cayden?"

"She helped out in the nursery today. I guess she'll be here any minute. Actually I wanted to talk with you about Cayden and myself. I was wondering if you could sit down with us a time or two and help us straighten some things out."

"Do you mean offer an opinion or something more along the lines of counseling?"

Cooper felt his neck grow warm. "Counseling, I guess. Cayden thinks I'm having a hard time turning loose."

"What do you think?" Pastor Matthew asked softly.

"Yeah, I am. I want to do the right thing, but I keep winding up at someone else's house asleep on their loveseat."

"Huh?"

Cooper blushed. "Cayden and I have had a few disagreements and she's managed to lock me out of the house on two occasions."

"That's why you were coming out of Kate's house in the morning hours?"

"Yes. The first time I was at Aunt Cynthia's, but then she sided with Cayden, so I had to beg for Kate's couch."

Pastor Matthew grinned. "So if we get a call one night soon, I should just put a blanket and pillow in the den?"

"You could be next. I'm running out of options. And I don't think Mrs. Peabody would be all that inviting." Cooper glanced up and saw Cayden entering from the other side of the church. "Here comes Cayden now. She doesn't know about this yet, but I'll speak with her this afternoon and call you. Is that okay?"

"That's fine." Pastor Matthew clapped Cooper on the back as he turned to go.

Cayden saw them and gave a wave. She picked up her Bible from the pew and came on over. "Ready to go? I'm starving." She looked around the foyer. "Where's Kate? Isn't she eating lunch with us?"

"Nah, I thought it'd be good for you and me to go it alone today. We need to talk."

Cayden narrowed her eyes. "What now?"

"It's not bad. I'm not going to boss you around, I promise. Nothing but good old brother-sister time."

"Uh huh." Cayden sighed. "Let's go. And you better not spoil my dinner." She whacked him on the shoulder as they walked to the car.

🐾 🐾 🐾 🐾

Monday afternoon found Kate exhausted. She struggled to her front door, laden down with spelling tests to grade, her satchel, and purse. Transferring all of it to one arm, she fished around in her purse for her door key. She had an odd feeling she was being watched. She saw Mrs. Peabody out of the corner of her eye, poised at the end of her driveway, shears in one hand, cut roses in the other. Kate couldn't see Mrs. Peabody's face, which was in shadow from the big brim of her floppy straw hat, but she figured it was screwed up in suspicion. "Don't worry, you old busybody, Cooper's nowhere around this afternoon." She muttered as she triumphantly stuck the discovered key in her lock.

Dumping her load onto the loveseat, she kicked off her shoes and headed straight to the kitchen, bidding the siren's call of chocolate ice cream. Smiling, she scooped until her bowl was full. Sticking her favorite antique soupspoon into the middle mound, she headed for the sunroom. Letting Clancy in through the French doors, she plopped into an armchair covered in a tapestry of a riotous array of multi-colored garden flowers. Clancy stretched out in front of her on the cold tile floor. Kate wiggled her toes and then stuck her feet underneath her, feeling the cool fabric. Closing her eyes for a moment, she relished the breeze from the ceiling fan, the freezing air coming off the ice cream blowing in her face. "Ahhh," was all she could muster. Just as she held her mouth open for the first bite heading her way, she heard the faint chimes of the doorbell. Her lower lip stuck out in a pout, besting any seven year old in her class. "That better not be Mrs. Peabody," Kate thought darkly as she headed for the front of the house.

It wasn't Mrs. Peabody, but maybe Mrs. Peabody was psychic, because there stood Cooper on her stoop, his head bent terribly to one side. "Cooper! For heaven's sake, what happened to your neck?" Kate exclaimed as she opened the door wider so he could enter. "Whose couch did you have to sleep on last night?"

"Very funny, Kate. I slept at home, thank you." He advanced carefully into the house. "One of the boys hit me square in the back of the neck with the football during practice this afternoon. When I turned my head to see who did it, the muscles froze and I can't move."

"Have you seen a doctor?" She squinted upwards at the odd angle of his neck. "This could be dangerous." She guided him onto her loveseat, and then handed him the bowl of ice cream. "Here, can you eat this? I'll fix me another bowl. I haven't touched it, yet." She looked at the chocolate longingly.

"Thanks." He grasped the spoon with an awkward gesture and guided it slowly to his mouth. Around a mouthful, he explained he had been to the doctor and they'd given him muscle relaxants. "Of course I haven't taken any yet, 'cause I had to drive. I came by here to see if you could take me to Dr. Mack, the chiropractor out on Orlander Road. I can't turn my head well enough to drive that far. Coach Rhodes said the chiropractor could fix me up and I wouldn't have to take dope."

Kate nudged his shoulder. "Muscle relaxants aren't "dope", ya big dope. Of course I'll drive you." She bent over and looked at him. "Does it hurt?"

"Oh, yeah. It hurts." He winced as he tried to straighten up. She took the empty bowl from him and he took his cell phone out of his pocket. "Coach Rhodes programmed the doc's number in here. Will you call, please?" He affected his most pitiful voice.

"Just hand me the phone, Cooper." Kate rolled her eyes and punched in the numbers. In minutes, they were on their way.

Kate never did get her ice cream.

CHAPTER FIVE

Cooper lay staring at the ceiling, unable to sleep. Although he was actually in his own bed, and no new arguments had broken out between himself and Cayden, the pain in his neck was just enough to keep him awake and his mind whirling. He decided to give it fifteen more minutes and if the pain didn't ease, he was going to pop one of those muscle relaxants the doctor had given him.

He could hear Cayden up and about, turning off the television, locking the front door and coming up the stairs. He expected her to sail right by his door, but instead she stopped and knocked softly.

"I'm awake. Come on in." He winced as he automatically started to raise his head. Gently easing back onto the pillow, he turned slightly. The hall light outlined Cayden; her hair seeming to catch sparks from it. He couldn't see her facial expression but thought by the set of her shoulders she was up to something. "Don't just stand there, come sit by the bed."

She padded over to the recliner and sat on the edge of it. Leaning forward, hands clasped between her pajama-clad knees, she said, "Cooper, can I ask you something?"

"Shoot. You know me, I'm a walking encyclopedia."

Instead of the sarcastic comeback he anticipated, she just vaguely muttered, "Um hmm," and stopped.

"Cayden?"

"Yeah?"

"Is something wrong? You seem a little distracted."

She shrugged. "I guess I don't know how to ask you this." She twisted a little in the chair. "So here goes. Are you gonna marry Kate?"

Cooper's face registered surprise. "I don't know. You think I should?"

"How would I know that? I've just been thinking. I mean, you want me to go to college and all, and I want that too, but, well, if you are going to marry Kate, I don't want to be in the way."

"How would going to college make you be in the way?"

"Do I need to go somewhere else, leave home, I mean, to go to school?" She dropped her gaze, as though afraid to hear the answer.

Cooper struggled to a sitting position, holding his neck. The pain was worse, and he figured he was looking at the reason. He clumsily stacked pillows against the headboard and scooted toward them, easing his neck to a resting position. "You're kidding, right? What in the world has made you think this? First of all, if Kate and I do get married, it won't be right away. We've not even talked about it. Secondly, neither she nor I would ever want you to leave. This is our home, Cayden. Kate isn't the kind of person who would ever ask or even want you to leave. I wouldn't be interested in a woman who would think like that."

"But, Coop, no woman wants a kid sister in the picture when she first gets married. Not even Kate."

"Come here." He patted the bed. Cayden slid over to the bed and Cooper put his arm around her. "You are full of nonsense. Don't worry about this. I mean it, Cayden. The problem resides only in your head. For all I know, if Kate and I do get married, we'd live at her house and you'd have this house. Ever thought of that?"

"No. This house is much bigger and nicer. Plus, it's our home. Why would you want to move out?"

"Why would you?"

Cayden huffed out a sigh. "I just wanted you to know I'm willing to live on campus somewhere if you need me to."

"Thanks, Sis, but no thanks. I want you right here at home. Plus, it's the biggest bang for our buck and for your education. Now, get some sleep. Frankly, I haven't even thought about getting married, okay?"

Cayden nodded. "Okay. Good night, Coop. Even though you're a royal pain and an embarrassment, I love you."

"That certainly brings a tear to my eye. Right back at you."

They grinned at one another. Cayden pecked him on the cheek and shut the door behind her.

Of course, afterwards, getting married was all Cooper could think about.

CHAPTER SIX

Two weeks later found Kate and Cooper on a brisk walk in the park with Clancy. With Cooper's neck healed except for tenderness if he turned it too far, and Kate being convinced Clancy was getting too fat, they had set a goal to walk every afternoon that weather permitted.

They waved gaily to Mrs. Peabody as Clancy jumped nimbly into the backseat. Attempting to back out of Kate's driveway, Cooper had to keep dodging Clancy's drooling mouth. "Kate, get his head out of the way! I can't see through solid brick."

Kate cooed to the dog who sidled over and dropped his head on the armrest between the seats. Cooper felt a gnawing anxiety in the pit of his belly, which had grown considerably since the conversation he and Cayden had about Kate and marriage. It seemed every time he was around Kate now, the word marriage blared around in his head loud enough to disturb all his rational thinking. Kate seemed oblivious that anything was changed, which irritated him a bit. Couldn't she see he was on pins and needles?

Glancing at her now, he saw a serene woman smiling down at her dog, humming absently. "How fat do you think he's gotten?" Cooper asked, a bit sharper than he meant to.

"Oh, I don't know. The vet just said to keep an eye on him. He'll eat anything that's not nailed down, you know."

"The vet?"

Signs From God

"You're so funny. Although Doc Branson is pretty chunky. However; I was speaking of the he between us." Clancy glanced up at her. She fondled his muzzle. "Don't worry, Clancy, you're still a handsome brute."

The day was crisp, the afternoon sun giving everything a golden glow. Clancy was eager for his leash, and after Kate snugged his halter, they set off at a fairly rapid clip. It wasn't long until Cooper and Kate were slightly out of breath, but Clancy was nowhere near tired.

They slowed anyway, and began to enjoy the walk. As they entered the path of the cutting garden, the fragrances were heady and bees lazily worked their way around all the flowers.

Cooper stared straight ahead, feeling as though he might explode. He took a deep breath and decided to take the plunge and bring up the subject. Why not let it torture them both? "So, Kate, have you ever thought about us getting married? To each other, I mean?" He turned a nervous smile toward her. She was nowhere in sight. Puzzled, he turned and looked back. She and Clancy were several yards away, Kate standing on the trail, Clancy half hidden in the bushes. "What are you doing?" Cooper grumped.

"Clancy is smelling flowers."

"Of course he is." Cooper rolled his eyes and walked back to them.

Clancy stood, frozen in place, one paw up, as millions of dogs have posed. But instead of on alert or treeing an animal, Clancy's nose was buried deep in a dahlia. His eyes were closed in ecstasy, whiskers trembling delicately.

"Good grief." Cooper couldn't believe his eyes. "Has

he ever done this before?"

"Yep. Every blossom his nose detects, he stops and, well, smells the roses, if you will."

"He looks totally ridiculous." Clancy turned to him and gave him a reproachful look. He moved onto the next bloom and resumed sniffing. "We'll be here for a month if he has to smell every bloom in the park. How do you get him to stop?"

Kate smiled at the dog fondly. "I just let him enjoy himself for a few minutes, then make him follow my lead. He doesn't like it, but he obeys."

"Good thing. He's as big as a house. Don't ever let him know he has a choice."

Kate laughed. She tugged the leash once. "Come, Clancy. Time to move on." He opened his eyes slowly, gave a regrettable gaze at all the blossoms, whined mournfully and then plodded forward.

"Drama queen," Cooper muttered.

He could have sworn Clancy knocked him down on purpose.

"Are you all right?" Kate asked, trying to stifle a giggle. Cooper had landed on his bottom on the side of the trail in the soft mulch between bushes. Clancy sat, smiling at Cooper, his big old tongue lolling.

"I'm not hurt. But Clancy pushed me."

Kate laughed. "Clancy stumbled and bumped you." She reached down and offered a hand to help Cooper up. As she pulled on him, she whispered in his ear. "But I wouldn't call him a drama queen again."

They had ridden back in companionable silence for the most part. Silence, if you didn't count the loud snoring emitting from the back seat. Clancy was propped up, paws dangling in the air, sound asleep.

"He could wake the dead. How do you sleep with him in the bedroom with you?" Cooper shook his head in amazement.

"Earplugs." Kate shrugged. "He only snores on his back, and most the time he's a side sleeper." Glancing at Cooper, she bit her lower lip, then asked, "Did you and Cayden talk with Pastor Matt?"

"Once. He took turns with us, then saw us together. I guess the whole thing lasted about two hours. Basically, Cayden is supposed to still ask permission to come and go and let me know with whom. Eighteen or no, she's under my roof and is still my responsibility. And I am to treat her with respect and trust, mindful that she is rapidly becoming an adult. Give her some responsibility, and when she proves she can handle that, give her more. By the time she graduates college, she will be ready to fly, I guess."

"No more arguments since then?"

"No." Cooper squirmed a little. He cleared his throat. "But Cayden did have a discussion with me the other night."

"Really? Well, that's good, isn't it? A discussion, instead of a fight?"

"Definitely an improvement." Wasn't Kate even going to ask him what the discussion was about, for heaven's sake? He took a deep breath. *'Here goes...'*

Kate shrieked. Clancy grunted as he slammed into the back of their seats and Cooper saw his life flash in front of his eyes as the car kept sliding long after Kate had applied the brakes. The semi in front of them was fishtailing like crazy and they watched as it hit a car in the oncoming lane. Cars were honking, tires squealing, glass breaking, there was chaos everywhere.

When they came to a stop, Cooper feared the worst was about to happen: were they about to get hit from the rear by approaching traffic? Wincing as he forced his sore neck to crane backward, he was relieved to see traffic already halting several feet away. He grabbed his cell phone to punch in 9-1-1 and was informed help was already on the way.

"Can you move the car over, into that parking lot so we can get to safety?"

Kate drew a shaky breath. "Yeah. Is Clancy all right?"

Cooper checked on the dog. Clancy was back up in the seat, head turned, looking behind them. "You okay, buddy?"

A wagging tail was his answer.

CHAPTER SEVEN

Kate sat at her desk, staring into space. A red pencil was poised above a stack of papers, waiting to be graded. The classroom was eerily quiet, especially after the ear splitting noise of ringing bells, desks scraping, kids chattering and parents arriving.

Everyone had been gone for about twenty minutes, and Kate had decided she could get a little work done before she left for home. But instead, she was motionless.

Ever since the wreck two days ago, she'd been jumpy. And Cooper had seemed unusually attentive. Now that she thought about it, the attentiveness had begun even before. He wasn't irritable, exactly, but something was different, she just couldn't put her finger on what it was.

A faint smile brushed her lips as she thought about him. She'd never felt about a guy the way she felt about Cooper. Sometimes she wondered where their relationship would go. It was obvious he was devoted to Cayden, and she was of the firm belief he should be. She thought Cayden liked her, even approved of their relationship.

But lately Cayden had acted differently, too.

It was true Cayden was almost grown. Cooper had confided his concern about Cayden's lack of devotion toward college. But it did seem to Kate that Cayden had warmed to the idea a great deal now that Stu was out of the picture. She'd heard a rumor that Cayden had started seeing a boy from church – um, what was his name?

Mickey, Mikey, something like that. As far as she knew, he was a good kid.

Kate leaned back in her chair and stretched a bit. She glanced at the wall clock. Ten minutes had passed and she'd accomplished absolutely nothing. "Katie, girl, you might as well go home." She muttered as she stuffed the papers into her satchel.

As she walked to her car Cooper re-entered her thoughts. Maybe she'd call him when she got home to see if he and Cayden wanted to come over for supper tonight. She could use the company.

Startled out of her occupation with her own life, she whirled around as she heard a frantic voice calling her name. It was John Donaldson, the principal. Surprised, she stood and waited for him.

He was a little out of breath when he reached her, his dark brown hair windswept, and tie askew. "Hey! Thought I'd missed you! I just got a phone call I need to talk to you about. Do you have time to come back in for a few minutes?"

"Of course. Is everything all right?"

"There's no emergency, if that's what you're asking." He lightly touched her back as he guided her into the building and down the hall. As they entered his office, he indicated a side chair for her. The other chair had books in it, which he removed and put atop his desk. He sat there, instead of behind his desk, as though he wanted this to be peer to peer instead of boss to employee.

"Would you care for some coffee or water or something?" He looked a little nervous.

"No, thanks. Too close to supper." She scooted to the

edge of the chair. "Are you sure everything's all right?"

John leaned forward and looked up at her. "Do you remember the little Ashe boy you had in class last year?"

"Thomas? Yes, of course. We all tried to help that family out at Christmas; the father had just been killed in Iraq, I believe. Wasn't Mrs. Ashe expecting another child at the time?"

"She was." He fidgeted with his tie. "I heard you talking about the wreck you saw. You were almost a part of it, weren't you?"

Kate gave him a puzzled look, doing her best in an attempt to follow his fragmented conversation. "Yes. It was a close call for us. The semi hit an oncoming car. I barely got stopped in time."

"The car that was hit was the Ashe family's."

"Oh, no!" Kate exclaimed. "Was Thomas injured?"

"Yes." He bowed his head. "Thomas nor his mother made it. Only the baby girl lived. The lady I talked to said 'Thank God for infant seats in cars.' From what they said, I don't think the baby was hurt at all."

Tears welled up in Kate's eyes. "This is terrible. Poor Thomas! He was such a sweet kid, too." She looked up. "Thanks for taking the time to let me know. I appreciate you doing this. Hearing it somewhere else would have been a big shock."

"There's more, Kate."

"Yes?"

"Apparently you made quite an impression on Mrs. Ashe when you taught Thomas. I guess, too, she found out you were behind the Christmas stuff as well as making sure Thomas had school supplies. Shoes too?"

Kate blushed. "How could she have found that out? I didn't tell anyone that I recall."

John shrugged. "Who knows? Doesn't matter, now." He sighed. "What matters is Mrs. Ashe has no family, there are no relatives. How this poor, destitute woman had the knowhow and resources to do this, I can't imagine."

"Do what? What on earth are you talking about?"

"She had named you sole guardian of her children, should anything happen to her. That may mean the little girl has been legally left in your hands."

"What?" Kate jumped up. "I don't even know the child. Can she even do something like that? The mother, I mean?"

John stood too. "I don't know. The attorney's office called me a little while ago and asked how to get in touch with you. They need to see you first thing in the morning. I'll get a sub for your class. I imagine you'll have to be checked out somehow before they'll let you take the child home with you."

"Home with me? Are you crazy?" She blushed. "Sorry. Look, I can't even process this. I'm totally shocked. I barely knew Mrs. Ashe. It's true I loved Thomas. I did everything I could to help him be successful in the classroom. But I didn't try to be his mother!" Kate finished earnestly.

John smiled. "Of course not. And I suppose you can refuse to do this. I just thought you needed a heads up before you walked blindly in on a meeting in the morning. If the secretary there didn't know me personally, I'm not sure she would have told me anything. As it was, she was practically whispering into the phone. I could barely hear her. So, try to look surprised, okay?" His smile turned into a grin.

"That won't be hard to do." Kate shook her head. "There's no way I can possibly do something like this. I can barely take care of Clancy."

John raised an eyebrow. "Who?"

"My dog."

"Oh. Well, go home Kate. I think you've got enough to think about now. And that dog would probably like supper."

As Kate arrived home, she realized she barely remembered getting there. She didn't see Mrs. Peabody wave at her, she didn't notice a pot of flowers had turned over on the porch floor; she stepped over the newspaper in the door.

What in the world was she going to do? She saw the message button blinking on and off the phone and knew it would be the attorney's office. She threw a fleeting prayer upward, kicked off her shoes and went to the back to let Clancy in, wondering: What will Cooper think?

❊ ❊ ❊ ❊

Cooper sat in Kate's driveway, stewing. He was as nervous as a long tailed cat in a room full of rocking chairs. He'd contemplated buying a ring, but, A: he didn't know what size Kate wore, B: he didn't know what style she liked and C: what if she said no, since they hadn't even discussed marriage at all?

He glanced nervously at her door, but the house looked deserted. He knew she was in there. A light shone from upstairs, her car was in the driveway and he usually knew if she wasn't going to be home. He was surprised she hadn't opened the door to ask why he didn't come on in. He rolled his eyes as Mrs. Peabody peaked out her living room window, again. She sure didn't miss anything.

He closed his eyes in prayer for a moment, asking the Good Lord to show him what to say and when to say it.

Slowly he climbed out of the car, smoothed his hair and dragged himself to the front door. If this was the right thing to do, why was he sweating?

He rang the bell and waited. Kate didn't answer. He rang again, and finally knocked. He heard a noise and the door suddenly flung open, making him jump. Kate stood there, her hair practically standing on end, her sweats soaked and it looked suspiciously as if she had been crying.

Cooper involuntarily took a step back. "Whoa! Have you been in a tornado?"

"Shut up." She turned and left him at the threshold. He followed her and then grimaced.

"Phew! What is that smell?" He waved his hand in front of his nose.

"It's Clancy. He got into some kind of dead something back behind the house."

"Then why does it smell like it's coming off you?"

"He's in the tub. I was giving him a bath."

"You left him there?"

"I told him if he so much as twitched a muscle I'd beat him within an inch of his miserable life."

"You must be a great teacher." Cooper grinned. "I can see why you have no problem with discipline in your classroom."

Kate didn't answer. She tromped up the stairs and he followed. As they entered the bathroom, the smell became almost overpowering. Clancy sat meekly, his hulking frame barely fitting into the tub. He glanced over at Cooper, then fixed his eyes straight ahead. He was covered in suds from his ears down and the expression on his face was of noble resignation to his plight.

Kate got on her knees and took a scrub brush to Clancy's back. The dog never moved.

Cooper leaned against the doorframe, thinking this was one of the funniest things he'd ever seen. He didn't deny the satisfaction of seeing Clancy humbled a bit, as Cooper still had feelings of resentment about being pushed.

Kate reached for the shower nozzle and began to rinse the dog. Just as Cooper was about to smart off, he thought he saw Kate's shoulders shake. "Hey, Kate, honey, are you all right?" He came forward and kneeled beside her. Tears were streaming down her face.

"It's not that bad. He won't smell this way forever."

Kate looked at him as if he'd lost his mind. "I'm not upset about Clancy, Coop. I had to put my feelings on the back burner and get him cleaned up."

Clancy's head drooped in shame. He gently licked the side of Kate's head, which explained her hair. A little sob escaped Kate, and she threw her arms around the dog, suds and all. Clancy rested his giant head on her shoulder and looked sadly up at Cooper. Of course, Clancy looked that way most of the time; his face was built that way. But that look was certainly appropriate now.

Cooper awkwardly patted Kate's back. "Want me to finish Clancy's bath so we can talk?"

Kate sighed. "No, just get ready to hand me those beach towels to dry him off." She put her hands on each side of Clancy's jowls. "Clancy Rupert the First, don't you ever do this again! Understand?" Cooper watched as Clancy batted his eyes at Kate.

She finished rinsing the dog and Cooper handed her towels as she dried the beast. Kate stood. "Stand back, Cooper." She hurriedly did the same, and Clancy shook for all he was worth. Satisfied, he grunted and trotted out of the bathroom. "Don't you dare get on my bed!" Kate yelled. Cooper heard a huff and then the monster trotted down the stairs.

Kate sprayed down the tub, gathered up towels and rugs and headed for the laundry room. Cooper followed her around, wondering if Clancy just didn't want them married.

Kate turned to Cooper. "I'm going to shower, then I'll be down. I've got some potatoes to bake and I was going to grill chicken. There's plenty enough for you to join me. If you want, you can get it started, and we'll eat together."

"Sounds good. I'll call Cayden and let her know I won't be home for supper. Anything else I can do?"

"Salad is in the fridge already made. Just start the potatoes, fire up the grill and set the table if you have time. I'll be down as quick as I can." Cooper nodded and turned to go down. "Cooper?"

"Yeah?"

"I really need to talk about something."

"Me too."

CHAPTER EIGHT

After supper, Kate and Cooper sat in sturdy rockers on her front porch. Clancy lay asleep on the floor between them, a faint, repugnant odor wafting from him.

Before the sun could set, the early October moon was impatient to rise, and in the East his round white face frowned at them in a menacing scowl. The evening was almost warm, and both of them were shoeless. Bellies full, they held glasses of tea, in which the ice was slowly melting.

Kate's face was tear stained, unable to hold back as she related to Cooper the telephone call that had so unsettled her.

"I don't know what to say, Kate. What a shock. And the poor little baby! What's her name, do you know?"

"I have no idea." Kate took a deep breath. "Here I sit, and some attorney is expecting me to take over a baby tomorrow, a baby whose name I don't even know!" Fresh tears started. "Cooper, what should I do? How can I possibly even consider this? I've never even thought much about having a family of my own, except in passing - you know - just assuming I would have children someday." Her chin trembled. "I've never been this confused."

Cooper reached and tucked a strand of Kate's hair behind her ear. He patted her cheek before he removed his touch. "I don't know, honey. But we believe God's Hand is in our lives and in everything that happens to us. I just don't know what you're response to this is to be. I know you've been praying," Kate nodded affirmatively, lower lip still trembling. "I'll be praying too. You're a good woman Kate, and you have a good heart. You desire what's right in your life, and we have to believe we'll know what that is by the time you have to give an answer."

"I'm just afraid what God wants and what I want might be two different things." She gave a watery laugh. "Except I have no idea what I want, really. I don't want a child in my life right now, but I don't want this child in the wrong hands either." She sat her tea glass on the porch floor and wiped her damp palms on her jeans. "Isn't it amazing how things can be rocking along so peacefully and them BAM! Everything's turned upside down?"

Cooper agreed. "And it could be worse by tomorrow."

"Thanks, Coop. I really needed to hear that."

"You know me, always trying to help." He sat his glass down too and stretched his arms over his head, then scratched at his hair. "It's getting pretty late. I guess I better go. I'm sure we're keeping Mrs. Peabody up past her bedtime."

"But I thought there was something you wanted to talk to me about."

Cooper stood. "Not tonight. What I had to say can wait. I just wanted your opinion about something. Believe me, in light of what has happened to you today, it's trivial. We'll save it for conversation when we're bored."

Kate stood too, and laid her head on his chest. "Okay. I look forward to bored again."

"Me too." He tilted her chin so she was looking at him. "Do you want me to get a sub tomorrow and go with you to the attorney's?"

She chewed her lower lip in thought. "I do. But I think it's better if I go alone. I'm in this by myself."

Cooper felt a pang in his chest at that remark. "Yeah, I guess you are. But Kate, maybe someday…I mean, I'll help any way I can if you decide to try this."

She hugged him tightly. "Thanks Coop. Believe you me, if I bring a baby home, I'll expect baby-sitting services free of charge."

Cooper looked down at the slumbering dog. "Hear that Clancy? Your bachelor days may be fast approaching over." Clancy opened one eye, yawned and started snoring. "He doesn't believe me. Poor slob."

"Pray with me before you leave, Cooper. Let's pray I make the right decision for this baby."

And they did.

🐾 🐾 🐾 🐾

Cooper pulled into his driveway and parked. He felt drained. How could the night have taken such a turn? How could their lives? Part of him was frustrated that once again he hadn't been able to speak of marriage, but another part of him was relieved. Did he really want to marry a woman who might suddenly become a mother of a baby? Could he shoulder that much responsibility, marry into a readymade family, and love a child not his own? Not even Kate's own? He honestly didn't know the answer.

Maybe God had kept the marriage conversation from happening because Cooper wasn't the man for the job.

Cayden looked up from the TV as Cooper walked in the front door. He strolled into the living room and tousled her hair. Annoyed, she slapped at his hand. He slumped into an armchair and stared mindlessly at the tube.

"What's the matter, Coop? You and Kate have a fight?" Cayden didn't take her eyes off the television, but obviously saw his mood.

"No. I'm just tired, I guess." He had decided not to share the baby news with Cayden until Kate made a decision. What was the point? Besides, he wasn't sure Kate would want him telling anyone, even Cayden. "Whatcha watchin'?"

"The end of a reality show. I got through with homework and decided to kill some time to keep from reading the most boring novel in the world."

"If it's so boring, why are you reading it?"

"Lit. class. Mr. Arnold is making us. I've attempted the first chapter twice. B-o-r-i-n-g. Why can't he have us read something that has some life to it?"

Cooper shrugged. "Beats me. Some of the so-called best literature leaves me cold. But for others it's a great read. You can't please everyone, I guess."

"That may be true, but you could try and please *someone*. I haven't talked to one person in the class that likes this book, and even Mr. Arnold said it was 'difficult'. No joke." She picked up the remote and turned off the TV. Glancing up, she frowned. "Are you sure everything's okay, Cooper? You look upset."

"Kate's got a little problem and I'm worried about her. But she's praying, I'm praying and we know it'll work out."

"Is she sick?"

"No, nothing like that. Life just throws us sometimes. It'll be fine." He stood. "Say a prayer for her, too. She needs the Lord's guidance in a decision she has to make tomorrow."

"Okay. Let me know how it turns out."

"I will. Good night, Cayden. See you in the morning. Lights out pretty soon."

"I'm coming up as soon as I get some water."

Cooper climbed the stairs slowly, wondering if he'd sleep at all.

🐾 🐾 🐾 🐾

Immediately after Cooper left, Kate called her friend, Anna Crawford. Anna had shared that she and Bailey, although newlyweds, were already considering a baby. Kate and Anna regularly swapped confidences, and both knew secrets were safe with each other. Anna had prayed with Kate over the phone, and both had shed a few tears. Anna volunteered to go with Kate, but once again Kate declined anyone's company. She knew this was something she had to do on her own.

Hanging up, she slid to her knees. "Father, I don't know what to do. Help me." More tears fell. "I know she's just a little baby, and she needs a Mama. But me? I still feel like a child sometimes, Lord. And what will this do to my relationship with Coop? I love him, God. I thought you were leading us to marriage, maybe. I can see it in his eyes, I can feel it in my heart. But is this more important? I know we aren't supposed to put our wants first, but to serve others." She pushed her hair behind her ears. "I need you to tell me what to do." She got up and plopped down on the bed. She reached for her well-worn Bible and turned to her nightly devotional.

"In Exodus we read about the poor Hebrew mother who had to give up her son in order for him to have a chance to live. It must have been a terrible thing for her to

have to do, but she loved her baby so much, she made sure he would be taken care of when she could not do this herself. To be a mother is to be selfless in love and devotion, as Christ has been selfless and devoted to us. Are you being called to be a mother? If so, do it whole heartedly, devoting yourself to God and His Glory."

Kate sat back, stunned. A chill ran up her spine. "Ask and ye shall receive, huh? Okay, God. Unless you do something to prevent this child from coming into my life, I guess I'm willing. I'll go into this meeting with an open heart. You lead, I'll follow."

Cooper sat on the edge of his bed, staring at the picture on his nightstand of himself and Kate, laughing into the camera. They'd been at a church picnic and one of their friends had been taking snapshots all day. This was a great photo. He'd had it enlarged as soon as he'd been able, and the framed image was the first thing he saw every morning. He picked it up and smiled back at the couple. "We look so good together, God. Happy, in love, a match made in Heaven. Right?" He looked upward. "At least that's what I thought. But now there's a baby in the way." He shook his head. "I know couples get the cart before the horse sometimes, and a baby results, but not like this." He sighed heavily and sat the picture back down.

He leaned back on the pillows and picked up his brand new Bible. His other one was old and fragile, and he had decided to stop by the bookstore last week and pick up a new one. But he kept glancing longingly at the old one. Finally he gave up and reached for his old friend. His hand slipped, and the Bible fell to the floor. As he reached down to pick it up, a whole section fell out. "Great," he muttered.

Signs From God

"Not only am I in a dilemma, I've torn up God's Word." He picked up the fallen section and his eyes were drawn to words in the book of Ephesians. As he read, tears welled up in his eyes. *"Predestined to be adopted."* He bowed his head. "Father, thank you that I am an adopted son of Yours. I know that adoption is a wonderful blessing. Not just for the child, but for the ones who adopt. I ask that You give me a heart for this baby if she is to become Kate's daughter. Show me how to love like You love. Help me to be to Kate and this baby exactly what You want me to be."

He sat there for a few minutes, feeling the peace wash over him. He reached for the phone. Kate answered after the third ring. "You asleep yet?"

"No. Praying and reading. And Cooper, God answered."

"He answered me too. You know in Ephesians where it tells us we are predestined to be adopted children of God?"

He heard her make a noise between a giggle and a sob. "How about Exodus where Moses' mother has to give him up so he can be taken care of? And Pharaoh's daughter adopts him?"

"Well, well. I guess we know now, huh?"

"I know I'm willing now. Whatever happens at the attorney's, I am willing."

"That's all He ever asks, isn't it? For us to be willing?"

"Yes. Maybe someday I'll learn." She was silent for a moment, then continued. "I don't know what this means about us, Coop. I care for you so much-"

"And I care for you too, Kate. This will work out. I'm

willing too."

"You are?" She asked timidly.

"Hey, if Clancy can handle it, so can I."

Kate laughed. "Well, I don't know if the Lord has spoken to Clancy yet." Her voice softened. "Thanks, Coop. I'll call you as soon as I get out of the attorney's meeting."

"Okay. I'll be waiting. And Kate? I do love you."

"Oh, Coop. I love you too. That means so much to me."

"Good night. Talk to you tomorrow."

"Good night."

Kate and Cooper hung up, each in their own house, in their own beds. But they were joined in their hearts, and both went to sleep with a smile on their face.

CHAPTER NINE

Cooper's morning had been anything but productive. He couldn't keep his mind on the students, and they were taking advantage of his distracted state. He finally gave up and put in a video, and determined to do it without guilt. He kept glancing at his watch, at the wall clock, and at the outdoors. He'd even kept his cell phone on, which was against school rules. But his mind was filled with so many questions that he didn't think he could wait one second longer than necessary.

Kate had been greeted warmly by the attorney's assistant and escorted into the office. She'd only had to wait a few minutes before Len Sherry had rushed in, briefcase in hand. He placed it on the desk and reached out his hand to Kate as she stood. "I'm sorry you had to wait, but there was a breakdown on the ramp, and traffic was backed up about five miles. I'm usually here long before now."

"That's quite all right. I've only been here a few minutes." She sat back down and nervously ran her hands down her lap. "You need to know I am completely in shock."

Mr. Sherry settled himself behind his desk, buzzed the secretary and asked for coffee. He raised an eyebrow in question to Kate, who shook her head no. "Just for me, Sally. And do we have any Danish?" At his crestfallen look, Kate surmised there was none left in the entire county.

"Are you a sugar addict?" Kate asked, smiling.

"Just about. They know I like sweets far too much, but sometimes they take pity and surprise me."

A light knock on the door, then Sally came in with one cup of coffee – and a Danish. Mr. Sherry grinned from ear to ear and told Sally she was re-employed. Everyone laughed, and she exited.

"I imagine you are in shock." He said, referring to her previous statement. "We were pretty shocked ourselves to find out you weren't aware of our client's intent." He took a bite of the pastry. "Mrs. Ashe completed this paperwork with my predecessor, James Black. There is paperwork in the files that indicates you were notified of Mrs. Ashe's wishes in case something happened to her, although I notice there are no signatures from you. Guardianship is usually a mutually agreed upon thing, not to mention within a family or close friendship."

"I never received anything. Thomas was in my classroom last year and I got to know his mother a little bit. I remembered she was pregnant at the end of the school year."

"Yes. She delivered in August." He shuffled through a folder as he spoke. "Mrs. Ashe was obviously a very bright woman, and from what I can find out, she loved her children very much. When her husband was killed, she got a pretty tidy sum and that helped her to get through the pregnancy and the last few months without having to work. Maybe her husband's death made her realize if something were to happen to her, the children would become a ward of the state if she didn't take action. And believe me, Miss Roe, she took a lot of action." He leaned back in his chair and took a bite of Danish with a reflective look on his face. "She took out a life insurance policy on herself and each child. If things work out as she wished, and you decide to become the mother, a little over a hundred thousand dollars will come to you."

Kate looked startled. "You mean from the life insurance policies?"

"Yes. Thomas had a twenty-five thousand dollar policy and Robyn's was one hundred thousand dollars. It didn't even take the twenty-five thousand dollars to bury them."

"Robyn." Kate repeated softly. "I'd forgotten that was her first name. She was a little thing, too. The name suited her."

"She must have liked the name herself. She continued the bird theme when she named the twins."

Kate tilted her head to one side. "What twins?"

Mr. Sherry raised his eyebrows. "I thought you knew the surviving children were twins."

"The baby is twins?" Kate felt the blood drain out of her face.

"Well, the babies are twins. Cutest things you've ever seen." He looked bemused. "You'd think if my secretary is going to leak information, she'd at least leak correct information."

Kate was stunned. "I came in here thinking I didn't know how I could possibly raise a child. And now you're telling me there are two. Not just two children, but two infants. I – I don't know what to say. Or do."

"I know this is a very difficult situation to be put in.

And frankly, I don't know what I'd do if I was in your shoes. But at least there's a tidy sum to help you begin to raise them. And the state would assist you during the foster care stage. Once you legally adopt the girls, of course, you'd be on your own as their mother."

Kate shook her head. "This is more than I can process. Give me a minute, okay?"

"Sure."

Kate stood and walked into the outer office. She told the secretary she'd be back in five minutes, then walked outside. There was a bench down along the sidewalk and she sat down, weak kneed. She stared into space for a few minutes, trying to pray. "Lord," she whispered, "What do you expect me to do with two babies?" She felt fear race up her spine. "I know if it's Your Will, things will work out, but I just don't know if something this hard is Your Will." She heard the wind begin to pick up and it felt like rain. There was just enough chill in the air to make her shiver a little. "I've got to go right back in there and tell the man something. What do I tell him, Lord?" She dropped her head and stared at her hands, listening, waiting. Nothing. She sighed heavily and raised her head. She stood, knowing she had to go back. Hadn't the Bible verses confirmed to her she was to do this? But two babies?

She let her gaze wander around the parking lot, at all the cars, all the people whose lives were trucking along as usual this morning. As she started back, something caught her eye. Staring, she moved a little closer to the car that was parked near the entrance.

And laughed out loud.

A bright yellow and black sign was suctioned onto the

window of the back seat. Someone had taped over the word 'Baby', and with magic Marker had written on the tape. The sign now said: 'Babies On Board'.

A few minutes later, Kate was sitting behind the wheel of her own car, cell phone in hand. She intended to leave Cooper a message since he was in class, but was surprised when he answered instead. "Are you not at school?"

"Yes," he whispered. She could hear kids giggling in the background. "The kids are in cahoots with me. They know I'm breaking the rules, but I explained it was for health reasons."

"Health reasons?"

"Yeah, I'm gonna have a heart attack if you don't tell me something." More giggles in the background.

You have no idea. Kate thought, a smug look on her face. "Well, I'm waiting on Mr. Sherry so I can follow him to the foster parents' house."

"To get the baby?" Cooper asked, excitement evident in his voice.

"Um, well, no. Today I just meet everyone. A date will be set, like in a week or so, for that to happen."

"I wish I could be with you. What's her name?"

Kate blinked. "Who?"

"The baby. What's her name?"

"Well, I think Mr. Sherry was about to tell me, but we got sidetracked," *I'll say!* Kate thought, "And I never found out. Mrs. Ashe's first name was Robyn, and he said something about her continuing the bird theme with them, I mean, with names, but, uh, I don't know."

"Kate, are you all right? You sound a little frazzled. Is something wrong?"

"No." she sighed. "But I am frazzled." She glanced in the mirror and saw Len Sherry headed her way. "Well, I have to go. Mr. Sherry is here. I'll call you back as soon as I can."

"I'll be waiting. The kids have promised they won't rat me out." This time she heard outright laughter from the class.

Kate flipped her phone closed and rolled down the window. Mr. Sherry poked his head in. "Ready?"

"I guess." Kate smiled weakly. "I'll follow you there. How far is it?"

"About ten miles or so. Children Services will have a caseworker meet us there. Sorry it took me so long, but I was on hold forever with them." He shook his head. "They are way understaffed." He grinned at Kate. "Maybe you will help lighten their caseload."

Kate nodded. Mr. Sherry hopped into his shiny black BMW and Kate, in her not so shiny black Chevy, followed, a huge lump in her throat, praying all the way.

They pulled in the driveway, directly behind the caseworker's car. Everyone exited their vehicles at the same time, and Mr. Sherry introduced Kate to Sharon Harrison from Children's Services.

Miss Harrison, swinging a briefcase as she walked, chatted as they headed toward the house. "I understand you were totally in the dark about the Ashe babies."

Kate nodded her head. "I didn't know a thing until a few days ago. And it was just a few hours ago I was told there were twins."

Miss Harrison stopped in her tracks. "What!" She looked at Len Sherry, who shrugged helplessly. "I can't believe you're still here. It's a wonder you didn't run like a scalded dog." She grinned at Kate.

Mr. Sherry spoke up. "I thought Kate knew there were twins, so I was surprised too."

"Well, I admire you for coming here today. But I'll tell you one thing," Miss Harrison said to Kate, as she placed her hand on Kate's arm. "Once you see them, you will fall in love."

Kate laughed nervously. "I am scared to death. I hope seeing them will help. I-I so badly want to do the right thing." Tears formed, uninvited.

Miss Harrison patted Kate's arm. "I know you do. Come on. Let's take the first step and see what you think."

They proceeded into the house after a light tap at the back door. A young girl, about twelve or thirteen flew into the kitchen. Her hair was a dark cloud framing her face, her blue eyes wide. She fluttered her hands toward them and exclaimed. "Ach, you're here to see the babes, are you not?"

Kate felt confusion war with amusement as she looked at this animated girl who spoke in a loud cockney accent. What in the world?

Miss Harrison leaned toward her and whispered, "Visiting niece," as a middle-aged woman came in behind the girl. She smiled warmly and headed straight for Kate. She took Kate's hand into both her own and grasped it.

Miss Harrison said, "Kate, this is Mary Stonefield. She's one of our foster mothers."

"Hello, Kate. It's so nice to meet you. This is Genevieve, my sister's daughter, who is visiting from England."

"Howda ya do?" Genevieve stuck out her hand. The handshake was so vigorous Kate felt like her arm was a hand pump.

"Genevieve is spending a year in the states as an exchange student. She's been so homesick we thought she was going to have to go back home. But then the twins came to visit and the homesickness vanished." Mrs. Stonefield smiled fondly at Genevieve. "She has twin sisters at home who had just turned two when Genevieve left for the states. We haven't taken in foster children in the past year or so because my husband wants to travel some, with our youngest now in college. But we just couldn't resist these babies."

Genevieve clasped her hands together under her chin. "They are simply lovely children! Plump little cherubs, they are." She turned to Mrs. Stonefield. "May I bring them out now, please, Auntie?"

"Not yet, darlin'. In just a few minutes, though, I promise." The contrast between the heavy cockney accent and the thick Southern one made Kate feel as though she were in a slightly skewed *'Monty Python meets Steel Magnolia'* play.

Genevieve, deflated for the moment, led them all to the family room, where she collapsed dramatically in the recliner. Others sat in chairs while Kate perched nervously on the end of the sofa. Miss Harrison opened her slim briefcase and took out a folder, which she laid open on her lap. Kate could see a photograph on one side, and papers on the other. Miss Harrison took the photo out of the folder and handed it to Kate. She explained, "This was taken about a week before the wreck."

The picture depicted a smiling Robyn Ashe. She was seated with an infant cradled in each arm. Thomas was standing proudly by her, his hand resting on his mother's shoulder. "Cor," Genevieve exclaimed, suddenly looming over Kate's shoulder, "You could pass for the woman's sister, you could. I'm astonished at the resemblance!"

Kate stared at the picture. She could see a resemblance, too. Although Robyn was sitting in the picture, it looked like they had the same build and bone structure. Same eyes. Same freckles. But her hair was more of a strawberry blonde, where as Kate's was a beige, medium color blonde. *'Robyn's is more the color of Cooper's hair',* Kate thought. She vaguely remembered thinking that same thing when Robyn had visited her classroom at the end of school.

Could the resemblance be the reason Robyn had done this? Did she think if the babies had a mother who looked like her it would be a connection of some sort? The babies were identically wadded up tiny bundles that she could tell little about. And Thomas. Her throat thickened as she looked at the small boy she had come to love that school year. It seemed impossible he could no longer be alive.

Kate looked up from the picture and offered it, wordlessly, back to Miss Harrison. She waved away the offer, indicating Kate keep it. "The twins were born August twenty-seventh, making them about eight weeks old. They are healthy and appear to be perfectly normal babies. They do have some clothing, but they are rapidly outgrowing newborn size. Robyn had purchased a Pack N Play, which they continue to sleep in. There are some blankets and two identical sweaters that should begin to fit them. I think Robyn purchased them the day of the wreck, as they were found in the car with the tags still attached." She dropped her eyes for a moment. "Anyway, we have a few things the girls might want later to help connect them to their mother and father. A couple of family albums, a few letters Mr. Ashe had written to Robyn during the war, Thomas's report cards, things like that. None of the furniture is worth keeping. There is a set of dishes that look like family heirlooms, but I don't know which side of the family. All the stuff can easily be packed in a few boxes." She leaned forward, looking Kate directly in the eyes. "If you are going to do this, we can do the background checks and assign a social worker to you within a week or so. Then you can pick up the babies along with a few diapers and some formula and bottles. You'll be supervised by our departmental social worker until a court date can be set. During that time, you will receive a small stipend check as a foster parent. Once the court declares you their legal mother, those checks would stop, but I understand from Mr. Sherry there is a sum that would be passed on to you."

Miss Harrison looked at him. He nodded and cleared his throat. "Since these are extenuating circumstances, Kate, when you take the babies home, we'll be willing to oversee any spending you need to make before you become the legal parent. Setting up two babies to live comfortably won't be cheap. After you are legally declared their mother, the rest of the money will be given to you in a lump sum, as was Mrs. Ashe's wish."

Kate's head was spinning. So much information! Yet, she knew, she knew. She smiled up at everyone, tears sparkling on her eyelashes. "This is a lot to take in. But what I really want to do is see them. Can I please hold the babies?"

Mrs. Stonefield jumped up. "Of course, dear. Come Genevieve, the moment you've been waiting for. Let's go get the girls!" Genevieve jumped up so quickly she almost knocked over a lamp. After righting it, she rushed from the room. They could hear her babbling all the way down the hall.

Kate spoke to Mr. Sherry and Miss Harrison. "I will do this. It seems as though this is the path God has chosen for me. I don't know if either of you believe, but I do. So do whatever you need to do, I'll be these babies mama."

They nodded in agreement and stood as Mrs. Stonefield and Genevieve came back in, each carrying a baby.

Genevieve proudly placed an infant into Kate's arms. "This one is little Sparrow." Genevieve explained.

Kate smiled down at the baby. "Do you mean her name is Sparrow?"

Genevieve gave a superior look to Kate. "Tis her name. Sparrow Leanne Ashe."

Kate looked at the baby, who stared back with dark blue eyes. Her hair was a pale blonde with a pink tinge to it and once again Kate thought of Cooper's thatch of strawberry hair. Kate touched Sparrow's fist, and caressed her tiny, dimpled knuckles. "Hello, little one. Do you think you can teach me a thing or two?" The baby kicked her feet a bit and made a noise down in her throat. "I guess that's a yes." Kate looked up and smiled.

" 'Ere, let me take her, and you can 'old her sister." Genevieve eagerly took Sparrow back and allowed Mrs.

Stonefield to step forward, repeating the steps with the second baby.

"I present to you Wren Elizabeth Ashe. She is the younger of the two by ten minutes. She weighed six ounces less than her older sister as of yesterday afternoon."

Kate was astonished that the babies looked so much alike. For the life of her, she could tell no difference. The same navy eyes stared at her, the same pale hair, the same dimpled hands. How on earth would she ever learn who they were? "Hello little Wren. I guess you'll have things to teach me too."

Before Kate left, someone thought of taking pictures with Kate's cell phone, so she posed with each baby before Genevieve took over the entire scene and drug the Pack N Play into the room to lay the babies in.

Miss Harrison and Mr. Sherry both reviewed information, and it was decided that Kate could be fingerprinted and complete paperwork the next day when she was finished at school. While all that was being processed, Kate could work out a plan with the school, figure out childcare and get her home ready for two babies.

On the drive home, she began the frantic process in her head of how to take care of everything, and quickly.

CHAPTER TEN

Cooper had waited so long he had officially declared himself a nervous wreck. So when his phone rang, he jumped dramatically, spilling the bowl of popcorn all over the kitchen floor. He quickly checked caller I.D. and saw that it was Kate. "Thank you, God!" he exclaimed as he hit the connect button. "Finally! I was about to give up!"

"I just got home, let Clancy in the back door and am now collapsed on my just delivered new sofa in the sunroom, wishing the fireplace had a fire going. But I'm way too tired to do anything but up the thermostat."

"You know I have to come over, right?"

"Right. Just don't expect a lot of lively movement. I'll talk, and tell you everything, but I may just barely be able to get off the couch to let you in."

"Even if I bring take-out?"

"I'll for sure crawl to the door if you bring food. Where from?"

"Bird of Paradise drive-thru."

'Bird – how appropriate.' Kate thought. "Sounds good. What's the biggest burger they sell?"

"The paradise burger, of course."

"Okay, I want one of those with cheese, an order of fries and an order of onion rings."

There was a respectful silence for a moment. "Did you say fries and onion rings?"

"Yep. And a large chocolate milkshake, too."

"Wow. You must have a lot to tell me." Kate heard a snicker in his tone. "I guess it is true what they say."

"And what would that be, Cooper?" Kate asked wearily.

"Expectant mothers do eat for two."

"Cute." She closed the phone, cutting Cooper off. "Your math is off by one." She muttered as she stretched out on the couch. Clancy came and put his big old head on her belly. "Oh, I almost forgot." She stretched over the dog and drug out a baby blanket from her purse. "Smell this, Clancy. Pretty soon these tiny little girls are coming to live with us, and they smell just like this. Get used to it, okay?"

Clancy put his nose into the blanket and snuffled. He looked up at Kate with a quizzical expression. She smiled down at him, and he put his head back on her stomach, the blanket underneath his jowls. Kate rubbed his head, and before she could remove her hand, she had dozed off.

From somewhere deep down in a sleeping fog, Kate was aware that the doorbell had been ringing for some time and that Clancy was pacing from the door back to her, excitement in every muscle. Kate sat up, yelled, "I'm coming!" toward the door and struggled to her feet. Clancy bumped her bottom with his head, urging her to go faster. "I know you can smell food through the door, but don't rush me. I just woke up, you big bully!"

She flung open the door and Cooper stood there grinning. His finger was paused on the keypad of his phone. "I was fixin' to call you. I thought maybe the phone would wake you up, even if the doorbell wouldn't."

"Lucky for you Clancy is bigger and better than either. Come on in." She pulled the door open wider and Cooper came in, handing her bags of food while he slipped his keys and phone into his jeans pocket. He shucked his jacket and hung it on the hall tree as they marched into the kitchen, single file. Kate looked back over her shoulder. "I hope there's a little something for Clancy."

"I ain't stupid. He has a big dog biscuit in there."

At the word biscuit, Clancy sat down abruptly. Kate almost tripped over him, barely stopping in time. "Sorry," Cooper muttered, having forgotten if you wanted Clancy to sit, all you had to say was – well.

Finally arriving in the kitchen, Kate sat out plates on the countertop. "Let's eat in the sunroom. I need light to wake up."

She pulled the coffee table toward the loveseat, Cooper said the blessing and Kate handed Clancy his biscuit. For a few minutes there was nothing but serious eating going on, but then Cooper could contain his curiosity no longer.

"What happens now? When do I get to see the baby?"

"What happens now is I go directly to Social Services tomorrow and get fingerprinted. I signed release forms today and they are doing a background check on me in the morning. Mrs. Stonefield, the foster mother, gave me a huge list of things I need to purchase to make this a baby house and Mr. Sherry says I can go purchase whatever I need and bring the bill back to his office for reimbursement from the estate I will be given once the adoption process is final."

Cooper's eyes widened. "Wow. There's money?"

Kate nodded, her mouth full of onion rings. "From life insurance policies."

"Oh."

"So, between now and next week I have to do some serious shopping, figure out my job, day care, and why in the world God has seen fit to do this to me." She sat down her burger. "Cooper, just talking about it wears me out. How will I ever do all this?"

He wrapped his arm around her shoulder. "First of all, you aren't alone. Aunt Cynthia said to tell you she'd be available to help you get settled for a few weeks, if you need her. Bailey said Anna wants you to call her, she's all excited too. Did you know they want to get pregnant?" Kate nodded. "Cayden has babysat before and she loves babies, so you can count on her some. The church has excellent day care, and then there's me. I don't know much about how to take care of a little baby, but I'm willing to learn. I do know how to run errands and mow grass, the usual stuff. And me and old Clancy here can keep each other company if he starts feeling neglected."

Kate reached behind her and showed Cooper the baby blanket. "I let Clancy smell this. They said if he associates the scent with me, he will accept whoever the scent belongs to."

"Clever. He's a big dog, but I can't imagine him being anything but protective and loving to a baby."

They picked up empty containers and wrappers and Cooper carried them to the trash while Kate pushed the coffee table back in place and stacked the dirty plates. She went to the living room, retrieved her purse and dug out her phone. Her palms were sweaty. How would Cooper react to the news?

"Come on in the living room. I have pictures to show you."

"Great! Can't wait." He settled himself beside Kate and waited expectantly as she found a picture.

"This is Sparrow Leanne Ashe."

Cooper looked at the picture for several seconds. "She's a little thing. You look like a natural holding her. Sparrow? Odd name."

"Yeah, but I like it. She's eight weeks old. I think she's gained two pounds since birth, so she was really tiny before." Nervously, Kate clicked to the next picture and handed the phone to Cooper.

"This looks like the same photo. Don't you have a different pose?"

"It's not the same photo, Coop. You're looking at Wren Elisabeth Ashe."

"Huh?"

"Wren." Kate's voice broke. "Oh, Coop, they're twins. Wren and Sparrow. Two babies instead of one."

Cooper sat, dumbfounded. He flipped back and forth between the two pictures, then clicked to see if there were more. The next picture showed Kate holding both babies in her arms.

"Lord, Kate! When did you find out?"

"At the attorney's office. He thought I knew. I almost ran out right then and there. But I didn't." Kate told Cooper about going outside to pray and the literal sign from God that said Babies on Board. "And now I feel like there's so much more to do. I don't know where to start."

"Well, you've certainly overwhelmed me, just hearin' about it." Cooper could only think of one thing to say; the thing that had held other Southerners steady for hundreds of years. "Bless your heart, honey. But it's gonna be all right. We'll take this one day at a time."

"Are you sure you want to, Coop? I wouldn't blame you if you said goodnight and good-bye."

"Kate. Look at me." She did. "What kind of man do you think I am? I can't guarantee this will work out for us, but I sure want it to. I wanted it to before the little birdies and I want it to no less now. If we are meant to be, one, two or five babies won't change that. Well, maybe five would…"

Kate whapped him on the arm. "Thanks. But stop while you're ahead." She grinned. "I'm gonna call Anna in the morning and see if she'll come over tomorrow afternoon and help me make sense out of the list Mrs. Stonefield gave me. She needs the practice if they want a baby. Then you can come for supper if you want to, and help me figure out stuff. And build a fire, please! It's turning cold."

"Be glad to. We need to celebrate with the first fire of the season." Cooper reached down and scratched Clancy's exposed belly as he lay sleeping on the rug. "He has no idea how his life is about to change."

Kate looked at Cooper and shook her head. "Neither do we, Coop. Neither do we."

CHAPTER ELEVEN

The next afternoon, as Kate was putting a big pot of spaghetti sauce on to slow cook, her doorbell began ringing. Clancy trotted to the door, came back and gave a small "whoof" to Kate, tail wagging.

"I bet that's Anna." Clancy wagged in agreement and followed Kate to the door.

Anna stood on the porch, shoulders hunched up around her neck. "Hurry up and let me in!"

"Surely a tough Yankee like yourself doesn't let a little spell of southern winter bother her."

"Ha." Anna slipped off her jacket, gave a perfunctory pat to Clancy, and flopped onto the couch. "I did everything right." She held up fingers as she counted. "I fell in love with a southern redneck. I married aforementioned. I moved down south with same. I did all this to avoid so called 'Yankee winters', thank you, and what do I get for my trouble? Skies spitting snow and threatening sleet tonight."

"I'll be sure and fill Bailey in on all the reasons you married him. One, right?"

Anna grinned. "More or less." She hopped off the couch and followed Kate into the kitchen. "So, tell me, how does it feel to know you're going to be a mother in a week?"

"Well, not near as bloated as I expected." Kate said dryly. "But otherwise, as scary as I figured it would be."

Anna hugged her. "You'll do great. Even though there's gonna be two of them and only one of you, you outweigh the both of them by a good hundred pounds, right?"

"Are you practicing to be a stand up comedienne?" Kate sighed. "Frankly, Anna, I'm terrified. How can I possibly take care of two babies?"

"I always say do everything one step at a time. Since you chose to ignore several steps before arriving at motherhood, we need to work on the list of purchases. At least we're good at shopping."

"Absolutely." Kate pulled out the list and they began to review, organize and divide. After two cups of coffee and a lot of giggles, they agreed they'd meet and shop Monday after school and work.

As Anna started to leave, she turned to Kate, eyes shining. "I have to tell you. This has been fun, and for more than one reason."

"Oh?"

"I found out yesterday! Bailey and I are pregnant! Due in July. We'll be mommies together!"

Kate squealed in delight and hugged Anna again. "What a relief. There'll be someone who can go through this with me for years." She grinned. "Does Coop know yet, or do I get the honors?"

"Unless Bailey has told him today, go for it." Anna glanced at the clock. "Speaking of the men folk, I gotta go. I'm meeting Bailey for dinner at the pizza parlor. We're celebrating with spices in case I get morning sickness soon."

With Anna's departure, Kate checked on the sauce and

settled on the couch to review the lists they'd come up with, and to await Cooper's arrival.

🐾 🐾 🐾 🐾

Cooper built the first fire of winter in the fireplace while Kate finished the spaghetti for supper. They moved the table into the sunroom and enjoyed their meal as the sun set and the fire blazed. Clancy lay sleeping by the hearth, his body stretched out on the area rug.

After admiring Kate's new sofa and bemoaning the fact she didn't have it when he was sleeping on the loveseat, he said, "I've got an idea, Kate. Do you have any marshmallows?"

"I think there's some in the pantry. You want to roast marshmallows?"

"Yep. I always crave something sweet after spaghetti and we've got the fire. Why not?"

Kate shook her head, but went to look for marshmallows while Cooper took Clancy out to search for sticks. After he sharpened the ends with his knife, he brought two long twigs in and Kate loaded them both with marshmallows. They sat cross-legged on the area rug, roasting the marshmallows as well as their faces. Clancy propped up behind them, and Kate or Cooper would occasionally give in and sneak him a marshmallow.

"Okay," Kate said, as she stuck her loaded stick into the flames, "Here's what I have so far. I'll work till Thanksgiving break, at which time I'm going on family leave. Mr. Donaldson says the School Board has promised me a job if I want to come back next school term. I figure I've got enough money to survive between accrued leave, savings, and the babies' money from insurance until then. The school has offered me a tutoring job two evenings a week, which will help with expenses too. Mrs. Peabody has volunteered to baby-sit those two evenings. It'll only be for about three hours each evening, and-"

"Whoa, there, little missy. Mrs. Peabody is going to baby-sit? Are you kidding me?" Cooper was looking at her with both eyebrows raised.

"Sure, why not? I know we tease about her Coop, but she's really a nice person. She's only sixty-eight years old. She's been widowed five years. Her husband was killed in a boating accident. She's raised three children, but they all live far away, and she doesn't get to see her four grandchildren."

"When did you become an expert on the life and times of Mrs. Peabody?"

"She came over yesterday afternoon. One of her Sunday School friends had heard about the twins and called her. She couldn't wait to find out about them. That's when she volunteered for the two evenings a week. I insisted I'd pay her something, but she was almost insulted." Kate popped marshmallows into her mouth and chewed for a few moments. "Also," she said, swallowing, "Mrs. Stonefield and Genevieve will keep the babies here during the day for me from now till the Thanksgiving break. They'll get here at seven in the mornings and leave when I get home. Social Services will pay them, although if Genevieve had her way, she'd pay to care for the babies, instead of the other way 'round."

"I guess you'll just lay around till then, huh?" Cooper was grinning at Kate as she prattled on about all to be done.

"Ha. Very funny. Monday is shopping with Anna, who by the way, is pregnant! Did Bailey tell you?"

"No way!" Cooper slapped his thigh. "That dog! He didn't tell me. Though I don't guess he's had much of a chance. But that's great!"

"Yep. She's due in July, so they just found out. After we purchase everything on Monday, I'll have four days to set up a nursery. I pick up Wren and Sparrow Friday afternoon." She made a disgusted noise in her throat as marshmallows dropped behind the fire screen, dripping down the glass. "How gross! I should have been paying closer attention."

"I'll clean it up." Cooper moved the fire screen to the center of the room. "When the glass cools down, I'll use something to get that mess off." He plopped back down on the floor. "Pray madam, continue your dialogue."

"Well, I was about to use all my feminine wiles to get you to agree to help me put together some baby furniture. Think that would work?"

"I'll do whatever your feminine wiles ask me to. When?"

"We're shopping Monday, so how about Tuesday after school? I'll fix a pot of soup and bake some cornbread."

"Sounds good to me." They both jumped as a loud crash shook the floor. They turned around to find the tail end of Clancy disappearing into the kitchen, the fire screen turned over.

"Clancy!" Kate yelled as she jumped up. Peering at the screen, she said, "He was licking the marshmallow off the glass. He is such a pig!" She stomped into the kitchen while Cooper picked up the screen.

"The screen's not hurt. Is Clancy?"

Kate came back into the sunroom. "I don't know. He

has disappeared under the bed. He won't come out, and I don't blame him. He knows he was a bad dog."

Cooper laughed. "You mean you are both just now figuring that out?"

Kate gave him a dirty look, but couldn't hold it. She giggled. "I've known for years."

Cooper stretched. "Let's get this mess cleaned up and call it a night. And don't forget to put the screen back in front of the fireplace." Kate nodded in acknowledgement. "Cayden has some math homework I promised to help with tonight, and I have to get up early in the morning to start getting the outside ready for winter. The way it felt today, I've just about waited too late. Do you need me to come over tomorrow afternoon and help you close up outside?"

"Nah. I've already put up the garden hose and closed the vents. I put the porch cushions in the garage yesterday afternoon. I brought in my plants two weeks ago. I always do that before Halloween. Around here you don't know if Halloween brings snow or shorts weather, so I play it safe. All I have to do now is get a cover for the spigot and I'm ready for winter."

"I've got an extra cover, I'll bring it next time I'm over. And before I forget, don't buy a whole bunch of stuff when you shop." Cooper looked a little sheepish.

"Why not?"

"Well, I'm not supposed to say anything, but I have it on good authority there might be a surprise baby shower at my house. So when you shop, don't go all out, okay?"

"Does Anna know?"

"Probably. Just let her be your guide. I hope I didn't spoil anything, but..."

"You didn't. You saved me frustration when Anna tries to stop me from buying stuff." She laughed. "I'll return the favor in a few months when it's her turn to have a shower."

"Sounds like a plan." He pulled her into his arms. "You're a mighty fine woman, Kate Roe. You're so organized even twin babies can't get you down. Walk me to the car and I'll give you a little kiss. Maybe Mrs. Peabody will be watching."

Kate showed Cooper she followed instructions well.

When Kate came back into the house, she went directly into the sunroom to put the fire screen back in front of the fireplace. Cooper had scraped off most of the melted marshmallow, but she got the Windex and did a little better job. She took her fireplace shovel and made sure all the dying embers were well away from the edge of the bricks, and half-heartedly scooped the dropped marshmallow and used sticks into the embers. She figured she could clean that up after the fire was completely cold, not wanting to risk a burn. Propping the fire screen back in place, she suddenly felt tired, and decided the table could be moved back into the kitchen in the morning. She just didn't feel like wrestling with it tonight.

Turning off the light, she did her nightly walk through of the house. She smiled slightly as Clancy joined her, looking shame-faced. "Couldn't resist doing our routine, could you, boy?" She fondled his ears and he leaned his head next to her. He turned for a moment, trotted into the sunroom and came back to her. "It's okay, you didn't break anything." She gave a cursory glance to the living room as she climbed the stairs to bed. Clancy sat down at the foot of the stairs. "Aren't you coming up with me?" He cocked his head, then laid down. "Okay, but you've gotta come up soon. I am not going to sleep wondering when you're going to try and jump on the bed." He thumped his tail twice, but remained where he was.

Kate shrugged and proceeded up the stairs, intent on brushing her teeth and getting on warm flannel pajamas. It really was cold tonight. She glanced into the soon to be nursery guest room and wondered, once again, how on earth she was going to manage her new life. Thank God she had a big enough house and a good job with a boss who was happy to cooperate until she could get settled.

Stretching, she turned down the covers, checked the thermostat and glanced back down at the stairs, where Clancy was curled up, asleep. Weird dog, but she loved him. Propping up on pillows, she picked up her nightly devotional and current novel. But before she could even start on her books, she was asleep.

🐾 🐾 🐾 🐾

Cooper found Cayden half asleep, as usual, watching TV. She greeted him by clicking off the show and saying, "Tell me more."

"Don't I need to tell you something before I tell you more?" Cooper flopped down into the armchair and kicked off his shoes. "Let's see. Spaghetti, fire in the fireplace, roasted marshmallows, Clancy knocked over the fire screen and hid upstairs. Same old, same old. Oh, yeah. And my girlfriend is shopping for baby furniture for twins on Monday with my best friend's wife." He shrugged. "Other than that, not much is going on."

"Twins!" Cayden laughed, astonishment clearly written on her face. "More than you bargained for, I bet.

How is Kate doing? I mean, is she in shock, or what?"

"I guess so. I don't think it's really sunk in, and how could it? This time next week she'll be bringing home two little babies, and she's scrambling to get everything ready. She's not really had time to get herself ready."

"What can I do to help? Besides baby-sit, I mean."

"Well, I'm going to put furniture together Tuesday, and I'm sure you could help there. I suggest you call Kate yourself, and volunteer whatever time you have. Even if everyone we know who is willing to help is running on all cylinders, it's gonna be a close call. Then when the babies get there, I think we'll really have to help for a while. Too bad I don't know what I'm doing when it comes to babies." He grinned at Cayden. "Now if they were spoiled teenagers, I could handle it."

"Hey! No fair. Here I am trying to be helpful, and all you can do is insult me." She threw a couch cushion at him and he ducked. "I'll call her in the morning. I can't wait to hold a baby, or maybe one in each arm. Meanwhile, we better get all the rest we can." She glanced at her watch. "Oh, I've got a date tomorrow night. I think you may actually like him."

Cooper yawned. "Is it that kid from church?"

"Yes. And I suggest you remember his name before tomorrow night." She walked out of the room.

Cooper yelled after her. "If you don't tell me, how will I remember?"

Cayden yelled back over her shoulder as she climbed the stairs. "I already told you. Use your head."

He grinned. "Casper? Seymour? Sven?"

The only answer he got was the slamming of Cayden's door.

CHAPTER TWELVE

The phone wouldn't stop ringing, no matter how far Cooper buried his head in the pillow. Finally, bleary eyed, he glanced at the clock as he picked up the receiver. Just a little after two a.m. He felt a nag of anxiety as he said hello.

A woman was crying hysterically on the other end, but he finally understood her to say "Fire and Clancy."

"Who is this again?" Cooper gripped the telephone, trying to hear what she was saying.

"It's Clara! Oh, Cooper, come quick, it's just awful!"

"Clara who, and what's awful?"

"Clara Peabody! Aren't you listening?!" She sounded as though she was going to start crying again. "Kate's house is in flames! I don't know where she is! Please hurry!"

Before he'd hung up, he was reaching for the sweat pants at the end of his bed. He was putting on moccasins and pulling a sweat shirt over his head when Cayden appeared in his doorway. "What's wrong, Coop?" She stood barefoot, flannel pajama's on.

"I think Kate's house is on fire. That was Mrs. Peabody, but she wasn't making any sense."

"Oh, no!" Cayden turned and flew down the stairs. She had her coat on by the time Cooper had the keys in his hand and they both ran out the door, Cayden with cell phones in one hand and Cooper's wallet in the other.

The car was backing out of the drive way before the

front door slammed shut.

They took turns praying out loud until their tires screamed around the corner. The whole street was roped off, so they could get no further than the end of the block. They could hear a siren in the distance headed their way. Flames shot up into the sky and red lights seemed to be bouncing off everything.

"Please, God, no, no," Cooper muttered under his breath, as he raced toward Kate's house. A fireman tried to stop him, but he saw nothing but the house burning. Where was Kate?

"Mr. McGuire! Cooper! Over here!"

Cooper turned to see a paramedic motioning him. Behind the guy, Cooper could see a stretcher and long blonde hair. "Kate!" He yelled. Relief washed over him. When he reached her, he dropped down to one knee, and stroked her face. "Are you okay?"

They were feeding her oxygen and she took the mask off for a moment. "Yeah. Fine. Have you seen Clancy?"

"No." Kate struggled to sit up, the paramedic gently pushed her back down. "Easy, Kate. I just got here. I'm sure he's fine."

She looked at the paramedic. "Have you seen a giant dog running around?"

"No, but lady, I ain't had a chance to look for a dog. I'm trying to take care of you. Put the mask back on."

Kate did for a second, but her worried eyes were looking frantically around. Tears began to stream down her face. She looked pleadingly at Cooper. "Find him, please Coop. What if he's in the house?" She rose back up, this time pushing the paramedic away. "If you don't, I'm getting up and doing it myself." She began coughing.

"Easy, Kate. I'll see what I can do."

He walked over to a smoke smudged firemen. "Have you seen a giant mutt roaming around?" Cooper knew the answer before the guy spoke. If Clancy was here, he would have attempted to get to Kate, or at least to Cooper.

"No."

"Could he still be in the house?" Cooper's heart sank at the thought. Despite their on-going battle, he found himself becoming fonder of the dog with each passing day.

"I doubt it. You say it's a big dog?"

"No, I said it's a giant dog. Close to your size. He's well over one hundred sixty pounds."

"I've been in there, just before the back roof collapsed. I didn't see anything. The lady got out on her own, just as we arrived."

"Okay, thanks."

He went back to Kate. "No dog in the house. He must have got out somehow."

"He saved me, Coop. He woke me up and dragged me out of the bed." She started crying. "I was fussing on him for waking me up, but he wouldn't listen. When I smelled smoke, I grabbed my shoes and sweats and got down the stairs as quickly as I could. I called him, but the smoke was so bad downstairs, I had to get out! When I opened the door the fire truck was pulling up. I told them to get Clancy out! Coop, did they do it?"

"The guy I talked to hasn't seen a dog. The man was in the house, Kate. He said there wasn't a dog in there."

"He's dead, I know he is. Cooper, it's my fault! I've got to get up and find him -"

Signs From God

"Kate you're not making any sense, lay back down!"

From across the yard Cooper thought he heard barking. He looked up. Mrs. Peabody was being pulled across the yard by Clancy. She had him tied with something bright pink, but no brighter than Mrs. Peabody's face. The roped off area stopped Mrs. Peabody's progress, but Clancy kept on coming, in spite of the two firemen who tried to stop him. He bounded over to Kate and began snuffling her frantically. Kate cried harder, but was smiling through the tears.

A paramedic hollered. "Hey! Get that dog offa her! He's going to smother her and she's having a hard time breathing anyway!" He started for Kate and almost lost a hand for his effort. Cooper had never seen Clancy even seriously growl, but this dog meant business. Every tooth was showing, and the hair on the back of Clancy's neck stood straight up.

"Are you crazy?" Cooper looked at the paramedic in alarm. "He's just checking to see if Kate's okay." He walked cautiously toward the dog. "Hey Clancy. She's all right. You saved her, boy." Clancy eyed him. "I know you can't be tricked. She's really fine. They've got to take her to the doctor and check out her breathing." Now everyone was staring at him as though he was crazy. Maybe he was. But he kept on talking. "Let Kate say good-bye for now. You can come home with me. I promise you can see her in the morning."

Clancy looked back at Kate. She slipped the mask off her face. "Go on, Clancy. I promise I'll see you in the morning."

Clancy sat down, and looked toward Cooper. Cooper

looked for Cayden and saw her standing on the fringe of the scene. "Go with Cayden and get in the car. I'll be there after I say good-bye."

"Come on Clancy. I'll sit in the car with you." Cayden called softly.

Clancy nuzzled Kate one more time, and with an uneasy whine, he obeyed.

Cooper stooped down. "Thank God you're safe. I was so scared."

"Me too." Kate began to cry again. "What am I going to do?"

"We'll figure it out in the morning. Just do what the doctors tell you to. I'll take care of everything, I promise."

He kissed her forehead, squeezed her hand and stood. He looked for a paramedic. "Is she really gonna be okay?"

"Yeah. Just a little smoke inhalation. They will want to keep her overnight, let a doc check her out to make sure. But if I were you, I'd show up by eight so she can go home." He glanced at the smoldering house. "Well, go somewhere besides the hospital."

Cooper's next stop was a fireman. "Do you know what started the fire?"

He squinted at the house. "All we know right now is it started in that back room."

"That's the sunroom."

"Right. Started at the fireplace. Probably a burning ember escaped."

Cooper remembered telling Kate to be sure to put the fire screen back up. He shook his head. No point in blaming anyone now. But she sure would be upset when she found out her own carelessness was the cause of her house burning down. Cooper thanked the exhausted fireman and headed for the car.

"Cooper!" he turned. It was Mrs. Peabody.

He smiled at her red sweatshirt and hot pink sweat pants. Her fuzzy blue slippers were ruined amidst the nasty water that was running down into the yard. "Hey, Mrs. Peabody. Thanks for keeping Clancy."

"Oh, he's the one that came barking to my door. Would not shut up. I was so mad at him by the time I got to the door I was going to smack him with my shoe. But then I smelled smoke and called the fire department instead. He was carrying on something awful and I was afraid Kate was still in the house. She's all right, isn't she?"

"They say she'll be fine. Just a little smoke inhalation, but nothing serious." He stretched. "Thanks again. I'm gonna call it a night."

"What is she going to do, poor thing?"

"I told her not to worry, I'd take care of everything. She'll just have to stay at my house until she can rent an apartment or something. Cayden's there too, so it won't be inappropriate."

"You're a fine man to take all that on, Cooper."

He shrugged. "Kate and Clancy won't be too hard to take care of."

"And the babies of course." Mrs. Peabody patted him on the arm and turned to leave.

Cooper couldn't move. He'd been turned to stone.

He had forgotten all about the babies!

Reaching the house, he told Cayden to take Clancy in and get him a bowl of water. "If he'll eat it, give him a dog biscuit. I keep a supply of them in the pantry to make sure he has a surprise when I take Kate food. I'm not going to be able to sleep anyway." He ran his hand across the stubble on his face. He smelled like smoke. "Look, I'll go to the grocery store and get some dog food, then I'm going to run by the hospital and check on Kate." His chin trembled a little and Cayden felt a thrill of fear go through her. She hadn't seen Cooper tear up much since their parents had died. "I can't stand thinking she'll be there all night alone."

"I understand," Cayden said softly. "Clancy and I will be fine." Clancy whined, looking anxiously back into the car.

"It's okay, Clancy." Cooper said. "I'm going to see Kate. I'll bring her back."

With that, Clancy stood at Cayden's side. Cooper made sure they were in the house before he drove off. He wasn't going to mention babies to Kate, but if that was on her mind with everything else, he had to let her know they would work it out.

Together.

CHAPTER THIRTEEN

Getting permission from the nurse, he slipped quietly into Kate's room, hoping she was asleep. But she turned a tear streaked face toward him as he walked in. Smiling weakly, he walked over and pushed a strand of hair behind her ear.

"What are you doing here?" her voice was raspy from the smoke.

"There's this bossy mutt at my house demanding dog food and I was just passing by."

"Uh-huh." She reached out for his hand. "I don't want you out in the middle of the night. I'm fine."

"I'm sure you are. But, then, what are these?" He traced the tear stains down her face.

"Just feeling a little sorry for myself. I can do that alone."

"Ah, I'm so thankful you're here to feel a little self pity." Cooper took a deep breath. "Nothing matters but that."

"I'm grateful." Her lower lip trembled and tears spilt out, once again wetting her cheeks. "But what about the babies?"

"We'll take care of them. All of us will help you."

"I don't mean that. I mean what if they won't let me have them now? I can't stand to think about it!"

Cooper hadn't even considered that a possibility. He looked bewildered. "Surely this won't make a difference. I mean, their mother said you were to have them, and you've agreed. She didn't say where you lived mattered. How could they say no?"

She gave a derisive laugh. "Where will I be housing them? How will I care for them now? I had all these plans and things in order, and all that's gone."

"That's not true, Kate. The only thing gone is your house. Nothing else has changed." He took a deep breath. "I have a big house. Two bedrooms are empty, so it's simple. One for you, one for the twins."

"Are you kidding me? If any of my house is salvageable, and I don't know if it is, it will take months to get it livable. Cooper, you're a bachelor, used to looking after a teenager and yourself. I can't imagine you're ready for a woman, a set of twin babies and a one hundred sixty-eight pound spoiled dog to move in."

"You're right. I'm not ready. But I'm not ready to let anything other than that happen, either. Kate, everyone has rallied around you; there will be plenty of help with the babies. You've already got time off coming, you've got all the financial things figured out. None of the babies' stuff had been brought over yet, right?"

"Thank God for that." Kate said softly. "There are only a few things they have left from their mother too, and I haven't been given any of it." She sniffed. "Wouldn't it have been terrible if they'd given me the few things left from that family and it had burned up?"

"Yes." Cooper thought of another thing. "And you and Anna haven't shopped. No nursery things have been purchased."

"That's true too. God was looking out after us, wasn't

He?"

"Yep. And don't think for a minute He won't continue to do so. Come on, Kate, let it be settled. Everyone's coming to my house." He smiled at her tenderly. "Please?"

She sighed. "All right. But first, I guess I need to find out if the adoption placement is still on. I've got Len Sherry's phone number somewhere." Suddenly she burst into to tears. "I don't have anything somewhere! It's all gone."

Cooper held her while she sobbed, her body shaking. "I'm so afraid, Cooper."

He stroked her hair. "I know. But I'm here. I'm not going anywhere. I'll sit right in this chair tonight, and take you home in the morning. And I mean that, Kate. Home. To my house. Home." She nodded slightly, and he held her till she fell asleep.

CHAPTER FOURTEEN

The doctor, after discharging Kate, exited the room. Kate was in the bathroom getting dressed when the door opened again. Cayden stepped in, grinning. "Does she get to go home?"

"Yes, she's getting dressed right now. What are you doing here?"

Cayden dangled keys in front of Cooper's face, annoying him, as only Cayden could do.

"These are Kate's keys. A fireman moved her car as soon as they got there and put it in Mrs. Peabody's garage. It's not hurt at all."

"Thank you God!" Cooper said. At some point in the night while he watched Kate sleep, it occurred to him she might not have a car either.

"And guess what I found in the front seat?"

"Just tell me Cayden. I'm tired."

She looked a little crestfallen, and he felt a stab of guilt. She was just excited about good news. He stood up and gave her a hug. "Sorry. I've been up all night and it's made me grumpy."

" More than usual." Cayden mumbled. She sighed, but continued. "I found pictures of the babies with their mother and the brother."

Kate entered the room. "Hey, Cayden. What brings you here?"

Cayden repeated the good news. Kate grinned and

reached in her sweat pants pocket and pulled out her cell phone. "I didn't even know I had this on me. Cooper, remember the pictures I showed you last night of me and the twins? They're in here! They didn't get ruined."

The door opened once again and a strange man stood just inside the door. "Miss Roe? I'm Captain Joshua Farmer from the fire department."

Kate walked over and shook his hand, then hugged his neck, much to the man's embarrassment. "Thank you so much for doing what you did for me last night."

"Well, you're welcome. It's my job." He cleared his throat, still blushing. "I wanted to update you on your home's situation. The back is totally gone. I'm afraid there may be so much smoke and water damage you won't be able to retrieve much of anything. I do have hopes for the basement area. We'll get everything cleared up today, and you can go over late this afternoon after we're sure there aren't any more hotspots or danger areas. Is there anything particular you want us to look for when we're going through the house? Valuables of any kind?"

Kate thought for a minute. "My mother's wedding rings are in a jewelry box in my bedroom, it's the only valuable jewelry I have. If you see any pictures..." she began to tear up, knowing that it wasn't likely. Kate cleared her throat. "The basement area is good news. I have an old cedar trunk down there with two quilts that were my grandmother's that I hadn't got out yet this fall. Maybe they'll be okay."

"We'll be sure to look for those things first."

"Oh! And my purse!" Kate's face fell. "But I have no idea where I might have left it."

"It was on the couch in the living room when I left your house last night." Cooper said.

"That's right. Can you look there, Captain Farmer?" Kate asked.

"Sure. But I doubt it will be salvageable. That's where a lot of water damage is. But maybe we can rescue it and there'll be enough of it left for you to identify things in it you will need to replace." He started to go, but then turned back. "The City Police have been guarding your house all night, and they'll stay there till my men get on the job, in about ten minutes."

"Thank you so much." Kate hugged him again, he blushed even more than the first time, and then he was gone.

She turned to Cooper and Cayden. "Let's get out of here. I want to see Clancy, and call Mr. Sherry about my babies." She looked at Cayden. "Cayden, you lifted my spirits so much about the car! I just assumed, when I finally thought about it, that the car was gone too. How did they get it moved?"

Cayden shrugged. "I guess the keys were in it, 'cause Mrs. Peabody had them."

"I must have left them in it when I got out my purse. I was so nervous about showing you the twins' pictures I didn't know what I was doing."

Cooper looked uncomfortable. "Kate, I'm afraid that's not all you forgot to do."

She looked puzzled. "What do you mean?"

"The fire started at the fireplace. The fireman I talked to last night said maybe an ember escaped."

"No way! I put the fire screen back, Cooper! I made

sure the Windex was dry, and then wiped it off again. I put our marshmallow sticks in there and decided I'd clean it all up when the embers were cold. But I made sure the fire screen was in place."

Cooper looked thoughtful. "So you left marshmallow sticks in the fireplace, behind the fire screen?"

They looked at one another and yelled, "Clancy!" at the same time.

"You two are just weird." Cayden said, gazing at them in fascination.

"Cooper, how could I have been so stupid? I knew he was up to something when I went to bed last night, because he wouldn't come upstairs with me. He just lay at the foot of the steps and curled up. That rascal was planning it the whole time!"

"I guess we'll know if the firemen can tell us where the fire screen was when they got in there. Now it makes sense that Clancy was able to get you awake and out in time. I couldn't figure out why he was at Mrs. Peabody's, other than to sound the call for help. But I think after he turned over the fire screen he hid out because he was ashamed. I guess fear overtook shame after a while and he was in a panic when he woke you and that's when he went over to Mrs. Peabody's instead of staying with you once you were both outside."

Kate let out an aggravated GRRRR. "That sounds exactly like that furry idiot. Lassie, he ain't. Wait till I get my hands on him!"

"Well, he is a dumb animal, Kate. He didn't know what would happen, any more than a little kid would have understood the consequences. And he loves you. At least he did the right thing, even if it was accidental. He's suffered from being so worried about you." Cooper looked shocked. "I cannot believe I just took up for that dog!"

Cayden spoke up. "He's stayed right by my side all night and whined in his sleep. He wouldn't even eat the dog biscuit." She looked alarmed. "Oh! He's in the car, waiting. I told him to be good and I'd be right out."

"I'm ready." Kate said. "And I'm not really mad at him. It could have been so much worse." She turned to Cooper. "If it's okay, I want Cayden to drive my car back to your house and I'll ride with you. Cayden, if you'll loan me some unsmokey smelling clothes, I'll get cleaned up and go see what's left of my house."

"Sure. But please let Clancy ride with ya'll. I don't think he could stand it otherwise."

Cooper nodded in agreement as they left to sign Kate out.

And Clancy was one happy dog to see his Kate.

CHAPTER FIFTEEN

On the way home Kate contacted Len Sherry and gave him the news. He expressed shock and sympathy, but assured Kate if she had living arrangements fit for babies, there would be no problem with the placement going through as scheduled. Kate gave him Cooper's address so the social worker could come there instead of Kate's home.

The next call was to Anna who promised she and Bailey would meet them at Kate's house when given the word.

As soon as they got to Cooper's, Kate took a quick shower in an attempt to wash off the smoky smell that seemed imbedded in her skin. Cayden found her some underwear, socks, old sweats and a ratty pair of sneakers. As Kate pulled her hair back into a ponytail, she looked at her reflection. She didn't look that different than she had twenty-four hours ago. But, oh my, things were sure different.

She bounced down the stairs and Cooper hollered at her from the kitchen. Clancy was lying at Cooper's feet, but jumped up running when he saw Kate. He leaned into her with his eyes closed, as though grateful for her presence. She smiled down at the dog and stroked his head. Looking up at Cooper, who had just taken a big bite of sandwich, she asked, "Are you ready to go?"

"No. And you're not either." He pointed to a plate

across from him with food on it. "I know when we get over there it will be hard for you to leave. So I want you to eat now."

"What kind is it?" She peered at the sandwich and glass of milk.

"Turkey. It's good, I made it myself."

"I guess you're right. I need to eat something." She pulled the stool out and sat down. "Where's Cayden?"

"Her new beau called and said if she'd come to his house and leave her car, they could borrow his dad's truck so we could haul some stuff over here if we needed to."

"That's sweet of him! Mickey, right?"

"Mikey. But I think he's growing outta that. I call him Mike. And he does seem to be a good kid." Cooper dropped a bite of sandwich, which Clancy caught in mid-air. "Good catch!"

"If you feed him from the table, he won't be able to get through the back door." Kate took another bite of sandwich. "This is good, Coop. Thanks."

"Eh, there's plenty more where that came from." He grinned. "I'm probably the world's best sandwich maker. I don't cook very well, but Cayden and I have made do over the years. We ain't starved, anyway."

"Well, you know I love to cook. I'll cook as much as I can while I'm here."

"Thanks. But with two babies, we might do sandwiches a lot more than we expect. Which will be fine." He reached over and put a hand over Kate's. "You know it's gonna be pretty bad over there," he said, changing the subject. "I've seen places the morning after a fire, and it's worse in some ways than when it was burning."

Signs From God

She sighed. "I know. I dread it. But I'm hopeful some stuff will be salvageable. If I get all emotional, cover for me, okay?"

"Sure. I'll tell 'em you got something in your eye."

Looking at her watch, she slugged down the last of her milk and pushed the stool back. "Let's go. It's not gonna get any better. Are Cayden and Mike meeting us there?"

"Yeah. I told them to give us a half hour and go on over. I called Bailey and let him know they could come on too. What do you want to do with Clancy?"

"Take him with us." Kate's voice trembled. "He's got to say good-bye too."

🐾 🐾 🐾 🐾

Parking across the street from her property, Kate began to choke up as soon as she stepped out of the car. Anna and Bailey were there, and Anna immediately took her friend into her arms.

"Pretty bad, huh?" Kate asked. Dabbing at her eyes, she stepped back.

"Oh, honey, I had no idea. They won't let us over there yet."

Both of them turned and gazed at the smoking remains. The front of the house was still standing, but half way down the roof line, the top of the house was gone. Smoke was curling lazily up toward the clouds behind the house. Shrubbery was trampled, the grass matted in places and dug up in others. The crime scene tape roped off the entire property. Kate saw a trunk and a covered clothes rack sitting on the driveway concrete pad and she felt a little surge of relief that something seemed to still be intact that belonged to her. Cooper and Bailey crossed the street and stepped over the yellow tape as Cayden and Mike pulled up in his father's truck.

"Oh, wow." Was all Mike said as they exited the truck. He looked shyly at Kate and bobbed his head. "Sorry about all this. I hope I can be of help with my dad's truck."

Kate smiled a little. "I appreciate your thoughtfulness, Mike. Maybe there'll be stuff to put in the back of it."

They all followed Cooper and Bailey across the street. Captain Farmer emerged from the back of the house. Taking off his hard hat, he shook hands with the men. Turning to Kate he sighed heavily. "We're gonna let you come in the front door. You can't go up the stairs or further than the front of the living room. It's okay to go into the kitchen area and see if there's anything you can salvage. It's pretty wet in there, but I think you might could save some pots and pans or something that didn't get broken." He glanced at the driveway. "We brought up the trunk you asked about. I looked inside and stuff's okay. The rack is zipped up, and the clothes stored in there seem okay too. Your purse is in pretty sad shape, but I laid it over there by the trunk. Maybe you can take it apart and let stuff air dry." He looked her eye to eye. "I wish there was more. We got here as soon as we could, and did all we could."

"You saved my life. I won't complain. I owe you gratitude." She looked at Cooper. "I want to look at the stuff they saved first, then let's go inside."

They were stopped dead in their tracks by an unearthly wail that seemed to come from the ground itself. "What the-" The hair on the back of Cooper's neck stood straight up.

Clancy's head was hanging out the car window. He howled. He looked at the house, and howled again. Kate rushed to him and opened the door. He sat on the ground and with his head thrown back. He seemed to mourn their loss and his mistake with grief stricken cries. For a moment, they stood frozen by the big dog as he cried his heart out.

When Kate stooped down by him, he looked in her eyes and placed one paw on her knee. "It's okay, Clancy. We all make mistakes." She took his head in her arms. "I love you still." He snuffled her hair and, resting his head on her shoulder, sighed deeply.

Kate looked around at everyone and saw that Mrs. Peabody had joined the group. She was wiping her eyes with the tip of her collar, which jutted straight out as though pointing the way forward. "May Clancy stay with you while we go in the house?"

"Of course, dear. He and I have become friends, haven't we, doggie?"

Freed from guilt, Clancy gave Kate an accusing stare before he ambled on over with Mrs. Peabody into her house. Kate grinned. She figured people could learn a lot from Clancy. Howl at the mess, then get on with life.

She squared her shoulders. "Let's get on with it."

"Is it okay if me and the guys go on in?" Cooper asked. "I won't touch anything."

"Sure. We'll be in, in a minute."

Kate opened the trunk and lovingly touched the old quilt. She picked the top one up and sniffed. There was a faint smoke odor, but not bad. She handed it over to Cayden and picked up the next one. No smell at all. To her surprise, underneath the quilts lay two flannel gowns and a pair of fleece lined moccasins. "This is a pleasant surprise.

I don't even remember putting these in here." She put the quilts back, thinking how her grandmother had worked so diligently on the double wedding ring and the log cabin designs. She sent a thankful prayer upward for their safety. She walked over to the rack and unzipped the liner. Two wool suits, with pants and skirts and her heavy winter coat. Draped over one of the jackets was her good slip. At the bottom of the liner lay her winter dress boots. "Well," she turned to Cayden and Anna. "I have more than I thought I would."

"Here's what's left of your purse." Cayden was pointing to a crumpled soggy mess. Kate squatted down and opened it up.

"Ewww. This smells awful!" She carefully took out the wallet and pulled three twenty dollar bills, a ten and two ones out. They were damp and smelly, but still in one piece. Her change purse had several coins in it and she spread them out on the concrete. Driver's license and credit card were not too wet, but other than that, all else appeared lost. Her brush stunk so much she didn't even want to salvage it. "Not bad, though. I don't have to get a driver's license." She looked at it carefully. "Great. It expired on my birthday. I can't believe I forgot to renew! And they didn't even say anything when they copied it for the adoption application!"

Anna laughed. "Have no fear, I'll take you this week and get it renewed."

Kate tucked the money under the trunk lid so it would dry and not blow away. "Let's go inside and see how bad it really is."

"Aren't you afraid someone will steal your money?"

Signs From God

Cayden asked.

"Nah." Kate nodded her head toward Mrs. Peabody's house. They turned and saw a curtain move imperceptibly.

Giggling, they walked toward the house.

Any lightheartedness Kate might have been feeling was cut stone cold as she gazed at the remains of her home. Cooper came toward her and put his arm around her shoulder. "It's gonna be okay. Don't forget that."

She nodded slightly, not believing it for an instant. The stench almost took her breath away. Everything was in ruins. How could she have even entertained a thought that she could come in and save something the firemen couldn't?

"Miss Roe?" She turned. It was Captain Farmer. "I went through an upstairs window and retrieved this." He handed her a soaked jewelry box.

She opened it slowly and saw her mother's wedding rings amid all the costume jewelry.

"Most of the cheap stuff will need to be thrown away, but I think your mom's stuff is good."

"Thank you." She whispered. She fingered through the junk and picked out the two rings. Slipping them on her own fingers, she was aware of how merciful God was being to her. Just when she was overcome with grief, a blessing was handed to her.

She put the jewelry box on the floor and walked over to the cabinets. Many of the doors had been flown open and broken dishes and glasses were everywhere. Opening the drawers, she pulled out all the flatware, spatulas, cooking spoons and knives. Stinky, wet, but salvageable. Pots and pans, ditto. Small electrical appliances, ruined. Cooper managed to get a warped lower cabinet door open. A few mixing bowls were intact. Much to her surprise, her favorite serving bowl was sitting, unharmed. She vaguely remembered sitting it under there instead of up on top and was glad she'd done so.

Her collection of hand woven baskets, pictures, paper goods, gone. All gone. She looked around her. What a mess! She closed her eyes and tried to focus on what was saved, not what was lost.

Cooper was loading stuff in a plastic laundry basket he'd found next to the couch. "I don't know where this came from, but it'll be good to use to haul stuff home." He patted Kate on the shoulder. "Anything else we can take?"

"I think we all need to take a good bath! I don't think I've ever smelled this bad." She wrinkled her nose. "Let's make sure none of this stuff goes straight into your house. Maybe we can use the water hose outside on this stuff first, and then put it straight in the dishwasher."

"Hey!" Cayden exclaimed. "Have you looked in this dishwasher?"

"No, I hadn't thought of that." She walked over and pulled on the door. As the rack began to slide out, she caught it. There were two glasses, two plates, two salad bowls and the same amount of forks. "So much for our supper we enjoyed." She looked at Cooper. "I didn't have enough dirty dishes to run the dishwasher, but I loaded what few we had used."

Cooper lifted the dirty dishes and added them to the top of the laundry basket.

They all surveyed the area, hopeful something else had been spared. Anna found a vase on the book shelf, Bailey found a soggy checkbook that was half way under the couch.

"I wonder where my book satchel is with all my school work in it." It was the first time Kate had even thought about it.

"It's in the back seat of your car," Cayden replied. "I thought I told you. Sorry."

"What a relief!" Kate sighed. "One less thing to worry about." Looking around one last time, she said, "Well, I think we're done here. Let's go."

Outside again, Captain Farmer waited on them. "Is there anything else you want to ask me?" He looked exhausted, and Kate knew he was ready to call it a day.

"I appreciate you staying and waiting. Will I be able to go upstairs?"

"No, Miss Roe. It's too far gone. I didn't dare walk on the floor, myself. I just saw the jewelry box on top of the dresser and used a hook to get it to the window."

"Is there any way to rescue the dresser?"

"If the floor goes, and I expect it to, you can come back and see what survives the fall. But I don't think there's anything in it. The back wall is burned pretty badly, and I suspect that means the back of the dresser is at least scorched. And the water damage is severe. Sheetrock from the ceiling is laying everywhere, on top of everything. I promise, if we see anything that even seems remotely salvageable, I'll call you."

"Thank you. This seems like a bad dream. I hate to keep asking you stuff, but my mind can't accept that one minute everything was intact, and the next minute it's in ruins."

"I know. I understand. Don't worry about it. Has your insurance agent called yet?"

Cayden spoke up. "She called earlier, and said she'd try to meet us here." She turned to Kate. "That's another thing I forgot." She dropped her eyes, waiting to hear Cooper light into her, but he didn't.

"Well, she's not here, is she?" Kate asked no one in particular. "I'll give her a call when we get back to the house. I'm too tired to stay any longer."

Mike and Bailey had just about finished loading the truck when the rest of them turned to the task. "Thank you guys so much," Kate said to them. "I can't seem to get it together enough to do anything."

"Here, Miss Kate." Mike handed her the money. "It was stuck in the trunk lid."

"We were drying it out. I can guarantee ya'll, this money will be spent quickly, it stinks!" She stuffed it in her pants pocket. "I'll retrieve Clancy and we can go."

She hugged Anna and Bailey, who insisted on stopping and bringing a pizza over. Mike and Anna left, saying they'd start the unloading as soon as they got there.

Cooper and Kate knocked on Mrs. Peabody's door, and she opened it quickly. Clancy was laid out in the floor, feet in the air, snoring loudly. "Come in, come in." She sniffed. "Never mind. You smell too bad. No offence. But you do!" She turned kind eyes to Kate. "Were you able to save anything, hon?"

"Not much." Kate reviewed what she had left. "But at least some of it was precious to me."

"Well, I certainly hope you have sufficient insurance."

"Enough to pay off my mortgage and a little left over, I

hope. To be honest, I can't even remember." Her voice started sounding wobbly, and Cooper gave Mrs. Peabody a warning glance.

She cleared her throat. "I'm sure it'll be all right dear, in the end. Now, even though we won't be neighbors, I still want to be a part of helping out with those sweet babies of yours. I mean that."

"I know you do, and as soon as we get everything figured out, I'll be calling on you."

Waking Clancy (who was fake snoring and watching her every move) and climbing into the car, Kate felt she had done all she could possibly do for the rest of the day.

CHAPTER SIXTEEN

As they were walking in the door, the phone rang, and Cooper immediately handed it to her. It was the insurance adjuster. Kate kept trying to focus on what the woman was saying. "It looks like you have enough to pay off the house with about eight thousand dollars left over. You also have coverage for the contents." She heard a frown in the woman's voice. "Not very much, though. Ten thousand dollars is all you have?"

"Yes," Kate answered. "I don't – didn't – have a lot of content. I've only lived in the house a few years, and started out with very little. I've gradually paid for a few pieces of furniture. I have pictures in my safe deposit box, like the insurance man told me to do."

"Excellent! That will help a lot. Perhaps you'll be able to get most of your content money because of that."

They talked on a few minutes, Kate feeling wearier by each of those minutes. They were agreeing to meet on Monday when Bailey and Anna arrived with the pizza. Kate quickly finished the conversation as her stomach growled in response to the aroma of the food.

"That smells so good!" Kate exclaimed. "Let me wash up a little and I'll be ready to eat."

As she exited, Anna turned to Cooper. "Who was that, if I may ask?"

"Insurance adjuster. Kate looks like she's gonna fall over and she's trying to talk business. I hope she can get some rest tonight. I'm going to suggest she stay home from church in the morning and sleep in. If anyone ever had a legitimate excuse, it's Kate."

"It's Kate, what?" Kate asked as she came back into the kitchen.

"Layin' out of church." Bailey said cheerfully. "Coop's just looking for an excuse not to go."

"I said Kate, not me, bird brain. You want me to miss so you'll win the perfect attendance in Bible Study."

Kate and Anna shook their heads. Kate said, "Can we bless this food so I can eat before my face falls into it?"

After the blessing, Cooper asked her about the insurance phone call. "She's coming over here Monday to discuss everything. Then I guess if I need to, I'll go back over to the house with her."

"Don't forget the social worker is coming Monday." Cooper reminded her.

"What time?"

"Cayden said she was coming at two. I wrote it on the calendar."

"Speaking of, where are Cayden and Mike?"

"They were gonna run by the hardware store and pick up some tools for me in case I need to put baby stuff together."

Anna asked, "When are the babies coming?"

"Well, first, I hope to see them tomorrow afternoon. I called and left a message for Mrs. Stonefield to see if I could visit. I want to see them, if only for a few minutes. I thought Cooper might like to go too." She hadn't meant to spring it on him in front of everyone, but she was so tired, it just came out.

He grinned. "I'd love to. I hope she calls back and says yes."

"Anyway, after the social worker visits Monday, I am hoping we can get them according to schedule."

"Are we still shopping for baby stuff Tuesday?" Anna asked.

Dismayed, Kate looked at her friend. "I'd forgotten all about it, but I still want to." She rested her head on Cooper's shoulder. "I feel like Thursday and yesterday were a million years ago."

"I called John Donaldson and talked to him," Cooper said. "He got hold of the superintendent and both said for me not to worry about Monday. That way I can run errands for you while you settle in."

"Thanks so much, Cooper. I'm a little overwhelmed right now."

Anna gave Bailey a meaningful glance. Bailey cleared his throat. "Well, we need to go. Got a lot to do." They stood. "If you make it to church, we'll see you tomorrow. If not, you know all of us will be praying for you."

Kate stood and hugged them both. "Thanks guys. That means everything to me."

As the door closed, Cooper turned to Kate. "You, my dear, need to go to bed. You're beyond exhausted. If Mrs. Stonefield calls back, she can tell me if we will be able to visit the babies tomorrow. If anyone else calls to offer condolences, I'll take the message. When Cayden and Mike get back, we'll unload your stuff. You can put your quilts and clothes upstairs in your room when you get up." He took her in his arms. "Have I left anything out?"

She snuggled close to him. "I have no idea. My brain

has shut down. I just want a bath and the bed." She looked up suddenly. "Even if I want to go to church tomorrow, I don't have anything to wear."

Cooper grinned. "Ain't that just like a woman? They never have a thing to wear."

"Smart remarks like that can get you locked out of the house."

"Tell me about it." They both laughed. "I'm sure Cayden can let you borrow something that doesn't look too adolescent. And don't feel bad if you don't go. Missing one Sunday won't hurt."

"I know. But I may need people."

"Understandable. Now, go take that bath and rest."

He kissed the top of her head and she left to do just that.

🐾 🐾 🐾 🐾

After her night's rest, Kate felt a need to see her fellow members. So, donning some of Cayden's 'less adolescent' clothing, they made it to Bible Study and the church services. Kate was glad she had made the effort to attend. Everyone was so kind and they had a special prayer time lifting her up to the Lord for strength.

When they arrived home, there was a voice mail from Mrs. Stonefield asking if they could come by and see the babies around four that afternoon.

On the way over, Kate warned Cooper about Genevieve. "She's – ummm – quite enthusiastic. And loud. And she also gets into your personal space. That may be because of her age or because she's not from this culture."

Cooper looked alarmed. "What culture is she from, exactly?"

"Mrs. Stonefield told me she has been raised in the

upper crust of London's finest. However; her nanny has a very heavy cockney accent, which she's picked up. Mrs. Stonefield stays Genevieve only uses it to impress people or really irritate her parents. And her little sisters' nanny was from Scotland, so she throws in some of that brogue occasionally."

"Good lord!" Cooper exclaimed. "What if the twins take after all that?"

Kate giggled. "Sparrow can take on a Scotsman's brogue and Wren can sound like a cockney street urchin."

"Boy, I'm really looking forward to this visit."

Knocking instead of using the doorbell, in case the babies were asleep, Kate felt excited to see the children again. Mrs. Stonefield welcomed them as she walked them into the living room.

"The babies are asleep, but they'll awaken within a few minutes." She smiled. "They rarely are late, they don't want to miss a meal. So, I thought it would be nice for you to be here and get the opportunity to help with feeding."

Kate looked around. "It's awfully quiet. Aren't you missing someone?"

"Ah, yes, Genevieve you mean. She's visiting a cousin for the weekend. They are about the same age and have become very close."

Cooper looked relieved and Kate nudged him in the ribs to keep him from saying anything. About that time two cries simultaneously arose from the back room. "And they're awake. Would you like to come back with me?"

Kate and Cooper didn't have to be asked twice. The babies were small enough that Mrs. Stonefield had them side by side in the same baby bed. They immediately stopped crying as soon as they heard them coming into the room. Kate looked down into the crib and her heart began to beat faster. "Hello, little girls. How are you this afternoon?" she crooned to them.

Cooper felt tears sting his eyes at the sound of Kate's voice. He looked down at the babies, who were staring at Kate, and he felt an incredible chill rush over his body. These babies looked so much like Kate! He thought. Then he looked again and swallowed big. Except for the hair. They had his hair…

🐾 🐾 🐾 🐾

The few hours they spent with the twins had been busy and fun. Mrs. Stonefield insisted Kate change their diapers, while Cooper looked on in mock horror at the mess. They each took a baby to feed, and when Cooper found out he was feeding Sparrow, he said he knew it all along.

Mrs. Stonefield expressed sympathy to Kate about the fire. She assured Kate, that as far as she knew, the placement was still right on schedule. "It looks to me, if the social worker visit goes well, these little ones will be in your arms on Thursday." She patted Kate's knee as she looked uncertain. "Don't worry, dear. I'm still going to visit and help out as promised, and I understand you have a built in baby-sitter with Cooper's sister."

"She's eager to help. I'll pay her, too, although she insists not. My neighbor, or rather my ex-neighbor, Mrs. Peabody, has agreed to help out too. She's raised her own children, but they live far away. She tells me this will help ease the loneliness of not having grandchildren close by."

"Everything will work out fine. You'll get the hang of being mama right away. I've seen it happen many times."

Kate looked down at the baby in her arms. Wren stared

back at her, eyes wide. Her little hands were wrapped around Kate's, who was holding the bottle. Kate smiled. "I can see how that happens, myself."

After a tearful good-bye and a slow trip home, Kate had taken a before supper nap. Cooper made sandwiches and they had coffee on the porch, Clancy between them. He had sniffed them thoroughly when they got home, and Kate had wished she'd remembered to get another baby smelling blanket from Mrs. Stonefield.

"Well, let's see, this is Sunday. Tonight and three more, then welcome to day care. So enjoy that coffee, sweetheart. We may be nearing the end of carefree evenings."

Kate smiled. "I guess you're right. I'm looking forward to it, scared half to death about it, and somewhat selfish to give this up."

They talked some more about what tomorrow entailed. Cooper agreed to go to the bank and get the house pictures out of Kate's safe deposit box for her, since he had to be out anyway to go by the school. He reminded Kate of the social worker coming at two. Kate could not honestly remember if the insurance lady had said she'd call or come by on Monday, so Kate made a mental note to call their office when they opened.

With a chaste smooch and a holler good-night to Cayden, Kate was asleep almost before her head hit the pillow.

Little did she know how much she was going to need a good nights' rest.

CHAPTER SEVENTEEN

Cooper was dreaming that he was in a dark hole and the more he struggled to move, the more entrapped he became. He awoke with a start and found that he truly could not move. Perplexed, he tried to sit up, and struggling with all his might, he managed an elbow up to peer about him. Clancy, dead weight and sound asleep, was on top of the covers, up against most of Cooper's legs and all his body. "You!" Cooper hissed. "You stupid mutt, get off my bed!"

Not even an eyelid twitched.

With a great heave, Cooper managed to sit the rest of the way up. He felt his temper boil. He got on his knees and pushed Clancy until he rolled him onto the floor. The dog dramatically fell over as if shot, then started snoring loudly.

"Oh, no, you don't. You are not sleeping in my room." Cooper became silent for a minute. "How the heck did you get in here? I had the door shut, I'm sure of it." He set his mouth in a firm line. "Who let you in here? I bet it was Cayden. I'm gonna kill her."

He got out of bed, and stepping over the 'sleeping' dog, he grabbed sweatpants and went to his bedroom door. It was slightly ajar. He opened it the rest of the way and peered into the hallway. No one stirred, and glancing at the hall clock, it was no wonder. It was three a.m. The house was quiet. Cooper stood there and scratched his head. He really didn't want to wake up anybody and do some sort of crazed investigation in the middle of the night. He sighed, resigned. He'd just have to let Clancy sleep on his bedside rug till in the morning.

Then somebody was gonna get it!

He turned and went back to his room, yawning.

Clancy was in the middle of the bed, covers drawn over him, snoring softly.

Kate stepped into the shower and closed her eyes. The water felt good, but she hardly noticed as her mind was in a whirlwind. She simply had to get hold of the insurance adjuster this morning! What was going on with that? She couldn't for the life of her remember what time the lady was supposed to show up today. She would have to call and check when she got out. She just hoped it wasn't at two. There was no way she could handle insurance and social work people at the same time. At least Cooper was going to pick up the pictures of the contents of her house from the safe deposit box. She hoped that would expedite getting an insurance check.

Oh, and she had to ask Cayden to make sure Clancy was at Mrs. Peabody's when the social worker came at two today. She didn't think she had it in her to keep Clancy and his opinions away from the social worker.

And what in the name of goodness was up with Cooper this morning? Going on and on at the breakfast table about Clancy being in his bed! She could not figure out how Clancy had opened her bedroom door. She was sure she'd closed it firmly so he couldn't wander the house during the night. And Cooper was adamant someone had to have opened his bedroom door to let Clancy in, because he knew for sure his door was fastened tight.

Kate's thoughts stopped cold. A dreadful picture entered her mind of Clancy figuring out how to turn a door knob with his big old mouth. She shook her head. Surely not! But she'd check for dried dog slobber on her door knob, just in case.

As she stepped out of the shower, someone knocked on the bathroom door. Wrapping a towel around her hair, she called, "Yes?"

"It's me." Cayden called. "The insurance adjuster is on the phone."

"Oh, thanks!" Kate opened the door. "I'll talk to them right now." Cayden handed her the phone and closed the door.

Kate adjusted the towel on her hair, and slipped into her heavy terry cloth robe. "Hello?"

"Hello, Miss Roe. This is Tina from your insurance company. I'm sorry to have to reschedule this afternoon, but I have a family thing that's come up. Could I come this morning instead?"

"Actually, that would be better, Tina. Cooper has gone to the bank for me to get those pictures, but he should be back in an hour or so. Would that be all right?"

"That would be fine. I'll see you between eleven and eleven fifteen."

Kate disconnected the phone and began to towel dry her hair a little. She was thinking about clothes when someone knocked on her bedroom door.

Cayden cracked the door. "Kate, the social worker is here."

"What?" Kate cried. She looked at the clock. "It's only

ten o'clock!"

Cayden had tears in her eyes. "It's my fault, Kate. I thought she said two when she must have said ten. And, um, Mrs. Peabody is here too. She was coming in the back door as the social worker was coming in the front. But she said she'd stay in the kitchen."

"To eavesdrop," Kate muttered. "Well, it can't be helped. I'll be down as soon as I finish dressing." She gasped. "Cayden, where's Clancy?"

"Ummm, he's sitting on the social worker's feet with his head in her lap. I couldn't get him to move."

"How's she taking it?" Kate chewed on her lower lip.

"Well, she looked a little alarmed at first, but she said she liked dogs and had one herself, so it was okay for me to leave the room and get you."

"All I can say is I'm thankful the social worker has a dog. What a relief. Tell her I'll be down in five."

"Will do." Cayden turned to leave. "Oh, and Kate, what's a 'teacup' poodle?"

Kate closed her eyes for a minute. "Oh, lord." She pulled a sweater over her head and grabbed her jeans. "Tell her I'll be down in two."

Practically flying down the stairs, Kate found the social worker cooing to Clancy, who looked at her moon eyed. He had one great paw resting by her, his head smack in the middle of her expensively skirted lap. Kate just knew without looking it was being slobbered upon liberally. As she turned the corner of the sofa, she could see Clancy's big old bottom sitting squarely on the lady's nice dress pumps.

"Hello," Kate said, trying to sound pleasant and not as

though she were about to have a coronary. I'm Kate Roe." She stuck out her hand. Realizing the lady could not stand up to shake hands she quickly sat on the sofa next to her. "I see you've met Clancy. I'd try to get him to move, but in all honesty, it probably wouldn't do any good."

The lady laughed. "It's because he knows a dog person when he sees one. Isn't that right, my little French man?"

Kate tried to refrain from rolling her eyes. "So you're familiar with Clancy's breed?"

"Ah, yes, the impressive 'Dogue de Bordeaux' the national guard dog of France. My dog is also French. A Poodle, and a mighty fine one at that. Jacque's won several awards at local dog shows. He'd probably do better than that, but I have an aversion to travel. The French can be very contrary, so I'm not surprised Clancy isn't always obedient." She patted Clancy on the head, then said, "Now scoot, darling, your mommy and I have work to do."

Kate's mouth dropped open as Clancy gave a heavy sigh, then got up and trotted off towards the kitchen.

"I haven't introduced myself properly, Miss Roe. My name is Jennifer Sanford. Miss Harrison assures me you are a fine young woman. After we chat a bit, I'd like for you to walk me around the premises. Of course, the health department will have to come out and do a water and waste check, as well as a few other things. But mostly, we have to be assured this is a safe home to bring the little ones to. Oh, I almost forgot!" Ms Sanford jumped up and walked toward the front door. "I have a few boxes just outside the door for you. If you don't mind assisting me, we can bring them in now."

Kate jumped up and helped her carry in the boxes.

There were two, one quite heavy that took both of them. "How did you get it from the car to the porch?" Kate inquired.

"The young lady that answered the door helped me. I didn't bring the things the rest of the way in until I could get a feel for you. It's important to me to know through intuition as well as facts about placement for adoption. I didn't want you to see all this stuff until I was satisfied."

She smiled at Kate and opened the first box as they sat down on the sofa again. "These are two photo albums that record the Ashes' life. A few snapshots of Mr. and Mrs. Ashe's wedding, baby pictures of the older boy and of course, a few of the twins. This little bundle, I believe are the older boy's report cards."

Kate stopped her. "May I see those for a second?"

"Of course." Ms. Sanford handed them to her. Kate gently took them and removed the rubber band. She ran her finger lightly over Robyn's signature found on Thomas's report card from her class.

"I was Thomas's teacher last year." She smiled. "He was a good student and a good boy. It's hard to believe he's gone."

"I can see you were attached to the boy. Perhaps that will be the link that will help you attach to the twins quickly." Ms. Sanford reached into the box. She removed a stack of envelopes. "These are letters from Mr. Ashe while he was in Iraq, written to Mrs. Ashe. I don't know if you want to read them, or save them for the children when they are older. I suggest you at least give them a glance before allowing the girls to ever read them, though."

Kate gave a nod. "I will. I don't know if I can do it

now. I have had so much trauma lately, I'm not sure I can handle that sadness yet."

"Understandable. Now, in this other box," Ms. Sanford reached and opened the flaps. "Is china. It looks pretty old, maybe heirloom china. We don't know which side of the family, unfortunately. But it seems to be the only thing of monetary value Ms. Ashe owned."

She and Kate carefully unwrapped a few pieces. "It's beautiful." Around the edges of the buttery cream china was Santa in his sleigh, the reindeer outlined in gold. The center of each dish depicted different Christmas scenes, all in Victorian style. "I believe there's a setting for eight." Ms. Sanford said.

"What a treasure! We can use these every year." Kate felt her eyes mist over. "I'm so grateful I didn't have any of this before the fire."

They re-wrapped the pieces, then Ms. Sanford leaned back and looked Kate straight in the eye. She smiled as Clancy quietly snuck back in and laid his head at her feet. "Tell me, Kate exactly how you're going to introduce those tiny babies to this big lug here." She leaned down and rubbed Clancy behind the ears. "It's obvious he's used to being the boss and having his own way. Am I right?"

"You are right. He's very gentle, but we've lived alone and he's never had very much excitement. Mrs. Stonefield suggested I bring a baby blanket to Clancy so he could associate their smell with me."

"How did that work?"

Kate laughed. "Very well. He immediately tucked it under his paws and slept on it. He liked the smell of babies. But unfortunately, it was lost in the fire."

Suddenly Clancy's head jerked up. He gave a soft "woof" and sprinted into the kitchen.

They heard a "here now!" exclamation from there. Clancy came running back with something in his mouth, Mrs. Peabody close behind.

"Oh!" Mrs. Peabody startled. "I'm so sorry!" She gave a stern look to Clancy. "I've been meaning to mention to you, Kate, that Clancy had this in his mouth when he woke me up the night of the fire. I washed it, but kept forgetting about it. It's a baby blanket, so I figured it was for the babies."

"Is that the one the foster mother gave you?" Ms. Sanford asked.

Kate reached down and got it from Clancy. "Yes." She said softly. "He must have saved it from the fire."

Ms. Sanford rose. "Well, I guess that answers my question, doesn't it?" She stooped for a last pat to Clancy's ears. "You're going to be a fine baby-sitter, Clancy. What a good dog!" Clancy wiggled all over at the praise, reached over to Kate and gently pulled the baby blanket from her hands. He laid back down, the blanket between his paws. Putting his head down, he buried his nose in the blanket and taking a deep breath, closed his eyes.

Kate thought she could collapse as soon as Ms. Sanford left, but while she was trying to make a proper introduction to Mrs. Peabody the door bell had chimed and Tina from the insurance company had arrived. Right behind her was Cooper. She made those introductions and Cooper led Tina into the den to get her started on looking at the photos while Mrs. Peabody once again exiled herself to the kitchen.

When Ms. Sanford had gone, Kate had rushed into the den. Tina was pleased with the photos of the interior of the house, and felt sure Kate would get an insurance check within ten days. This would indeed pay off the mortgage. The extra eight thousand would be a separate check than the content money, but both should be dealt with quickly.

When everyone was gone, including Mrs. Peabody (Kate could never figure out why she was there to start with, except God had sent her with the baby blanket), she filled Cooper and Cayden in about the social worker's visit. Smiling brightly, Kate said, "She was a little eccentric, but very warm. She said she'd do the interview work up tonight, so that Wren and Sparrow can be picked up Thursday. She'll contact me as soon as she knows for sure."

Then Kate burst into tears.

CHAPTER EIGHTEEN

Tuesday morning Anna called to make sure the shopping trip was still on. Although it was spitting snow, the weatherman had promised clearing and a high of nearly forty degrees. Kate agreed they should venture out by ten a.m.

"And the first stop is getting your driver license renewed." Anna said. "You have enough stuff going on without getting a ticket."

So after a lengthy wait at the DMV, they had shopped for an hour at Target and then on to Babies R Us. Kate had skillfully pretended she didn't know about the baby shower, and had tried to keep from purchasing a lot of things Anna had steered her away from. She had been adamant about a few things, though, things she couldn't resist, and things she had to have the moment they stepped in the house with the twins. The check out girl had raised her eyebrows when she saw two identical frilly dresses, two tiny blue feminine coats, and caps to match. "Twins", Kate had said, hardly believing it herself.

Anna had treated her to an expensive Italian restaurant at lunch, and they both had eaten too much. Chatting over coffee and desert, the conversation turned to Thanksgiving. "Bailey and I are saving extra days for when the baby comes. He/She will be old enough to travel when Thanksgiving rolls around next year, and we can spend holidays with family. But this Thanksgiving needs to be spent with friends. Kate, why don't we get together and all celebrate? We could share cooking responsibilities. If I'm able, I'll do most of the cooking. If I'm not urping, that is. I'll be about eleven weeks by then, I should be okay. Ya'll will have your hands full of babies!"

"That sounds wonderful, Anna. I'll check with Cooper to make sure they don't have any plans."

Anna looked embarrassed. "I'm sorry, Kate. I guess I keep thinking you and Cooper are already an official couple - like married - I guess. I know you're not," she hastened to add as Kate's face reddened. "I guess it's living in the same house, babies coming Thursday..." she trailed off, looking sheepish.

Kate burst into laughter. "Gee, I wonder why you'd think that?" She reached over and grasped Anna's hands. "I know from the outside it looks like we've settled in like an old married couple, but it's not that way on the inside, Anna. We're struggling with the relationship we had before the fire. And now babies!" She shook her head." I don't know if we can survive all this. Maybe so, because I'm crazy about Cooper. But we just have to wait."

Anna squeezed Kate's hands. "Fine. Check and see if they have plans and we'll go from there."

When Kate got home, all seemed quiet and peaceful. No one was home but Clancy, so she lay on the couch with him by her side, feeling like things had returned to the way they had been for so long before the fire. She dozed and didn't awaken until Cooper drove up and Clancy jumped up to greet him.

Kate took the last few minutes of quiet to thank God for the roof she had over her head, for Cooper, whatever they might become, for now.

She remembered Jesus saying not to worry about tomorrow, that today had enough worries of its own. She nodded her head in agreement and stood to unlock the door for Cooper.

She greeted him with a hug. "Hey," her voice sounded raspy. "I went to sleep."

"No wonder. You've been going non-stop for days. Take it easy this evening. I'll call for pizza and Cayden can run get it. I'll make tea and we'll be all set."

Kate nodded gratefully. "Speaking of food, Anna wants us to all get together for Thanksgiving. She says she'll do most of the cooking since the babies will be keeping me busy. I told her I'd check with you."

"Sounds great. I'm sure Aunt Cynthia will whip up some of her desserts. She'll be happy to have a big crowd, too. She has said over and over she wished we had more people."

"You don't think she'll be hurt?"

"No. She already mentioned having it here instead of her house. Just tell Anna and Bailey to plan on having it here, too. She and Aunt Cynthia can prepare a lot of the food, and I'll help with food or babies or whatever I need to do." He looked happy and Kate thought the more they talked about it the more he liked it.

"Okay, you talk to Cynthia, and I'll talk to Anna. Now, come on. I want to show you the dishes the social worker left."

The dishes sat in the corner of the dining room. Kate bent and unwrapped the first dish and handed it to Cooper. "Wow." He traced the gold outline on the reindeer. "These are fantastic. Are we gonna be allowed to use them at Christmas?"

Kate laughed. "I think that would be a good idea." Her voice softened. "I'm so happy we can start a tradition right off the bat with the girls that include their parents and Thomas."

"Me too." Cooper sat the dish back in the box, wrapping it carefully. He also examined what he was feeling carefully. All the plans, the making of traditions, all the uses of the word we. He stood. "You are going to be a fantastic mother, Kate."

She cocked her head and looked at him intently. "Thanks, Cooper."

"Well." He cleared his throat. "Let me find Cayden and assign her pizza duty. Then I'll get the kettle going for tea." He smiled at her. "Why don't you take a shower, or lie down or walk the dog - whatever you wish?"

Kate smiled. "I'm heady with freedom. I think I'll walk Clancy."

As she leashed the dog, she couldn't help feeling that Cooper was being more than just helpful. She was sure he'd wanted to be alone for a little while. She didn't blame him, though. This was pretty overwhelming for them all.

But she still didn't like the way it had made her feel.

CHAPTER NINETEEN

When Kate awoke on Wednesday morning, she felt anxious. She waited for a moment to see what that was about, and realized this was the last day before the babies arrived, and the last day she would see her classroom with the children she had taught these past few months. She was going to talk to them today about why she'd been absent the last few days, and why she would be absent the rest of the year. It made her feel guilty that these children had only had her there for a few months and now would be in the hands of someone else. She heaved a sigh. It couldn't be helped, and she had talked at length with the substitute teacher who had been hired to finish out her year. He was a great guy, and she knew he'd do a fine job.

She sat up in bed. Clancy wasn't in her room. Her door was slightly open and she could smell coffee. She yanked on sweatpants and a sweatshirt, grabbed her heavy socks and took a quick look in the mirror. "Ugh. Brush your hair or Cooper will run screaming." She did so and then crept to the door. She slowly put her hand to the knob and felt it. Yep. Dried dog slobber.

Now what? Lock and key her room?

She rounded the door to the kitchen and found Cooper propped up with the newspaper, coffee in one hand. Clancy was chewing on a bone. They looked like the picture of contentment.

"Morning," Kate spoke, hoping Cooper wouldn't start

in again about someone putting Clancy in his room.

"Good morning to you. I solved the mystery." Cooper said, giving a nod toward Clancy.

"You did? Did it involve a big old sloppy mouth turning door knobs?"

"How'd you know?" Cooper took his feet off the chair and put his paper on the table. "I can't believe you figured it out."

Kate shrugged, pouring herself a cup of coffee. "It just came to me in the shower Monday, but we've been so busy I forgot. Then night before last he stayed in my room, so I really forgot. When he was gone this morning, I tested. There was dried dog slobber on my door knob." Glancing down at her hands, she set her mug on the counter and went to the sink for some hot soapy washing.

Cooper grinned. "I think the noise woke me up this time. I was ready to pounce on whoever was letting him in. I couldn't believe it, Kate! He marched right in, and pushed the door partly closed with his rump and sashayed right over to my bed. Just as he started to jump I sat up. Scared him to death! I got up and discovered the same thing you did. Dog slobber on the door knob. Except the slobber was fresh." Cooper shook his head. "Clancy didn't seem to mind he'd been found out. By the time I turned around to go back to bed, he was in the middle of it."

"Oh, Cooper, I am so sorry! He knows to never get on a bed."

Cooper snorted. "You mean he knows to never get on *your* bed."

"So, any suggestions how to stop Houdini?"

"Not yet. But surely two intelligent adults can figure

out how to thwart one dog."

"Surely." Kate stretched. "You sure make good coffee, Mr. McGuire."

Thank you kindly, ma'am."

"I guess I'll go up and get ready to go to the school. Today's the day I talk to my class for the last time this school year."

Cooper stood up too. "You'll do great, Kate. I gotta get going too. Duty calls." He walked out as Kate was rinsing her mug. "Oh, and I took Clancy out. We had a good walk."

"Thanks," she called to his retreating back. She looked down at her dog. "And you," she said, pointing her finger at Clancy, "Are in big trouble. I just have to figure out how to fix this."

She bent down and rubbed his head. "You sure do make life interesting, Clancy. As if my life wasn't interesting enough."

Clancy cocked his head, listening to her. As she walked out of the kitchen, he went back to gnawing on his bone.

🐾 🐾 🐾 🐾

Kate felt a pang of regret mixed with nostalgia as she entered the school building. She took a deep breath in of the way only a school can smell. The principal's office was the first door on the right. She stepped in to the secretary's office and waited for Angela to get off the phone. As the secretary hung up, Kate spoke. "Hi, Angie. Is Mr. Donaldson busy?"

"There's Kate!" John Donaldson walked through the door before Angela could answer. "How does it feel to be back in the salt mines?"

"Kind of sad, actually," Kate answered. "I really haven't had a lot of time to miss it yet, but I'd rather have been here."

"I bet that's the truth. We were all so sorry to hear about your house, Kate." Angie said.

"Thanks. Your prayers sure have been appreciated."

"Come on in and give Mr. Bennett a minute to get role called and lunch money collected. He's still adjusting and the scamps take advantage first thing in the morning."

Kate laughed. "Oh, I imagine they do!" She settled into a chair in front of Mr. Donaldson's desk. He handed her a cup of coffee and settled into a chair himself.

"So, tell me how all this is effecting you."

"Well, I'm tired. But I'm very excited about tomorrow. The babies finally come home with me." She shrugged. "Or where home is for now. Cooper and Cayden have been wonderful, and they seem excited about the babies too. It just seems unfair, putting them through this so unexpectedly."

"From what I've seen out of Cooper, I'm sure he doesn't mind helping you. He seems crazy about you, Kate."

She smiled. "Let's hope so. I just don't want to *drive* him crazy!"

Donaldson laughed. "Well, if twins can't do it, nothing can." He leaned back in his chair. "I hear there's a big to-do planned Sunday. Do you want to know, or did I just spoil it?"

"Oh, I've heard about it. I'm going to try and act surprised. I'm very grateful. Let's just hope I can get some sleep between Thursday when the babies arrive and Sunday when the surprise party arrives."

Thanking the principal for the coffee and bidding Angela good-bye, Kate took a deep breath and headed for 'her' classroom. She'd asked Angela to let Mr. Bennett know she was on her way, so he could prepare the children, if he chose.

Before opening the door, Kate paused, said a heartfelt prayer and knocked lightly. She heard, "And here she is!" as Mr. Bennett opened the door. He was so young! She knew he'd finished school last year and done a great job student teaching, as well as substitute teaching all last year, while looking for a job. This long, temporary job would give him good experience, and she was glad for him. But for a second, she felt possessive of this particular class. It was *her* class.

However; that was quickly forgotten as joy filled her heart when all seventeen children stood up and cheered as she walked in the door. She stood for a moment in front of the class, beaming at them. As they finally quieted down, she leaned against her old desk and smiled at everyone of them. She sensed anticipation in the air, looking at their little faces. She had already become fond of them and recalled all the special things she remembered about each child.

Taking another deep breath, she began. "Well, you guys know about my house, right?"

Julie Simpson raised her hand. She was smaller than any other child in the class, had flaming red hair and so many freckles they melted into one another. She always wore bright blue. Kate guessed her mother wanted to play up the child's best features - stunning, huge, blue eyes.

"Yes, Julie?"

"It burn-ded down, didn't it?" She asked solemnly.

Kate loved the language of the seven year olds, and wasn't about to correct them today.

"That's right. But I want you to know I'm fine. Clancy saved my life!" She heard several gasps in the room. They were all familiar with Clancy from the many stories she shared with them, mostly about his naughty side. "He got out of the house and ran for help. I guess he's a hero!" Kate failed to mention that Clancy probably started the fire, too. She walked around the front of the room a little. "That's why I haven't come back to school, and why Mr. Bennett has been kind enough to take my place." She stopped for a moment, bowing her head, getting her thoughts together. "But I have something else to tell you. You see, I was going to teach you guys until Thanksgiving break, but I wasn't going to come back for the rest of the year anyway. I just didn't have a chance to tell you, because of the fire."

Several "Why Miss Kate? and oh, no's!" rang out.

"Well, you see, I'm going to be the mother of twin girls!"

Sammy Ralston jumped out of his chair. Kate braced herself. She mentally called him 'Sammy the Stinker' because, well, because he was a stinker. "No, you ain't, Miss Kate, I know that for a fack!"

Kate tilted her head toward Sammy. "Is that right, Sammy? And how would you know that for a fact?"

"Cause when you're gettin' a baby, you look like this." He proceeded to stretch his arms out in front of him like he was carrying a beach ball, and waddled down the aisle between the desks.

Several giggles broke out, but others looked shocked and glanced nervously toward Kate.

Kate felt herself blush violet to her roots, but never let her eyes stray from the little boy. "You may sit down, Sammy." He strutted back to his seat, looking satisfied. "It is true when mommies carry babies in their body, they grow big around their tummy, because the baby has to get big enough to live outside the mommy's body. But I'm not carrying the babies in my body. These babies are still very little, but they were born almost six weeks ago."

Rudy Patterson's hand shot up. He was the cutest kid she'd ever seen, and one of the smartest in the class. "Yes, Rudy?"

"They weren't in your body, were they Miss Kate? Cause you weren't big when school started."

"That's right, Rudy. Unfortunately, these babies mommy died in a car accident." In the corner of Kate's eye, she saw Bonnie Sumner get tears in her eyes. She was a very sensitive child, so Kate wasn't surprised. "I know this is a very sad story, and it makes me sad to tell you. But these babies had a very good mommy and she loved them very much. So she made sure they would be taken care of, no matter what. I am very blessed to get to be their mommy now."

Todd Daily's hand rose. "Miss Kate, will you be their mommy forever?"

Kate smiled at Todd. "Yes, that's right Todd. I'll be their mommy now, forever."

Todd smiled broadly. "Then they'll be like me, right?"

Kate lifted a brow. "What do you mean, Todd?"

"'Cause I'm abdobted. They'll be abdobted, won't

they?"

"Yes they will! I didn't know you were ab -er - adopted, Todd!"

"Yes, ma'am. My mommy and daddy got me when I was brand new."

"Well, Todd, tell your mommy and daddy I think they are very blessed!"

"Yes, Miss Kate. I'll tell 'em, but they already know."

She heard Mr. Bennett try to cover a laugh with a cough. "I'm sure they do, Todd." Kate nodded at him. "I'm going to miss you all very, very much. I already do. But I wanted to come today and tell you in person, that although I didn't get to be your teacher for very long, I hope you learned some things from me. Because I learned something from you. I learned to love you all so much." She gave them a wink. "I'll tell you what. If Mr. Donaldson and Mr. Bennett here, don't mind, I'll bring the babies by for a visit after Christmas vacation. How does that sound?"

A collective "YAY!" went up. She hugged each child good-bye, shook Mr. Bennett's hand and went home.

CHAPTER TWENTY

Kate did a load of laundry and started supper. She knew Cooper and Cayden loved lasagna and she'd made a big salad to go with it. She was rummaging in the freezer for garlic bread when the phone rang. She picked up the kitchen extension to answer. It was Pastor Matthew. "Just wanted to let you know Kate, that our Bible Study team meets tonight and we will be in specific prayer for you and the babies."

"Thanks, Matt. I appreciate it. Everyone is being so supportive. I'm excited and scared too."

"Do you know Patricia Hawkins?"

"Her name sounds familiar. Doesn't she sing solos at church sometimes?"

"That's her. Anyway, she had a set of twins about three years ago. I mentioned to her your situation, and she said she'd be more than happy to come over in a few days and maybe offer you a tip or two."

"That sounds like a wonderful idea. I keep trying to imagine what it's going to be like with two babies, and I draw a blank. To be honest, Matt, I was having a hard time imagining one!"

Matt laughed. "That's very normal Kate. Anyone about to be a parent feels that way. A lot of things you'll feel and go through won't be because of the odd circumstances, but will be because of it being a new experience. Always remember that, and remember somebody fairly close by has had a similar experience. Don't forget to call on them, either."

"I'll try and remember that. You may have to remind me."

"What are friends for? I'll let you go now. See you in a few days."

By the time Kate had discovered the garlic bread and had it in the oven, Cooper had driven up. Clancy trotted to the door, a big grin on his face.

Kate shook her head. Clancy was happy one minute and the next minute seemed to be in mourning. She knew he was trying to adjust, too. But there had been a couple of times in the last few days she'd really been worried about him. He didn't want to go on walks; he just pulled on his leash to go back in the house. He still greeted everyone, but then kept to himself a lot more than ever before. Kate sighed. Was there any such thing as a doggie psychiatrist?

Cooper found her in the kitchen and gave her a kiss on the cheek. "What's the glum look about?"

"Worrying about Clancy and his depression."

"He's a dog, Kate. He's adjusting. Give him time. He'll come around."

"I guess you're right. Supper will be ready in about ten minutes. Where's Cayden?"

"Beats me. She should be here shortly. She didn't tell me she had other plans."

"Then I'll set the table for three."

"I'll wash up. Was you day good at school?"

Kate smiled. "Interesting. I can't wait to tell you."

Supper had at first been full of laughter and talk, Kate sharing all the things that had happened at school, acting out the scene with Sammy waddling about. She shared Matt's phone call, too.

Cayden talked about her day and her ever deepening romance with Mike.

Cooper groaned over ball practice and the inept sports team he was expected to turn into pros in just a few weeks.

Finally, they all spoke excitedly about tomorrow, trying to imagine how it would be, but they were at a loss for words.

Each said their good nights and went to their respective bedroom. Clancy for once seemed happy to go with Kate and not look back longingly toward Cooper's room.

It took a long time for Kate to go to sleep, as she lay there making lists in her head. It had turned colder in the afternoon and she didn't want to forget the sweaters, caps and warm blankets.

But finally exhaustion set in, and she slept, deep and dreamless.

🐾 🐾 🐾 🐾

Snuggled under covers, she felt a gentle shaking. She moved her shoulder away and sunk deeper down, but the shaking continued and then she heard her name whispered. Rousing, she saw Cooper's outline standing over her and she sat up so quickly they almost bumped heads.

"What's wrong?" she said, louder than she meant to.

"Nothing's wrong, Kate. Clancy and I have something we want to show you."

"What time is it?" Her eyes widened. "Have I overslept? Are we going to be late?" She exclaimed, beginning to clamber out of bed.

"No, we're not late. It's barely five."

Kate narrowed her eyes suspiciously. "Has Clancy

done something bad?" She gave him a dirty look and he whined, leaning into Cooper's leg.

"Nope. Not that either. Here." Cooper handed Kate the robe that lay across the foot of her bed. "Put this on and come to the window."

Looking puzzled, she did as Cooper instructed. He pulled the blinds open and Kate gasped. At least six inches of new snow covered everything and it was coming down straight and hard. "Oh, my," she breathed. "It's so beautiful!" Then panic seized her and she turned to Cooper. "How will we get to Wren and Sparrow? We can't drive in this!"

"Calm down, Kate. I've got it covered. I woke up about three and saw what was happening. I called Pastor Matthew and asked to swap cars. We now have a four wheel drive in the garage."

Kate hugged him. "I can't believe you called Matt at three in the morning, but I'm sure glad you did."

Cooper grinned. "Actually, he thought I was calling to ask to sleep on his couch."

Kate giggled. "That's certainly understandable with your reputation." She did a little dance and Clancy woofed softly. She bent down and put his head in her hands and rubbed his ears. "We can get the babies, Clancy!" He woofed again, tail wagging.

"I know it's early, but want some coffee? I don't think I can go back to sleep."

"Me either! Do we still have some of those really sinful doughnuts?"

"Yes'um, we sure do. Uh, I think. I mean, I know we have one left."

"Uh huh. I'm feeling generous this morning. I'll split it with you."

"Good. And then I'll fix oatmeal, because we have to be fortified to pick up the twins."

Kate looked up at Cooper and tears filled her eyes. "Thanks, Coop. You are a blessing."

Cooper blushed. "Me? I'm just here to help." He tilted Kate's chin. "Because I want to, Kate. Got it?"

"Got it. Race you to the doughnut."

Seat belted in, four wheel drive engaged, they rolled very seriously down the drive way. Kate held onto the blankets, caps and sweaters as though her life depended on it. Squinting out the windshield, she watched the snow pour down. She had called Mrs. Stonefield and let her know they were coming, however slowly.

"It's beautiful, isn't it?"

"I was just thinking what a story you can tell the girls when they get older – about the day you brought them home."

Kate laughed. "Kids love that story, don't they? I remember asking all sorts of questions when I got old enough to be interested."

"Yeah. And I remember Cayden's homecoming too. I tried to make it special even after Mama and Daddy died. I figured it was something to keep as a very important memory."

Kate reached over and patted Cooper's heavily clad arm. "You are such a sweetie."

"Whatever you do, don't tell the boys on the team. I can hear it now: 'Coach Sweetie' this and 'Coach Sweetie' that."

Kate grinned. "That's something I'll consider as blackmail material if I ever need it."

They came up on two cars that had landed in the ditch on each side of the road, in an apparent attempt to keep from hitting each other. Cooper slowed and rolled down his window.

"Need help?" He asked the fellow nearest him.

"Nah. Tow truck is on the way. We ain't hurt, just embarrassed. Ya'll don't need to be out in this mess."

Cooper grinned. "Well, we have to pick up our twin babies and bring them home."

"Well, son, in that case, get goin'!"

Everyone waved and they continued on their way.

"You enjoyed that, didn't you?" Kate asked.

"Sure. It isn't every day you get to brag about picking up twins. Made his day, too. He'll go home and tell his wife about it."

The snow had almost stopped by the time they got to Mrs. Stonefield's. As they got out of the car, Kate slipped and almost fell. "Careful little Missy," Cooper said in his best John Wayne voice. "I can't tend to you and the little 'uns, too."

Kate rolled her eyes. "That was bad, Coop, very bad."

Cooper faked a hopeful look. "You should hear my Rocky Balboa."

"I'll pray for you."

They stepped up to the porch, and clutching the posts, stomped their boots to get the snow off the soles. Mrs. Stonefield opened the door.

"Come in, before you freeze! Isn't it beautiful?"

They turned and looked at the pristine world. The

evergreens bowed low, heaving with a full coat of snow. The bare branches of the oaks were lined with white, and Mrs. Stonefield's black wrought iron fence looked as though someone had capped it with whipping cream.

Kate gave Mrs. Stonefield a hug. "I couldn't believe this snow when Cooper woke me up early this morning. I almost cried. I thought there was no way we could get here."

"Our pastor swapped vehicles with me at three this morning so we could use his four wheel drive." Cooper explained.

"Now that's a man of God if I ever heard of one!" Mrs. Stonefield exclaimed.

The house was warm and inviting. Mr. Stonefield had a fire going in the den and the house smelled of coffee. Kate and Cooper took off their coats and stood by the fire for a few moments. They declined coffee, sudden excitement overtaking them.

Wren and Sparrow were in carriers on top of the kitchen table where Mrs. Stonefield had been feeding them warm Pablum cereal. They were kicking their little feet in anticipation of each bite, focused only on the spoon headed their way. "The pediatrician just started them on some very watered down cereal this week because they were taking in so much formula." Mrs. Stonefield laughed. "They absolutely love it! You'd think it was ambrosia or something."

Kate walked over to the babies and took over feeding Wren. She cooed to her with each spoonful.

Mrs. Stonefield turned to Cooper. "Ah, love at first sight. And you?"

"Fear." They laughed. "But I'm also enamored. They are so beautiful. Like china dolls."

Mr. Stonefield patted him on the shoulder. "Very loud, demanding, china dolls. But I am truly going to miss them. I'm afraid I've fallen in love with the little dears myself. We do get visiting rights, don't we, Miss Roe?"

Kate turned. "Oh, yes. You visit anytime. Your wife and Genevieve are going to help baby-sit for a few weeks to get me accustomed, so you come with them."

"Oh, no. I'll come when the little ones are fed and dry and ready to play. Grandpa stuff, you know."

"Speaking of, where is this famous Genevieve I hear about but never meet?" Cooper asked.

Mrs. Stonefield said, "She was pretty upset over the twins leaving. She knows, of course, this is the right thing, and she's happy about it; but she's very attached. She asked not to be here this morning, so she's at her cousin's. But she'll be with me when we come to help out."

Stepping back outside after a drawn out good bye and wrapping of babies, the cold air hit them with a force. The snow had stopped, and the sky was totally blue except for a few small white clouds that looked more like puffs of smoke. In the far field birds were on the ground, like tiny, moving black buttons against the white of the snowy ground. Kate held Sparrow close, and waited while Cooper fastened Wren into her car seat. Gently passing Sparrow on to Cooper, he did the same for her.

Kate straightened and looked Mrs. Stonefield square in the eye. "I'll do my best. I know this is God's will, and I'm already in love."

Tears began to form in Mrs. Stonefield's eyes. "Go on, or I'll be a mess. God is with you, who could ask for more?"

CHAPTER TWENTY-ONE

It was lunch time when they got back home with the babies. Cayden threw open the door the minute they pulled into the driveway, dashing outside with Clancy. Cayden squealed at the cold, darted back in as Clancy barked furiously, wagging not only his tail, but his 'all overs'.

Cayden came back out, pulling on her coat. She held onto Clancy as she slipped and slid over the sidewalk to get to the car.

Kate opened the door. "We're home! Whew! I was scared to death. Even with a four wheel drive; it's scary out there. We saw a wreck on the way and two on the way home."

"How are you going to get them in the house? Everything is so slick!" Cayden was peering in the back seat. The babies were wrapped up, with big blankets folded beside them to finish covering them up for the trip into the house.

"I'll sit the car seat on the ground and push. They can just slide in the house."

"Cooper! That is not funny!" Cayden gave him her most sisterly look. "Tell me what to do before we all freeze to death."

Clancy poked his nose in the back seat as Kate opened the door. He sniffed carefully and then back pedaled, watching as Kate unfastened Wren from the seat. She picked up the blanket and put it over the baby and with mincing steps, headed for the house. Cooper did the same with Sparrow.

Cayden rushed to the door and held it open for them. They came in single file, Clancy the last to enter. He sat down in the entry way and raised a paw, expecting his feet to be wiped free of ice and snow. He was totally ignored. He cocked his head in puzzlement, gave a canine shrug and made wet paw prints all over the floor as he trotted into the den to sniff some more. His heart sped up a little. He recognized the smell the blanket had given off before the fire.

Kate sat on one end of the couch, Cooper on the other, the babies lying in between them. Cayden was on the floor on her knees, awestruck at the sight before her. Clancy nudged her, and she scooted a little so he could see too.

Kate smiled at him and rubbed the top of his head. "Well, Clancy, what do you think?"

He carefully placed a paw in her lap. "Ewww! Wet dog feet!" She put his paw back down. "We didn't wipe your paws, did we? Sorry about that!" She rubbed his head again, and let him get a little closer to Sparrow. He gently sniffed her, and she stared at him, her little hand rested on his nose. He moved on to Wren and sniffed her too, but she paid little attention. Clancy trotted off suddenly and came back with the blanket that he now claimed. He laid it in Kate's lap.

"That's right, Clancy. That's the blanket that smelled like the babies. They're here to stay, so we have to get used to it all, okay?"

He woofed softly and took the blanket back, and laid down on it.

"Um, Kate, something smells over here." Cooper looked alarmed.

"This may be our first diaper change at home."

"Ugh, clean up on baby two. She is stinking just like her sister!" Cayden held her nose.

"Boy, I can tell you two are gonna be a lot of help." Kate laughed. "Sit in my place and I'll go get diapers and wipes. Do ya'll think you can stay conscious long enough for me to do that?"

"It's doubtful, Kate. But I'll try to man up and do it."

Kate rolled her eyes and ran upstairs to the nursery.

❈ ❈ ❈ ❈

The first night could not have been better. Everyone stayed up till midnight, Cooper and Kate doing the feeding together. The babies slept until five and Kate was thrilled. She stood in the nursery alone and prayed over each baby as they stared at her, wide eyed. She changed them and carefully carried them both down to the kitchen, putting them in the carriers that had been left there the night before. They watched her solemnly as she prepared the formula, then she sat between them on the couch and held a bottle in each hand as they fed contentedly.

Clancy came in and put his head on her lap, eyes half closed.

"If it's this easy all the time, Clancy, we've got it made." She smiled at his furry, sleepy face and felt at peace.

By seven, Kate was feeling a little tired, but proud of all she had accomplished. She'd put a load of laundry in, bathed both babies and had breakfast cooking when Cayden stumbled sleepily into the kitchen. "Good morning!" Kate smiled at Cayden, who had propped herself up on the counter, holding one tiny foot in her hand.

"Mornin'" she mumbled. "Whose foot is this?"

Kate peered over at the babies. "Wren's."

"How can you tell them apart already?"

"I can't. I'm careful to remember what they have on and which seat they're in. Their names are on the back of the seats. See?" She pointed to the pieces of tape with the babies' names scrawled on it. "Wren has a small birthmark on the back of her neck, too. I just don't want to look at it all the time and give her a complex."

"Right." Cayden yawned. "Something sure does smell good. Whatcha cookin'?"

"Bacon and pancakes. Is Cooper up yet?"

"Yeah, that's what woke me up. He's singing in the shower."

"Oh, dear." Kate laughed. "Just be glad we can't hear him downstairs."

"Why do you think I came down?" Cayden rolled her eyes. "He has the worst voice I've ever heard."

"Who does?" Cooper asked as he walked into the kitchen. He smelled like shampoo and soap, making the kitchen all the more aromatic.

"You, dope, who else?" Cayden said with a smirk. "Whereas, I sound like a bird when I sing."

"Yeah, I expect a record deal to be made any day." He reached over and kissed both babies. "Kate you have this kitchen smelling like heaven. How long have you been up?"

"The girls got me up at five. I've got laundry going and them bathed, so I thought breakfast would be helpful to ya'll before you leave for school. I listened to the radio and the roads are cleared, so no snow day off for you two."

"All you've done sounds great, but don't wear yourself out before the sun comes up. You'll have a long day today." He warned.

"Mrs. Stonefield and Genevieve are coming at some point today. Besides, I can nap when the girls nap."

Cooper looked doubtful. "Well, okay. But I'll at least take Clancy out for a good walk before I leave."

"Thanks, Coop. He needs some attention. He's sulking under the table now."

Cooper glanced underneath the table. Clancy was laying there, head on paws. "Hey, boy! Want to go for a walk after breakfast?"

A limp wag was all the response Clancy had. "Maybe a walk will perk him up." Cayden said, bending down to pet him. "He's had a lot of adjustments lately. I'll try to be more attentive too."

"Thanks, Cayden. He's a smart dog. The smarter they are the more they need."

A little after nine that morning, Kate put the girls down for a nap. She fell across the bed, having a hard time believing it was only nine o'clock. At school she would have barely begun to teach! She reached over and turned the monitor on, then fell back on the bed, eyes closing. Far away, she heard a ding and realized the dryer had cut off with the third load of clothes for the day. Too bad, she thought, let 'em wrinkle. She felt herself begin to drift.

The phone rang, jolting her out of her bliss. She grabbed it before it woke up Wren and Sparrow. It was Mrs. Stonefield. "I'm so sorry to tell you this, Kate. But my husband fell and we're in the emergency room. I'm afraid his arm may be broken."

"Oh, no! How terrible!" Kate sat up, running her hand through her hair. "Can I do anything?"

Mrs. Stonefield chuckled. "Dear, you can't possibly do anything. I'm calling to tell you I can't do anything for you. I know you were expecting Genevieve and me at ten."

"Oh. Well, this can't be helped. I'll do fine. After all, it's the first day. I'm not overwhelmed yet."

This time Mrs. Stonefield laughed outright. "That's good to hear. If Robert's arm isn't broken perhaps we can make it tomorrow. Genevieve is heartbroken and pouting a bit. But I've promised her we'll get there as soon as we can."

"Of course you will. Tell Genevieve the babies can't wait to see her again. I hope Mr. Stonefield is all right. Please let us know."

"I will. Here's the nurse now. Say a prayer it isn't broken."

"I sure will."

They hung up and Kate once again lay down. She did indeed pray for Mr. and Mrs. Stonefield and threw one in for herself and the babies while she was at it.

She rolled over on her side, thinking she could at least rest, even though she was no longer sleepy. As soon as she did, Clancy appeared, whining and doing the 'I gotta go out' dance. "Okay, okay. Give me a minute."

Sitting up once again, she searched for shoes. Carrying the monitor with her, she leashed Clancy and walked him into the back yard. As usual, he sniffed around more than he relieved himself, but finally found the perfect spot in the melting snow.

Re-entering the house, Kate got the dryer emptied, gave Clancy fresh water, mopped up after him, and looked in the freezer to see if anything jumped out at her to prepare for supper many hours from now.

The phone rang again. "How's it going so far?" Cooper asked. She could hear what sounded like a million kids in the background.

"Are you outside?"

"Yeah. Recess. I told my aide I had to make a quick phone call. Did you nap?"

"Ha, ha. No, I did not get to visit Nappy's house at all." Kate told him about the phone call.

"Well, that's just great. Did you call Mrs. Peabody and ask for help?"

"She's already volunteered to baby-sit Sunday evening so we can go to Cayden's chorus recital. Plus, it's my first day. Surely I'm not so old I can't do this alone."

"I promise as soon as I get home after practice I'll do whatever you need me to."

Kate's heart sunk. She'd forgotten Cooper had team practice. He wouldn't be home till supper time! "What has Cayden got this afternoon?" She tried to sound casual, but she was beginning to think this day was going to be very long.

"Beats me. I can't keep up with her. Want me to call her and leave a message?"

"No, don't bother her. She'll come straight home if she can." The baby monitor began to come alive with a soft whine. "I hear one of the babies. It's wake up time. I better go see about them."

"Okay. See you around six or six thirty. Don't worry

about dinner. We'll think of something."

"Thanks, Coop. See you then." They hung up and Kate ran upstairs, listening as one soft whine turned into two loud wails.

By five thirty Kate had done two more feedings, six diaper changes, one more dog walk, talked to seven well wishers from church, received a UPS package for Cooper while fending off Clancy, done one more load of laundry because Sparrow had soiled her bed during her last nap, and forgotten all about her own lunch until her stomach growled so loudly it startled Clancy.

As she was reaching for the peanut butter Cayden came in and insisted on making supper.

Relieved, Kate laid on the couch, the babies in carriers in front of her on the floor. She dangled plastic keys, cooed and goochied, and was delighted when Wren smiled at her with a big gummy grin. She didn't realize she'd dozed off until she heard Clancy barking excitedly as Cooper walked in the door.

"What's this?" he cried. "My sister in the kitchen! Has a natural disaster occurred? Are we in for some cataclysmic event that will be on the evening news?"

"Shut up, Coop. I'm trying to help. Kate's about done in. Where have you been?"

"Cayden, Cayden," he tsked. "You sound like a fisher wife. I've been at work, ball practice after school."

"Oh. I forgot. Wash up and set the table."

"Yes'um. What are we having?" He asked as he walked over to the couch. He kissed Kate's cheek, patted Clancy's head, and randomly picked up a baby. He held her over his head as she kicked and waved her arms, then he gave a wet lip smack loudly on the forehead, and did the same for her sister.

"Mac and cheese, baked potatoes, fish sticks and loaf bread. I can't cook, so leave me alone."

"That's okay, Cayden," Cooper said kindly. "We'll just all sleep standing up tonight because of all the starch."

"Coop, leave her alone. I'd eat fried grass if she makes it. I'm starved and pooped."

"What'd you have for lunch?"

"Nuttin'. I forgot. Let's get these young'uns on the counter and eat."

After supper, Cooper and Cayden insisted Kate lay down for a while. She slept for an hour and awoke to barking and crying. It turned out to be just routine stuff, but she was up again until after the midnight feeding. Afterwards, she fell into a deep, dreamless sleep until crying awoke her again at four thirty.

Thus was the story of day one.

CHAPTER TWENTY-TWO

By six Friday morning, Kate had put in a load of clothes after feeding the babies, then slept on the couch till Clancy had re-awakened her at seven to go out. She'd stood barefoot in the remaining snow on the back patio to let him do his doggie business. Clancy was not a happy dog at this turn of events, straining at the leash to no avail. He grudgingly used the nearest bush and slunk back inside as Kate hurried to fetch socks for her frozen feet. She quickly dried off Clancy's paws too, and thought briefly about cooking breakfast. Instead she got out cereal bowls, slapped some bananas on the counter, and hoped for the best. The dryer dinged at the same time the twins woke up. Just as she was mixing the girls' cereal, Cayden came down and stared at Kate.

"What's wrong?" Kate asked.

"Just your hair. I've never seen it so, um, tousled."

"I haven't even thought about my hair! Here, stir this. Don't let it get very hot." Kate ran into the half bath and groaned when she looked into the mirror. It couldn't have been worse if she had concentrated on it with a tease comb. She looked around for a brush, but found nothing but a pony tail holder. She tried to comb her hair with her fingers and pulled it through the holder.

Coming back into the kitchen at the same time Cooper entered, she saw his eyes widened slightly at the sight of her, but he said nothing, just kissed her cheek and poured cereal, cut up bananas, and poured milk. Cayden fed the twins and Kate quickly got out the clothes from the dryer, folding them and hoping that was good enough.

Cooper said the blessing and they ate silently for a few minutes. Cayden and Cooper were both eying Kate with quick sideways glances, until she put down her spoon and sighed heavily. "Look, guys, I'm okay. Really. I know I look a mess but I'm just a little tired and feeling disorganized this morning."

"Do you want me to lay out of school and help today?" Cayden asked hopefully.

"Nonsense, Cayden, you're not missing school. I'll call in a sub and help you." Cooper scooped up dirty bowls and started filling the dishwasher.

"Nonsense is right, Coop. Neither of you are missing school today. I can handle this. I may not look like I can, but the twins are great. Cayden, if you'll walk Clancy again, I'd appreciate it. Cooper, if you'll take the laundry with you upstairs, I'd appreciate that too. The girls will be ready for a change by now, and a nap soon. I'll nap with them and be right as rain."

Cooper tilted her chin up so she had to look him in the eye. "Promise?"

"Absolutely. And Mrs. Stonefield said she and Genevieve would probably be able to come today, so I'll have plenty of help if they're coming."

The phone rang.

They weren't.

And thus began the second day.

Cooper had been worried sick about Kate all morning. He found himself pacing the classroom as the kids took their weekly exam. His eyes lighted on James Hillside. The boys' head was bent over his paper, his tongue stuck out slightly as he wrote an answer. Cooper hurried over to him.

"James." The boy jumped as though he'd been shot.

"Sir?" He looked up, his blue eyes wide.

"You're a twin, aren't you?" Cooper whispered, trying not to disturb the others around them, but it was obvious the whole class was beginning to notice.

"Yes, sir."

"Your twin sister is Jane, right?"

"Um, yes, sir." James glanced nervously at his paper, knowing time was limited, and so was his knowledge of this week's history test.

"Did your mom ever mention if it was hard to take care of two babies?"

"Oh, yes, sir!" James brightened considerably. "My brother Michael was only two when we was -er, were- born and my mom said she almost lost her mind trying to tend to all of us."

His chest puffed out a little. "In fact, she says I was a colicky baby and didn't sleep for weeks!" He lowered his voice. "My mom lost twenty pounds then gained forty back the first year and had to start wearing glasses."

Cooper cocked his head. "Why'd she have to start wearing glasses?"

"She said it helped her see the light. My dad always laughs."

"Oh." Cooper nodded. "So I guess you don't have any other brothers or sisters?"

"Nope, we're it."

"Did your mom have anyone come in and help her out

when you guys were little?"

"Yes, sir. My mom says if it wasn't for Nana she couldn't have made it."

"Well, thanks for the talk, James. Oh, by the way, if you don't have time to finish the test, you can stay in a few minutes. I'll make it up to you, somehow." Cooper glared at the rest of the class, who quickly ducked their heads.

"Thanks, Mr. McGuire." James replied, relief obvious in his voice.

🐾 🐾 🐾 🐾

Kate was up to her elbows in soapy water when the doorbell rang. "Oh, no, please don't ring again!" She flung soapy water everywhere racing to the door before it made a baby waking sound again. Clancy stood, shook soap bubbles off his nose and trotted to the door, standing behind Kate in curiosity. When the door opened, it was Anna Crawford. She had her arms full of deli sandwich bags, plus a doughnut bag. Kate and Clancy's eyes widened in anticipation and he gave a soft woof. "Don't you dare bark!" Kate admonished him. He looked indignant, then totally ignored her, and went straight for the goods.

"Knock it off, big fella or you won't get your share." Anna warned him. He sat immediately.

"Anna!" Kate hugged her, trying not to crush the bags. "Why aren't you at work?"

"Doctor's appointment. I told them I wouldn't be back today. I have sick leave coming out the wazzu. I figured you needed some company and I need some experience." She grinned and peaked around Kate. "So, where are the little darlings?"

"Asleep, thank God. But not to worry, we have about twenty minutes, thirty on the outside and they'll be winding up their lung capacity."

Anna laughed. "Then let's eat while we can." They walked to the table, and Anna sat the bags down. "I was feeling generous, so Clancy has some turkey meat all for himself."

Kate got down the plates and glasses and poured them milk. "Sorry I don't have anything else to offer to drink, but Cayden is going grocery shopping this afternoon."

"Milk's fine. I need it anyway." She patted her tummy.

"So how are you?"

"Great. I'll tell you all about the doctor's visit while we eat."

Kate said the blessing. Anna chatted excitedly about her sonogram and the absence of morning sickness. She asked many questions about taking care of babies. Kate was amused and wondered if Anna was going to whip out a notepad any minute.

"Now, Kate," Anna said, pushing back her plate, "I am staying the afternoon. You are going to take a nap, then a bath, and for Pete's sake, wash your hair! If you'll tell me what to start for supper, I will. If I need to do laundry, or just play with the babies, I will. But I'm not taking no for an answer. This will be my only chance to really help out until we do our Thanksgiving thing."

Tears formed in Kate's eyes. "I'd tell you we could just sit and talk instead, but frankly, Anna, that all sounds so wonderful, I'm taking you up on it."

"I figured with the shower coming up Sunday and Mrs. Stonefield out of commission, I needed to do this."

"Mrs. Peabody is staying after the shower so we can go to Cayden's chorus concert." Kate chewed her lower lip.

"Do you think she'll be okay?"

"Sure. And if there's any doubt, I'll stay too. That is, if you still want me to after I baby-sit today. If you wake up and their diapers are on their heads and I'm feeding them dog food, you may change your mind."

Laughing together, they stood from the table and heard the first whimper off the monitor. "And the show begins!" Kate said.

CHAPTER TWENTY-THREE

By the time Cooper and Cayden arrived home, supper was a delicious smell coming out of the oven, Kate looked rested and coiffed, the twins were clean, and lying in the pack n play with Clancy eying them contentedly.

Cooper looked around and whistled. "I was gonna guess the good fairy, but I don't think she'd be up to the job."

Kate laughed. "Anna came after her doctor's appointment and took over. She let me sleep three hours! Then I got up, showered, washed my hair, put on clothes that don't have spit up on the shoulder and feel like a new woman."

"I told you a little help wouldn't hurt, Kate. See what a helping hand can do?"

She hugged him, and holding onto his embrace smiled into his eyes. "You're right. But I feel pretty worthless to not be able to last even two days without collapse."

"You were doing great. It was just too much for one person."

He walked over to the babies and leaned over to grab one. He snuggled the sweet smelling neck and made her giggle. "Good afternoon, Wren."

"Sparrow."

"I knew that. Just testin' to see if she knows her name yet."

"And guess what else? Mrs. Stonefield called. She and

Genevieve will be here early tomorrow afternoon to help out so we can get ready for the baby shower. Genevieve is spending the night to help with the feedings. She's looking forward to going to church with us Sunday. And remember after the baby shower Mrs. Peabody is staying to baby-sit while we go to Cayden's chorus concert. Your Aunt Cynthia called and said she'd help with the clean up after the shower and stay if Mrs. Peabody needed her, so Anna won't have to do that. She also told me she's going to come every Monday from one to four to give me a break. Mrs. Stonefield and Genevieve are coming Tuesdays and Wednesdays from ten to three and Mrs. Peabody has promised Thursdays, eleven to five. That will give me time to grocery shop so you and Cayden won't have to, do housework, cook and bathe!" she finished with a flourish.

Cooper laughed. "Well, things are certainly looking up." He had deposited Sparrow and picked up Wren. "When I left I thought I was gonna have to take the bull by the horns and insist we get you some help. Now it looks like the problem has been solved." He reached down and scratched Clancy behind the ears with one hand while he doddled Wren on his knee with the other. "That means we can play more in the evenings and spoil these two."

"And as soon as the twins are a little older I won't need so much help. Once they aren't quite so demanding I can manage on my own."

"Like when they turn twenty?"

Kate smacked him with the dish towel. "Thanks for the vote of confidence." She opened the oven. "Looks like the roast is about done." She lifted her head and listened. "I think that's Cayden pulling in with groceries. Help her unload and I'll make the salads."

Kate hummed and smiled to herself. A great relief washed over her and she figured even if her sleep was interrupted some tonight, she'd be able to get a lot done tomorrow.

🐾 🐾 🐾 🐾

Kate had snuggled under the covers a little after eleven, having fed the babies and given Clancy one last back yard walk. She had gone to sleep remembering the pleasant evening the family had shared.

She awoke with a start and looked at the clock. It was five fifteen and the babies had not awakened her! She grabbed the monitor. It wasn't on. Fear gripped her heart and she flew to the nursery. Stopping at the door, she saw Cooper in the rocking chair, a baby on each arm. Two empty bottles were on the table, along with two neatly folded dirty diapers. The monitor was turned off and he was talking to them softly. She strained to hear.

"What happens is, the Sandman comes driftin' into the window, lookin' for babies who need their sleep. He sprinkles a little sleep in their eyes and before you know it, he's floatin' them off to The Land of Nod. He zeroes in on Sleepy Town, lookin' for Nappy's house. There it is! And, boy is it a great place to be. Clouds are the ceilings with beautiful, sparklin' stars as night lights. Your cradles are in the bows of giant trees and humming birds sing you to sleep, 'cause they know the words in this land. You girls should be there right now." He yawned mightily and blinked. Then he muttered, "No wonder Kate is half dead doing this by herself all night and day."

"Need some help there?" Kate asked softly.

Cooper looked up and grinned. "Take your pick,

Mama. I have two fine little ladies who need putting to bed."

She walked over and scooped up Sparrow and laid her in the bed. Cooper did the same for Wren, putting them within touching distance of one another. He reached over and turned the monitor back on, and they slipped out of the room.

"I turned that thing off hoping you could actually sleep through the night."

"What got you up?"

"I was headed back from the bathroom and heard the first stirrings. I hurried in and turned off the monitor and took care of business. Didn't help much, did it?"

She smiled at him. "It helped a lot. Plus, I heard a new story."

"Aw, my mama used to tell that to me when she was trying to get me down for a nap. It always seemed like a great adventure."

They were at Kate's bedroom door. "I loved it. I'll have to remember it, unless you want to keep it special for the three of you."

An awkward silence followed, and Kate wanted to kick herself for suggesting this long future with Cooper in it.

She cleared her throat. "Well, we have a big day ahead of us tomorrow. You finally get to meet the mysterious Genevieve."

"From what you tell me, that will be a great adventure." He turned to leave. "Good-night, Kate. See you in the morning."

"Night, Coop. And thanks for doing night duty."

"Any time."

Kate closed her bedroom door and sat on the edge of the bed for a moment. She wondered, really wondered, what the future held for her romance with Cooper McGuire.

Cooper walked into his bedroom and barely kept himself from slamming the door in frustration. What was wrong with him! How could he have frozen Kate out like that? Because he was scared, that was why. He was liking – no loving – the kids and wife feeling that had been dropped into his home. It was good for Cayden too. Kate was like a big sister, a female influence Cayden had needed. She'd settled down so much since Kate had moved in, and talked more about church and God.

But was he ready, really ready, for marriage? To be a real daddy, not just someone who was helping out for now? He bowed his head. "God, I haven't taken the time to pray or read Your Word in days. I've lost touch with You and I'm feeling pretty embarrassed right now at how I handled the situation a minute ago. First, I ask You to forgive me for my absence, and secondly, I say, HELP!"

"Fear not, for I am with you."

Cooper expelled a sigh. "Thank You for being with me. Teach me what I need to do in these circumstances. Do I ask Kate to marry me, or what?"

"Wait on the Lord."

Cooper felt chills. Why did he put off talking to the Holy Spirit, when all he had to do was ask? "Thank you, Father. I won't stop reading Your Word again. I'll ask for guidance from You every morning. I want to do what's right by these babies and by Kate. I love her, but I don't know if it's Your will for us to marry. I'll wait."

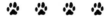

Kate had opened her eyes a little after seven,

anticipating the awakening of a baby or two. Opening her bedroom door she smelled coffee and bacon. With a smile on her face she tiptoed downstairs to see who was up early cooking. It was Cooper. "Hey, Coop. What got you up and going?" She reached and rubbed Clancy behind his ear as she passed him.

"Good morning. I woke up and thought I heard one of the babies." He shrugged. "I guess I was dreaming, because they were sleeping like little angels. I figured I'd take a turn at cooking this morning so when they do wake up you can be free to take care of them."

"Thanks." Kate walked over and gave him a hug, and lingered, her cheek resting on his back. "You feel so good. We don't get to hug as much lately."

"True. But once the chaos dies down a little, I'm gonna catch up. I miss our dates. We need to start that again so we can study our feelings more." He smiled her way, then handed her a mug. "Get yourself some coffee while you can."

Just as she poured a cup, the first little grunt came through on the monitor. "Ah, well. Those gals have their timing down pat." She sat the mug down. "I'll warm it up in the microwave in a little while."

"Do you need help bringing them both down?"

"Nah, I've got it covered."

Ten minutes later Kate came back down with a baby in each arm. "There's my girls!" Cooper said, putting the bacon and eggs on the table and coming to them. Taking Sparrow in his arms, he nuzzled her, making her smile. "I love it when they smile at me. Makes me feel ten feet tall."

"I know," Kate said. "It's the sweetest thing in the

world." She put Wren in her seat and got the bottles ready. She positioned herself between the two carriers and took Sparrow from Cooper.

"Kate, let me feed one of them. That gives us each a hand to feed ourselves."

"You sure you don't mind?"

"Nope, not a bit." He glanced at the clock. "Cayden needs to be up in about fifteen minutes. Help me watch the clock. I can't afford to start late this morning, and she wanted to ride with me today to pick up the groceries and supplies for the shower tomorrow."

Finishing up breakfast, Cooper went to wake Cayden and Kate started on the dishes.

Clancy jumped up suddenly from his place under the table and trotted to the door expectantly.

"I'm coming," Kate told him. Looking out the window, she saw a vehicle pulling into the driveway.

It was Mrs. Stonefield, and Genevieve was scrambling out of the car as quickly as she could.

CHAPTER TWENTY-FOUR

"Who just drove up?" Cooper asked as he came back downstairs.

"It's Mrs. Stonefield. She has Genevieve with her." Kate craned her neck to get a better look. "Genevieve is getting something out of the back seat."

"I thought you said they were coming early this afternoon, not early this morning."

"I did. Maybe I misunderstood." Kate patted at her hair and turned to Cooper. With a sincere look in her eye, she asked, "How does my hair look? Do I look okay?"

Cooper smiled tenderly. "You look fine. Why are you worried?"

Kate looked down. "I want Mrs. Stonefield to think I'm a good mother."

"Oh, honey, you are. I'm so proud of you."

The doorbell rang and Clancy let out a woof as Kate and Cooper hurried to the door.

"Come in, come in!" Kate exclaimed. "What in the world do you have there, Genevieve?"

In her arms was one of the biggest white rabbits Kate had ever seen. "This is Professor Parsley. We've just taken him to the vet'nary. We thought he had a cold."

Mrs. Stonefield smiled. "The vet said it was allergies. We came on here instead of going back home. Since Genevieve can't stay the night as planned, I knew this would give her some extra time with the twins, too. I hope you don't mind."

"Of course not. The vet sure is open early!"

"Yes, they open at seven. So people can come and go before they have to report to work, I suppose." She turned to Genevieve. "Now that you've shown them Professor Parsley, I think you need to return him to his carrier."

"No, Auntie, he'll get cold and lonely out there!"

"It's fine to bring his carrier in and put him in the corner of the den, isn't it Coop?" Kate asked.

"Sure thing." Cooper answered.

"Oh, well, then, I'll do it straight away." With that, Genevieve set the rabbit down and scooted out the door.

"Genevieve! I meant for you to take the Professor with you!"

But the Professor was making a getaway, hopping hurriedly toward the kitchen, where his twitching nose smelled food. He stopped abruptly. Staring him down as he rounded the corner was the forgotten dog. A deep rumble erupted from Clancy's chest. He splayed his feet and barked loudly, making the rabbit skitter on the hardwood floor, straight under the table. Clancy went after him, barking all the way.

"Oh, dear!" Exclaimed Mrs. Stonefield, taking off after Professor Parsley. "I forgot all about your dog!"

Kate stared wide eyed at Cooper before jerking herself away from his own shocked gaze. "Clancy, no!" And she, too, rushed to the kitchen.

"What's going on?" Cayden asked, coming down the steps, looking as though she'd just been awakened rudely in the middle of the night.

The door banged open as Genevieve tried to wedge the

large carrier through the opening.

Clancy tried to dive under the table, causing a clatter of everything on it, and the babies, who had been looking merely interested in the melee, simultaneously opened their little mouths in perfect circles and began to wail.

Genevieve brightened when she heard the babies. Pushing Cooper aside with the carrier, she exclaimed. "Let's take a keek at the wee bairns!" With a shocked look on her face as she saw the giant dog's rear end trying to stuff its way under the table, she admonished Kate. "I do say, Kate, you should keep that great beastie under better control!" Then she joined the rabbit and front end of the dog under the table. "Come here, Professor! I demand your obedience immediately!" And with that, she dragged the rabbit out, opened the carrier and snapped the door closed. "There!" Then turning to Clancy, she shook her finger in his face. "And shame on you, Mr. Dog! Professor Parsley is a great deal smaller than you are, and company to boot! Mind your manners!"

Clancy looked shocked, then mortified. He glanced at Kate, then slinking away, cowered in the corner of the den. Genevieve lugged the carrier right behind him and put Professor Parsley in the other corner.

Cooper stood, slack mouthed. Kate's hair stood on end. They each grabbed a baby and began to comfort her. Mrs. Stonefield looked embarrassed, and Cayden was trying her best not to burst into laughter.

"There now, we're all set." Genevieve said, coming back into the kitchen. She clasped her hands under her chin as she looked from one baby to the other. "What little darlin's they are! I'll wash up quick like, because I can't wait to hold the dearies in my arms once again." She dashed to the kitchen sink and began to scrub her hands furiously.

Kate turned to Mrs. Stonefield. "Professor Parsley?" She asked weakly.

"It's the name out of an old German Primary Reader Genevieve purchased off e-bay. I'm terribly sorry about all this."

Genevieve walked up to Cooper. "Let me properly introduce myself." She stuck out one very pink, slightly damp hand. "I'm Genevieve Cuttlebuck."

"Oh." Cooper looked as though he'd been permanently addled. "Uh, nice to meet you. I've heard a lot about you, Genevieve, but I dare say none of it has done you justice."

She smiled, obviously pleased. "Thank you. Now, may I please hold Wren?"

"Sparrow." Kate said.

"Really? You can tell already?"

"Most the time, yes."

Cooper looked terrified to actually hand over a helpless baby to this - this - whirlwind of destruction, but glancing at Kate, he knew he had to.

"Oh, she's much heavier than I remember! Hello, dear one! I've missed you so." Genevieve cooed to Sparrow. She looked up with tears in her eyes. "I love them both, truly I do!"

Kate felt herself softening. "I know it's been difficult, Genevieve. I'm hoping you'll find time to help out with them for a few days."

Genevieve beamed. "Oh, yes! Absolutely!" She turned to Mrs. Stonefield. "That is the plan, isn't it, Auntie?"

"Yes, Genevieve, it certainly is." Mrs. Stonefield looked around her. "Where do you want me to start?"

Kate said, "I didn't expect you till this afternoon. I was going to mind the babies and clean house while Cooper and Cayden shopped for the groceries and stuff for the baby shower."

Mrs. Stonefield looked startled. "Isn't the baby shower a surprise?" and then added, "And if not, shouldn't you be picking things out to your liking?"

"That would be nice, but I knew I couldn't handle the twins and concentrate on shopping." Kate's eyes twinkled. "It was decided a few days ago that since it was here it was becoming close to impossible to keep it a secret. They let me in on it so I could help out."

"Well, then, now that Genevieve and I are here, you're free to go along with them and get exactly what you like for the shower!"

"Or I can stay here with Genevieve and Mrs. Stonefield and help out, Kate. That will give you and Cooper a little alone time." Cayden said. She took Wren from Kate. "Come on, Wren let's join your sister at the table."

Kate looked, and Genevieve was spooning breakfast into Sparrow's open mouth, talking to her a mile a minute. "Well, okay, I guess." Kate bit her lower lip. "I'll write out the schedule. We shouldn't be gone longer than a few hours."

"Take as long as you want, Kate. All the girls and I will be fine. We'll clean whatever you tell us to, and the babies are no problem. Remember, I'm used to it."

Kate blushed. "Of course you are! You had them

longer than I have. I just haven't left them yet."

Mrs. Stonefield laughed. "I understand completely. That's the way all new mothers feel. But it will be good for you to get out and explore the world a little without them. Now, shoo, go get ready!"

Kate walked up stairs, still a little surprised at the turn of events. Then she realized she was getting out of the house! A thrill of joy shot straight through her and she ran up the stairs the rest of the way.

"Kate, I'm gonna walk Clancy and then I'll finish getting ready." Cooper called from downstairs.

"Okay, thanks." She picked up a pad and pencil and quickly jotted down the chores that needed done before the baby shower tomorrow. Then she made a separate list of Wren and Sparrow's usual schedule. She took a deep breath and grabbed her toothbrush.

Just as she finished dressing, Cayden poked her head in Kate's room. "I came up to get a couple of diapers." Cayden grinned broadly. "One thing I'll never worry about again."

"What's that?"

"Being a stressor on your relationship with Coop. If ya'll can survive Genevieve Cuttlebuck, you can survive anything!" Laughing, she closed the door.

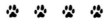

Kate and Cooper entered the door burdened with bags of supplies. Mrs. Stonefield hurried to help them, calling for Cayden and Genevieve to assist.

"Where are the babies?" Kate asked, as all three came to the rescue, unloading the vehicle.

"Asleep. They've been down for about thirty minutes, I guess. Your timing is excellent. Maybe we can get all this stuff put up before they awaken." Mrs. Stonefield held the door for Cooper as he made the last haul into the house. "Oh, and Kate, by the way, a gentleman called from the bank. His name is," she pulled a paper out of her pocket, "James Hulsey. The bank's closed now, but he left a cell phone number for you to call."

Kate looked puzzled. "I wonder what that's about. The mortgage is paid and my bank account is in good standing."

"Maybe you won the toaster of the week or something." Cooper volunteered.

"I'm sure that's it, Coop. After all, a busy guy like Mr. Hulsey would want to make sure I got that information a.s.a.p."

Cooper grinned. "Go ahead and call him. We'll get the groceries put up and by the time you're off the phone, you can start looking at all this stuff for the shower."

As Cayden zipped by Kate's room, putting up bathroom supplies, she heard Kate say, "I see. Well, thank you for calling, Mr. Hulsey. I'll get back to you at the first of next week." She was still standing in the hall, looking troubled when Cayden came by back by.

"You okay, Kate?"

"I guess. Someone has contacted the bank wanting to buy the lot my house was on."

"Well, that's good news, isn't it?"

"I'm not sure. I can't stay here forever, Cayden. Somewhere in the back of my mind, I must of thought I would build there again."

"Why can't you stay here? I can't stand to think about you and the twins leaving! I never thought of you actually leaving!"

Kate smiled at Cayden's vehemence. "I appreciate the way you feel, Cayden. Actually, that's a blessing to me. But Cooper and I have made no commitments to one another. I should be looking at living independently like I would have been if there had been no fire."

Cayden thrust her chin out stubbornly. "But there was a fire. I think God allowed it to happen so you would move here. And Cooper loves you, Kate."

"All the more reason I need to live somewhere else. The community has been very forgiving about our living arrangements because of the twins, and I can't leave yet. But once I am more adjusted and can make some decisions, I have to leave, Cayden."

"Maybe I'm the one who needs to leave, Kate." They both turned to see Cooper standing at the top of the stairs. "I didn't know it was bothering you."

"Coop, it's not bothering me. At least not till the last few minutes. And I certainly won't stand for you to leave. Why would you leave your own house?"

He shrugged. "That sounds a lot simpler than you and the girls leaving." He came to them and put his arm around each of them. "Let's not worry about it for the next few days, okay? We have a party tomorrow and we will be celebrating those two wonderful babies that are sleeping down the hall. Kate, you've got baby-sitting arrangements next week, so you and I can get away together and talk. How's that?"

"Nobody ever asks me anything!" Cayden pouted.

"Well what do you think, Cayden? Lord knows your opinion is pivotal in this discussion."

She stuck her tongue out at Cooper. "I think ya'll need

to cave and get married and then when the adoption court date comes, the babies will have a married mama and daddy."

Kate laughed. "Cayden, it's not like we had them out of wedlock and Cooper needs to make an honest woman out of me."

"I know," Cayden sighed. "But this is all so complicated." Tears pooled in her eyes. "And I love you and the girls so much, Kate. I don't want you to go."

"Thank you, honey. I love you too. I don't know what I would have done without your help these last few days. Even though I may leave this house, I promise I'll never leave your life, okay?"

She sniffed. "Okay. I guess."

"How about you running on down and we'll be there in a few." Cooper said.

"Sure. As usual, I'm relegated to 'the little sister run away and play' role." She mumbled down the stairs.

Kate grinned. "You have to give that girl credit for speaking her mind."

"For sure. Look, Kate, you've been under terrific stress these past few days. You can't possibly make a sane decision about moving out yet."

"I know. The phone call just jolted me into realizing I wasn't even thinking about the future."

"And no wonder. The present has been pretty full, don't you think?"

"Oh, yes. In fact, I think I heard the present whimper a little."

"No doubt. But before we go check on them, I want to say one thing. Promise me you won't look at moving out for at least a month. The girls will be older, you'll be more adjusted. In fact, why don't we look at this right after Christmas?"

"That's more like seven weeks. But okay. I'm pretty overwhelmed to think about moving the girls out before Christmas." She ducked her head. "I've been looking forward to having a real family Christmas in a real house for their first Christmas. Their dishes and all…"

"Good. Me too. And I'm going to ask Aunt Cynthia if she'll stay late one day next week and help Cayden get the babies to bed. I want us to go out on a real date so we can talk." He winked. "And smooch. Smooching would be good."

Kate laughed. "I'm all for both if you'll feed me good food."

"Done. Now let's get down there and decorate. I just love pink."

"Yes sir. But first we have to pick up a baby or two. I hear them again."

"Like I said, I love pink."

CHAPTER TWENTY-FIVE

Everyone sat around the table after supper. The babies had been put to bed after a stressful day of being handled a lot, frenzied housecleaning, and decorating. Clancy lay under the table, looking depressed, occasionally casting sour glances toward the caged Professor Parsley. Mrs. Stonefield had just mentioned having to go home when the doorbell rang.

Taken by surprise, and a bit embarrassed by it, Clancy lunged straight up, banged his head on the table, and began to bark viciously. While everyone tried to catch half full glasses, and Kate tried to shush Clancy before he awoke the babies, Cooper went to the door.

As Cooper opened the door, Clancy continued to overreact, almost knocking Cooper over. The dog stood splayed footed, back hair up, growling menacingly at the person who had rung the bell.

A very terrified young man stood there, a huge bouquet of fresh cut flowers grasped to his bosom. Clancy stopped barking instantly, whined a little, then jumped the man. A small yelp escaped the guy. He squeezed his eyes tight, and his lips moved in silent prayer. Clancy put a paw on each narrow shoulder and buried his head in the blooms. His delighted snuffling could be heard all over the house.

"Clancy! Get down!" Kate scolded. She yanked him down by the collar. "I'm so sorry! He was startled by the bell and over reacted. I have no idea what's gotten into him."

The deliveryman dropped the flowers to his side, where Clancy continued to blissfully inhale their scent. His tail wagged slowly.

Recovering, the young man smiled fondly down at the dog. "I reckon it's all right," the fella drawled. "A dog ain't nothin' but a nose and a tail with stuff in between, anyway."

Kate felt weak kneed over the whole thing. She signed the delivery ticket and tipped the guy – heavily. While Kate went in search of a vase, Cooper allowed Clancy to continue deep breathing into the flowers. He bent down and whispered in Clancy's ear. "No wonder a rabbit thinks he can get the best of you, ya big sissy."

"I heard that, Coop. Clancy may be ignoring you now, but you know how he likes revenge." Kate took the bouquet from him.

"I'll risk it."

Taking the flowers into the kitchen and pouring water into the vase, Kate was so tired she wondered how much more she could take tonight.

"Does this much codswallop go on all the time?" Genevieve asked.

"You got me there, Genevieve. I don't know what that means." Kate shrugged, grinning down at Genevieve.

"It means nonsense." Mrs. Stonefield said. "And Genevieve, that was rude. Apologize."

"I'm sorry. I didn't mean to be rude. It's just that - "

"Enough, Genevieve. Kate, honey, we must be going. We're tired, and I know you're beyond that. Now, what time do you want us here tomorrow?"

"Well, the shower is at four. Would three be okay?"

"Absolutely." She reached over and kissed Kate on the cheek. "I know saying get some rest is a silly thing with twin babies, but do try."

Kate smiled. "I will."

Kate got an amazing amount of rest that night. The babies slept till their four a.m. feeding and went right back to sleep. She awoke well rested at eight, ready to take on the day.

Cooper, however; had a rough night. He was awakened shortly after he went to sleep, as Clancy landed on his bed. After a brief struggle to get the dog off the bed, Cooper gave up. Clancy had him pinned across the legs and slept there the entire night. And snored. Loudly. Cooper swore at first light the dog was sleeping with a contented smile on his face.

Because, after all, revenge is sweet.

CHAPTER TWENTY-SIX

The second Sunday in November arrived. Having totally dressed the babies up for the first time, all three adults had fallen completely in love again, gazing upon the dresses, the socks, the ribbons. Arriving at church, Kate was suddenly sure she couldn't leave them in the nursery, until finally Cayden agreed to stay with them.

After church, both Kate and Cooper were surrounded by people adoring Wren and Sparrow, amazed at how identical they were, oohing and ahing over each move or sound. Cooper received a fair amount of nudges and winks, until finally Pastor Matt called him over. He handed Wren to Cayden and shouldered his way through the crowd.

"Fine looking babies."

"Thanks. Everyone seems to think so, Matt."

"Are you handling all this okay? I mean, I see all the innuendoes going on. Feeling a little pushed to be a married man and daddy all of a sudden?"

Cooper grinned, then sighed. "Frankly, Pastor, the only time I feel like a bachelor anymore is when I go to bed at night and I'm alone."

Matt patted him on the back. "Need to talk?"

Cooper sighed again. "Maybe. I love Kate. I'm starting to love the babies. Heck, I'm head over heels! I'm beginning to be unable to remember what life was like just a few days ago. Not that I mind, but I'm wondering if I need to leave or Kate needs to leave so we can get a grip on how strong our relationship is. Kate mentioned leaving yesterday, and I talked her out of it. Told her to wait till after Christmas. But do you think I need to leave sooner?"

"Whoa! You do need to talk!" Matt paused for a moment. "Look, Cooper, why don't you drop by Monday after you get out of school and let's just chat and pray for a while. How's that?"

Cooper nodded. "Unless I have to do something at the house. If I can't come, I'll call you."

Cooper walked back to all 'his girls' as they were walking out the door. He took Sparrow from Kate so she didn't have to wrestle both the diaper bag and baby to the car. Matt watched Cooper bend down and kiss the baby on the forehead as they walked out, then slip his free arm around Kate.

"Poor guy. He's got it bad. And not just for one woman. But for all three!" Matt said a quick prayer for them before turning his attention to someone else.

A quick lunch, down for a nap, last minute sprucing up of the house, then Mrs. Stonefield and Genevieve's arrival followed closely by Aunt Cynthia and Mrs. Peabody. Kate was making sure both the girls had on dry diapers when the doorbell rang. It was Anna.

"Kate Roe, do not peek in here! I mean it. I've got the cake and it's a surprise."

Kate laughed. "Okay. Just tell me when we can come down." She held Wren, Genevieve held Sparrow, and it was killing Genevieve to have to stay upstairs and not see the cake.

"Okay," Anna called. "But don't go in the formal dining room."

Kate looked at Genevieve. "I don't think I've been in there more than twice the whole time I've been here. Come on, let's show off our pretty babies."

The doorbell rang, and continued to do so for the next fifteen minutes as friends arrived.

Cooper had set up chairs in the den before he and Bailey had left with Clancy and Ernest with a promise of saved pieces of cake.

Many pictures were taken, everyone wanting theirs taken with at least one of the twins in their arms. The moment came for Kate to see the decorated cake, and it took her breath away.

On a flat piece of cake colored grass green, a giant chocolate bird's nest sat. Cupped inside were two baby birds, one with a grasshopper and one with a worm, both made from gummy candy. The lettering read "Welcome home, Wren and Sparrow!"

"I don't know whose idea this was, but it's great!" Kate exclaimed. "I just hate to be the one to cut it."

"Oh, Miss Kate, may I please have one of the dear birdies to eat?" Asked an over eager Genevieve.

Everyone laughed. "Pictures first, from every angle. Then I guess we'll eat it."

After refreshments, they all gathered in the den and began passing gifts to Kate. Genevieve sat on one side to hand them to her, and Cayden sat on the other, recording the giver's names.

Two last gifts remained. John Donaldson's wife, Patsy stood. "Kate, your class all wanted to be a part of this. Since it would have been difficult to contain over twenty second graders, we asked them to compile what they wished, and John promised them he'd make sure you got it all. As you can imagine, we didn't want them to think they had to spend money, because frankly, many of the families don't have a lot. But we did encouraged them to make a card. In this bag are several cards, some homemade gifts as well as a few purchased ones. The ladies here decided to save this bag till next to last."

She handed the large gift bag to Kate, not answering the question in Kate's eyes – *'So, then what's been saved for last?'*

Inside were numerous, carefully colored creations that were sweet and funny. Some had purchased tiny socks, rattles or bibs. Each gift had a name attached to it that brought joy to Kate's heart.

When finished, Patsy presented her with the last gift. "This is from Todd Brown – well really, from his mother, Clarice. I'm sure you remember Todd was adopted as an infant, so she recognizes this as a pretty special time for you." Patsy smiled down at Kate. "And I will tell you, it's grand."

Puzzled, Kate reached into the bag. What looked like a picture was wrapped in pretty paper. She gently pulled the paper away, and turned the picture frame over. Beautifully embroidery depicted a tree limb, sitting upon it a bird's nest with a wren and a sparrow inside. On each of their tiny wings was their name, Sparrow or Wren. They were looking up beseechingly at two large birds – one on each side of the nest. To the left was a robin, the name Robyn embroidered on her wing. With a clawed foot holding a scroll, she was reaching across the babies nest and a beautiful yellow bird was also reaching across to accept it.

On her wing was embroidered Kate.

Under the scene was an unfurled scroll with the poem:
A mother's love is greater than
The strength of many giant men.
It tarries not when called to sacrifice
Her heart, her soul, her very life.

As Kate read the poem with a shaky voice, there wasn't a dry eye in the place. Genevieve blew her nose loudly.

Kate looked to Patsy. "Where is Mrs. Brown?"

Patsy laughed. "She said she didn't know you well enough to come. But I think the real reason is she was embarrassed for you to see and read her art. It's a masterpiece, isn't it?"

"I think it's the most beautiful thing I've ever owned."

"When Anna saw the piece, she knew the shower had to have the same theme. That's where the idea of the cake came from."

Shortly thereafter, guests began to leave. Patricia Hawkins reminded Kate that she had her own set of twins at home and would be glad to offer advice or just a listening ear anytime. Mrs. Peabody, Aunt Clara, and Mrs. Stonefield began cleaning up, shooing Cayden and Kate upstairs to get ready for the chorus concert. Cooper, Bailey and the dogs arrived, boisterous and hungry. Anna fed them. Genevieve was in charge of guarding babies (mostly to keep her out of the way).

And then it was on to the concert. A very beautiful Cayden left early when Mike picked her up. After a near panic attack, Kate left (sans babies) with Cooper. Both their cells phones on, with promises that they would be called if necessary.

The concert was a polished performance, and Cooper had actually remembered the camera. Cayden looked like an adult in her formal attire. Cooper felt a stab of panic when he saw the look in Mike's eyes, and a sudden rush of guilt. He hadn't paid enough attention to Cayden lately. She'd been behaving and the twins had kept him occupied. He vowed to get a little more inquisitive starting tonight.

When Cooper and Kate arrived home, they found Mrs. Stonefield alone downstairs, watching TV. She greeted them warmly, Clancy by her side.

"How was the concert? Do we have a budding star in Cayden?"

Kate answered, "She looked beautiful. She had a two line solo and did nicely." She rubbed Clancy's ears. "Where is everyone?"

"Your Cynthia and Clara left about an hour ago. They stayed till everything was spic and span. Genevieve is upstairs, sound asleep with the twins."

Kate smiled. "Let her spend the night, if that's all right."

"Are you sure you don't mind? She's so tired, I hate to disturb her."

"That's fine. Since it didn't work out for her to sleep over last night, it's only fair. Cooper's Aunt Cynthia is coming over from one to four tomorrow, and I'm going to try and get in touch with the guy who is interested in purchasing my land to see if he can meet me during that time. Since I have to leave anyway, I can bring Genevieve home, if you'd like."

"That's all right, dear. I've grocery shopping to do

around eleven. I'll pick her up then."

Mrs. Stonefield left shortly afterwards, Cooper and Kate chatted briefly until Cayden came in, walking on cloud nine.

"So, how is Mike treating you?" Cooper said suspiciously.

Cayden narrowed her eyes for a moment. "He treats me very well. I don't like your tone, Coop. It sounds like you want to fuss."

"Sorry. You just looked so grown up tonight, and he looked like a puppy mooning over you. Worried me, that's all."

Cayden leaned down and kissed his cheek. "Stop worrying. We're fine. He's a great guy. I promise."

Kate stood and stretched. "It's almost midnight. If I'm lucky I can sleep four hours before the girls wake up hungry."

She was wrong.

So very wrong.

CHAPTER TWENTY-SEVEN

At two a.m. Kate sat straight up in bed, heart pounding. She immediately capped her hand over her ears. What was that noise?!

She got quickly out of bed, ramming her feet into her slippers, keeping her ears covered at all times. She glanced over at the monitor. The audio light was running up and down. She figured the babies were screaming in terror.

She fled her room. The noise in the hall was louder. She met Cayden running down the hall as she ran toward the nursery. "What's going on?" Cayden yelled. Kate shook her head and kept on going, with Cayden right on her heels.

The babies were screaming and they each took one into their arms. She covered one of Sparrow's ears with her chest and the other with her hand, motioning for Cayden to do the same for Wren. Cooper opened the door and motioned them downstairs. "It's some kind of house alarm. Let's all get downstairs and I'll call the police."

As Kate turned she nearly fell over Genevieve, who was looking at her with big eyes that held unshed tears. She had her hands over her ears too, so Kate motioned her to follow them.

Clancy was in the hall, running around in circles, barking. When he saw Kate, he swiftly fell in line and ran down the stairs.

Kate saw Cooper on the phone, the other ear covered. She wondered why he didn't go outside so he could hear, than thought maybe someone had tried to break in the house. Underneath the loud *"Wah, wah, wah,"* she thought she could also hear a *"Wonk, wonk, wonk,"* but had no idea what anything was.

Cooper snapped his phone shut, motioned for Kate, and they stepped out in the hall. He put his mouth to her ear. "I've called the police. They're on their way. We have a burglar alarm system, but I had no idea it would do this. I looked at all the doors, I don't see where anyone has tried to break in."

"Cooper, what's the other noise?"

"Huh?" He listened intently, then an incredulous look came over his face. "It's the car alarm!"

Cayden came out to the hall and yelled, "Coop, the cops are here."

There was a uniformed officer and a guy with some kind of tool box. He held up the box with a questioning look and Cooper nodded yes and tilted his head toward the laundry room.

The man disappeared and in a few moments they were in silence except for the *"Wonk, wonk, wonk"* coming from the garage. They were also in total darkness.

"Hold on, people, we won't be in the dark but a second," came a disembodied voice from the laundry room. "And if you can find a flashlight and car keys, could somebody kindly stop that dang noise?"

The police officer immediately snapped on his flashlight. Cooper went to the counter and picked up the car keys. He opened the kitchen door, aimed the remote and the *"Wonk, Wonk,"* stopped.

The electricity was restored quickly, but the twins were

still screaming and Clancy was still barking furiously. Cooper yelled, "Biscuit!" which made the policeman jump. Clancy stopped barking and immediately sat, an expectant look on his face. Cooper took the baby from Cayden to shush her and Cayden collapsed on a stool.

"Okay folks, the alarm is shut down. I have no idea why it did this. Actually, I've never seen one quite like it. Musta bought it from The Acme Home Alarm System Company." He laughed at his own joke.

"Why'd the car alarm go off?" Cooper asked.

The repairman shrugged. "Sympathy pains, I guess. Probably the high velocity of sound triggered it."

The policeman spoke up. "The alarm didn't send anything to us at the station. My partner has looked around outside and there is no evidence that anything has been tampered with, which makes us think it was a false alarm. Did your dog act like he was suspicious?"

"He was sound asleep until the noise." Cooper answered. Clancy wagged his tail.

"I advise you to have it checked out in the morning." The policeman nodded to Cooper. "Well, we'll leave you folks and hope you have a better night from here on out."

Cooper thanked them and showed them to the front door. The repairman cooed to the twin Cooper held, which made her cry louder.

He walked back to the dazed women in the kitchen. Cayden and Kate were both crying quietly, both babies were crying not so quietly.

Genevieve, who had stood silently through the whole thing spoke. "I am completely gobsmacked over this whole endeavor." She walked up to Cooper, who was mutely surveying them all. His hair stood straight up, his unshaven face sleepy and his bleary eyes blank. His robe was barely hanging from his shoulders and his feet were bare. Genevieve tiptoed, trying to be face to face, and whispered reverently, "Are ye suffering in silence, now?"

Cooper blinked. Squinting, a strangled noise emerged before he spoke. "No, Genevieve, no I'm not." He reached over to the dog food tin, handed Clancy his long awaited biscuit, and handed Wren to Cayden. "I'm going back to bed." And he left them standing there.

"Well, of all things -" Cayden looked as if she were about to go after him in righteous indignation, but Kate stopped her.

"Let him go. That's what we all need to do. Help me fix the babies a bottle and we'll get them back to sleep. Genevieve, go on back to bed, honey. You'll be exhausted in a few hours when your aunt comes to get you."

"All right, Miss Kate, see you in a bit." She turned to Clancy. "Come, ye great beastie. I'm in no mood to walk the stairs alone." Clancy got up, tail wagging, and followed.

Kate gave a wan smile to Cayden, who smiled back, shaking her head at the retreating Genevieve.

CHAPTER TWENTY-EIGHT

The babies had slept till seven the next morning, which had given Kate more sleep than she had bargained for. By the time she got them changed and downstairs, Cooper had toast and oatmeal on the table. Cayden looked so sleepy she was almost in her bowl, and Clancy was on his back, paws up, snoring.

Cooper looked up, a bit sheepishly. "Morning, Kate. I see our little birdies let you sleep in."

She smiled. "Yes, and I'm grateful. Coffee smells good."

"I'll pour you a cup while you fix the bottles." He nudged Cayden. "Wake up before you burn your nose in the oatmeal. Is Genevieve still asleep?"

"Sleeping like the dead, as they say. The babies didn't even get a movement from her. She slept right on."

"What time does she have to be up?"

"I'll wake her about ten. Mrs. Stonefield will be here by eleven. I'm going to call that Mr. Hulsey at the bank as soon as ya'll are gone and I get the girls settled, to see if he can arrange a meeting for me with the guy who is interested in the property. I'm hoping for this afternoon while Cynthia is here to stay with Wren and Sparrow."

"I really don't like you meeting with some guy alone. We don't know anything about him."

"Don't worry. I'll ask Mrs. Peabody to keep a watch out."

"You mean look out her window or something?"

"Yeah," Kate grinned. "Or something like that."

"Do you think she'll be comfortable spying on you like that? I mean, won't that go against her nature?"

There was a moment of silence, before they both burst out laughing, startling Cayden into full wakefulness.

🐾 🐾 🐾 🐾

Cynthia arrived right on time. After a brief rundown of what to do to whom and when, Kate set off to meet with a Mr. Hansard. She called Mrs. Peabody to ask her if she would dog sit Clancy while she showed the property, and asked if she would mind 'glancing out the window' from time to time to make sure everything looked okay with Mr. Hansard and herself. Mrs. Peabody readily agreed.

Kate pulled up to the curb in front of her yard. Tim Hansard was already standing there, looking toward the remains of the house. He was a tall, slender, dark haired fellow who appeared to be in his late twenties. At the sound of her car, he turned, a smile on his face. A very nice face.

"Hello," Kate called. "I'll be with you in a minute. She went around to the passenger side and leashed Clancy, then both she and the dog walked into the yard. "This is my guard dog. The next door neighbor is going to keep him while we look around."

Tim Hansard just nodded his head. His lips twitched slightly at the "guard dog" mention, as Clancy was grinning a big old dopey dog grin, tongue lolling out, rear end swaying to the beat of his tail.

Kate hurried across Mrs. Peabody's lawn. The door opened before she could knock. "Here you go." she said, handing the leash over to Mrs. Peabody. "Holler if you need me."

"Your Mr. Hansard is very nice looking. I bet he's a gentleman. But I'll keep a lookout."

Mrs. Peabody winked and closed the door.

Kate smoothed her hair and once again headed toward her property. She held out her hand and introduced herself.

"It's very nice to meet you, Miss Roe. Quite a handsome dog you have there. I have a Bull Mastiff at home. She'd probably fall in love instantly with your dog."

"Thank you. It's good to know you're a big dog lover too." She glanced up at the house and sighed. "Well, let me show you around and tell you about the house fire."

He listened sympathetically, a lot of sorrow on his face. "I know this must have been a nightmare. Are you sure you are okay with us doing this?"

"I am. I can't shy away from it all the time."

"Can you tell me how your house was laid out? I'm thinking if I buy the land, I might be able to use your basement and foundation to build on. I haven't checked that out, but it would save a lot financially and time toward building."

"It sure would! We can get close to the house, even step in the front part, but we can't go in further."

After some time of looking and asking many questions, they stood at the kitchen counter. He talked about an offer, and Kate told him she would consider it. As they turned to leave, he looked down.

"What's this?" He bent to pick up something from the trash on the floor. "It's a spoon."

"My favorite antique soup spoon! Thank you!" As he gave it to her, his hand brushed hers slightly. Kate felt color rise to her face and thought *'how silly for that to embarrass me!'* She laughed nervously. "I always saved this spoon for eating my ice cream." She smiled at the young man. "It's interesting that every time I feel really sad about the house, God gives me a present."

James smiled. "I'm glad I was able to be God's Hand."

They turned and headed for the door. He stopped abruptly and turned to her. "This may sound presumptuous, but I know you're not married and I wondered if you'd like to go to dinner with me."

Kate looked at him, surprised. "Thank you for the offer. But I am involved with someone." She laughed. "And I'm in the process of adopting twin babies."

"Wow!" He laughed. "If you ever get uninvolved, call me. I'll take all three of you out to eat. How's that?"

Kate joined his laughter and promised him she would.

After James drove away, Kate had the oddest feeling that he had been more of the hand of God than he realized. She was flattered he had asked her out, but it made her realize how much she truly loved Cooper. She sighed. Hopefully Cooper cared enough to take on babies, a dog and her own complicated self.

She could only hope.

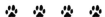

Cooper got out of his car and walked slowly up the church steps. He really wanted to talk to Pastor Matt, but he didn't want to almost as much.

Matt met him at the door. "Come on in, Coop. My office is cluttered but warm." Over his shoulder he asked about Cooper's day.

"It was okay. The kids are getting anxious about the Thanksgiving holiday coming up. We get four days plus the weekend, so it will be quite a treat."

"What are you and Cayden doing for Thanksgiving this year? Going to your Aunt Cynthia's as usual?"

"As a matter of fact, we're doing it a little differently. Aunt Cynthia is coming to our house to cook, and Bailey and Anna Crawford are joining us too. Anna will help cook and Kate is going to have a couple of desserts ready beforehand. While all the women cook, I'm to tend to the girls. I think Cayden has invited Mike, but he may have family plans."

They sat down in Matt's office and Matt folded his arms on the desk. "So, have you been praying about this whole situation you have on your hands?"

Cooper squirmed in his seat. "A little. But to be honest, between babies and school, I pretty much just function. I don't have very much quiet time anymore. I still try to read my Bible every night, but more often than not, I go to sleep before I finish praying."

"You're up with the babies too?"

"Not exactly. But I hear Kate sometimes. And if I don't hear her, I get concerned and open my door to make sure the babies are all right. And Clancy has found a way to open doors with his mouth, so half the time I wake up with him in the bed with me."

Mike laughed. "Sorry. But that is one smart dog."

"Yeah, too smart for his own good sometimes. Don't tell him, but I've grown very fond of the mutt."

"How is Cayden adjusting to all this?"

"She absolutely loves it. She got all upset when Kate mentioned moving out. She wants the situation to be permanent."

"What do you want, Cooper? Where does your heart

live?" He looked intently at Cooper. "If your heart resides with Christ, then He will provide these answers. If your heart belongs to someone or something else, you can't trust it. The Bible says our hearts are wicked. So, I ask you this: if your heart resides with Christ, what do you want?"

Cooper sat back in his chair. "I don't know. I think I want to get married at some point." He was quiet for a moment. "The weird thing is, on a day to day basis this is great. There's not much I dread or dislike. But when I try to look into the future, marrying with two babies, I panic. Truth is, I had just started thinking about discussing marriage when all heck broke loose. Kate finds out she's got a baby on the way, then it's two babies, then her house burns and she's living with us. And then the babies come home."

"Cooper, frankly I'm surprised you haven't run away from home!" Matt shook his head. "Do you realize how much stress this has put you and everyone else under?"

"Yeah. I guess we've done pretty well in spite of it all."

"How about sex?"

Cooper looked startled. "Huh?"

"Have you and Kate had a lot of sexual temptation, living under the same roof?"

Cooper threw back his head and laughed. "Preacher, when Kate moved in she was suffering from smoke inhalation and shock. Then the real shock came in the form of twin babies. I've had less sexual temptation in the last few weeks than since I was a little boy and didn't even know what that meant." Cooper leaned forward. "It's easy to see how couples have a first baby. But I'll be honest with you, Matt. I don't see how they ever have the energy, much less the time to create another baby."

Matt grinned, then laughed out loud despite his best effort not to. "Well, that's good, I guess. So, why are you thinking of moving out? To get away from it all? To look proper in the eyes of the community? Is God leading in this decision?"

Cooper sighed. "I don't know. Kate thought maybe they should leave because if people see how much we care about each other they'll start talking about us living together. I really don't want people to think badly of any of us." He chewed his lower lip. "And maybe I need to get away to see more clearly. I love Kate, but do I love her enough? Is this what God wants us to do? And then I think, if He doesn't, why in the world did He allow all this to happen? I love those babies. Talk about where my heart lives! I can hardly stand to think about being away from them. And it's only been a few weeks! How will I feel in a few more weeks? I made Kate promise to stay till after Christmas. That way Wren and Sparrow will be a little older. But the real reason I wanted her to stay was because of the fantasy of a Christmas with Santa coming. The tree, the presents, the food. And the girls' mother left heirloom Christmas china we'll use for Christmas dinner."

Matt smiled. "Quite a picture you paint." He leaned forward in his chair. "I'll tell you what I see, Cooper. I see the love you have for Kate and the twins. The only negative thing I see is your doubt, or maybe really, it's fear. And I don't blame you at all. After Thanksgiving, why don't you rent a cabin somewhere quiet for a couple of days and really pray and study? I feel confident God will make

Himself heard. It's hard to listen with all the chaos you're living in. He wants you to listen, Cooper. He will instruct you if you'll take time to listen."

Cooper looked thoughtful. "That sounds like a good idea." His face began to light up. "Yeah, that's a great idea! At least I'll have time to listen. I could go up to Lake August the Sunday after Thanksgiving and come home Monday evening. That would give me time."

He stood. Matt shook his hand after they had a brief prayer, where Matt asked God to remind Cooper that his heart should really live in Christ wherever God has placed him.

Cooper felt lighter than he had in weeks. He knew God always answered prayer, and boy, did he need some answers!

CHAPTER TWENTY-NINE

Cooper pulled into the driveway and noticed everyone was home but him. As he opened the door, Clancy greeted him happily. Cooper bent down to scratch the dog's ears. Straightening he sniffed, smelling food in the air for supper.

He ambled on into the kitchen. "Something sure smells good."

Kate turned from the stove. "I've got steaks out on the grill, potatoes frying and salad in the fridge. Cayden said if you were too tired, she'd watch the steaks. Mike's eating with us, so I figured they could grill outside and talk since the weather has warmed up a little, and we could cook inside and smooch."

Cooper grinned, and grabbed her by the waist, kissing her soundly. "You're my kind of chef."

As they settled into the getting supper cooked routine, Cooper told Kate about his talk with Pastor Matt. "I made the reservations for Sunday afternoon, coming back Monday afternoon since there's no school until Tuesday. I figure I'll head out as soon as church is over. It's just a forty-five minute drive, so I'll have plenty of time. Monday I can stay until about six, and if ya'll wait supper, I can be home to eat by seven."

"That's a great idea, Coop. We all need times like this. I'm glad Matt recommended it."

They chatted some about the upcoming Thanksgiving

feast. Cooper said he'd put the turkey in before they went to bed Wednesday evening. Kate had talked to Cynthia, who would come over about nine Thanksgiving morning and help set up tables. Anna and Bailey would show up about eleven with their share of the food. Cooper agreed to baby-sit while Kate did some serious baking on Wednesday, since there would be no school that day.

"And what about that date we've been talking about?" Cooper asked. "Why don't we plan a night out the Tuesday before Thanksgiving. There's no school the next day, so Cayden will probably readily agree to baby-sit."

"Cayden baby-sit when?" She asked as she came through the French doors, steaks piled high on a platter.

Kate reached to brown the rolls and get salad fixings out of the refrigerator. "Tuesday night before the holiday. No school the next day, so what do you say?"

"Can I help her?" Mike asked, as he came in with tongs, garlic, and other paraphernalia from grilling.

Cooper scowled. "Only if you help with the babies and don't forget they are even here."

"Cooper!" Cayden scolded. "How could anybody in their right might forget the twins? Don't be so condescending."

Cooper looked thoughtful. "Speaking of, where are they?"

"Look in the floor." Kate said, smiling toward the den.

They were in little swings, which had been wound up. Both of them were wide eyed at the adventure, and Clancy sat between them, head going back and forth as though he was at a tennis match.

"You know," Cooper said, "Clancy could just raise

'em and save us a lot of trouble. They'd be speaking French in no time."

"Very funny, Coop." She walked over and gazed fondly at the three. "But he does take his job seriously, doesn't he?"

Sparrow made a grab for his whiskers every time she swung by, and Clancy never even flinched. Wren watched her sister, then, she too made an effort. Both of them fell short by a few inches.

Cooper grinned down at the dog. "Won't be long buddy boy before you are going to be in a heap of trouble. When these little girls get mobile, watch out!"

"Bread's ready. Let's eat! Come on, Coop and say the blessing before the steaks get cold."

The amen was said soon enough and the evening was as pleasant as any Cooper had ever had. He began to have second thoughts about going away, even for a night. What if one of the babies got sick? What if they did something for the first time and he missed it? He sighed to himself. He figured he knew the answer to his commitment before even going. But he knew he and God still needed to talk.

🐾 🐾 🐾 🐾

The following days ran like a well oiled machine. The only glitch had been when Professor Parsley cornered Clancy in the dining room. The Professor had apparently chewed threw the cage latch and had freed himself. When Clancy ambled into the room, the Professor wasted no time in running straight at him. Because of the scolding Genevieve had given Clancy the last time, he sat humbly in the corner until someone found them.

All the women voted not to tell Cooper.

Clancy was forever thankful.

The Tuesday before Thanksgiving dawned cold and clear. Kate found herself anticipating an actual date with excitement and a little anxiety. She smiled to herself. She wondered if she could remember how to really fix up without a baby on each shoulder.

Cooper fidgeted all day at school. The kids were on the verge of being out of control, as they always were right before any kind of school break. This one was no different. He caved for much of the day, which amazed the kids, but they took only a little advantage of his preoccupied mood.

He showered and shaved after making sure each baby got lots of tickles and hugs. He picked out Sunday trousers and even put on a tie. He shined his shoes using the back of each pant leg after he put the shoes on, checked his teeth in the mirror, shook out his wool jacket and ran down the stairs.

And waited.

He looked at his watch. Okay, he was ready ten minutes early. He got a glass of water and sat down to talk to Clancy. Clancy put both paws over his ears and tried to go back to sleep.

Finally Cooper heard Kate coming down the upstairs hall. He walked to the foot of the stairs to wait. "Wow." was all he could say as Kate came down the stairs. He felt like he was in one of those cheap love story movies where time slows down and the beautiful woman walks toward her man until she reaches the foot of the stairs.

Cooper reached up and touched Kate's hair. "I never knew before what the Bible meant when it says a woman's hair is her crowning glory." He swallowed hard. "I've never seen you look so beautiful."

Kate smiled. "It's only because you haven't seen me without baby spit up and sweats for weeks."

"Not true. We've been to church."

"That's different. Tonight I'm trying to look like a woman with appeal."

"Well, teacher, you get an A+."

"Thank you. Let me get my coat and we'll go."

They both stuck their head in the den where Cayden and Mike were watching television, the baby monitor next to them.

"We're gone guys. Listen to that monitor carefully."

"We will, Coop. Don't be such a mother hen. I've got it turned up as loud as it can go. We can hear both of them breathing."

"Thanks you two." Kate said as they walked out the door.

"No prob."

They were treated like royalty at the restaurant. Only a few people were scattered about, so they were given a seat right in front of the fireplace. There was a piano player on the other side of the room playing very softly.

After the waiter took their orders and left, both seemed a little embarrassed.

Finally, Kate laughed. "I feel so shy. Like this is our first date."

"We've been in utter chaos and now the calm. We usually can't hear ourselves talk unless we shout. I don't think the folks here would take kindly to that."

Kate laughed. "I agree." She took a sip of water. "So, tell me about your planned trip. I bet you are so excited to get to be by yourself."

Cooper grinned sheepishly. "To tell you the truth, I've thought about backing out a hundred times. I don't know if I can stand being away from you and the girls. I feel like such a wimp. I've sold out. What will my bachelor buddies think of me?"

"I won't tell if you won't." Kate said. "You know you'll love it once you get there. And it's less than an hour's drive. If we needed you, you could be home quickly."

"But what if one of the girls says her first words or something and I miss it?"

"Cooper, they're not quite three months old. I wouldn't expect a polished speech on some complex subject for several months. You've seen them smile. I know they're changing every day, but nothing monumental is likely to happen."

Cooper sighed. "I guess I just feel reluctant. But I know I have to do this. I have to have some time alone with God. I haven't in a while."

"I manage to squeeze some of that in when ya'll are gone and the girls are asleep. You have been so busy I can see why you need it."

The waiter brought their salads and drinks. Cooper said the blessing over the food and they ate silently for a few moments. Cooper finally laid down his fork. "I want to discuss something."

Kate tilted her head. She felt anxiety rise up in her throat. "Okay, shoot. What is it?"

"Not too long before the house burned, Cayden asked me if you and I might get married. I told her we hadn't even discussed it, and that was true. But after we talked, I couldn't get the idea out of my head. I tried to mention it a couple of times, but would get interrupted. Remember the night Clancy rolled in something dead?"

"Yes. That's the night I told you about the baby, which turned out to be babies, as you might have noticed."

Cooper snorted. "I've noticed that from time to time. I had fully intended to discuss the possibility of marriage with you that night. But first it was Clancy being bathed, and then you had something to tell me, which was the baby news. Later, I thought maybe that was God's way of stopping me from talking to you about getting married. I thought maybe I wouldn't be able to take on the responsibility of fatherhood so soon." He looked down at his hands. "I even thought I might not be able to love someone else's child as though it were my own."

"And?"

Cooper gave a short laugh. "And, how can I resist? You know I'm head over heels about those babies. But it does change everything. I admit I've felt confused and have even tried to divorce myself from emotions some. Plus, who has had time to know what God wants of me? Are you and the girls in His will for me to become husband and daddy? Or is this just a time of helping out?"

"So this is why you're going off to pray?"

"Yes. I spilled my guts to Pastor Matt. He believes I know the answer and just need confirmation." He took Kate's hand. "I need to make absolutely sure before I even ask you, Kate. I think it's only fair."

Kate nodded. "It is only fair for all of us. I'll be praying too."

Their food arrived and they ate, mulling over the

conversation.

""Kate, do you know what you'll say if I do ask?"

She smiled. "We'll cross that bridge when we come to it. It's not fair to ask me that."

Kate's cell phone rang. "We're almost finished." She hung up. "I guess we skip desert. That was Cayden and she thinks Wren has a fever."

"See? This is the kind of thing I worry about when I plan on leaving."

"She didn't say *Typhoid* Fever. It's probably nothing." But the worried look in her eye gave her assurance away as false.

Cooper got the waiter's attention, explained their need to leave and was able to pay quickly.

He drove just slightly over the speed limit, but only because Kate kept insisting he slow down.

🐾 🐾 🐾 🐾

Kate looked closely at the thermometer. "Wren's got a fever of one hundred-three degrees." She held the fussy Wren close to her.

"I have a friend I graduated high school with. His name is Jeff Stiles. Let me see if I can get him on the telephone. He made a doctor and was really smart – doubled up on everything in college, and I'm pretty sure he made pediatrics his specialty." Cooper dashed out of the nursery.

Cayden and Mike hovered over Sparrow, who seemed fine. She was sleeping peacefully.

In just a few moments they could hear Cooper on the phone with someone. When he finished, they heard him bounding back up the stairs.

"God is good, folks. I got hold of Jeff's wife and she

gave me his beeper number. He is at the hospital, just about to finish up stitches on a kid's head. He said to come on over and he'd wait on us. I explained there were twins, but only one sick, he said bring them both anyway." He turned to Kate. "Let's go."

Kate looked at Cayden as she began to bundle up Sparrow. "You want Mike to stay with you until we return?" She absently pushed Clancy's head away as he tried to sniff Wren.

"Yeah. We'll walk Clancy and wait for you to call or come home." She looked at Mike. "Do you think your parents will be okay with that?"

"I'm sure they will. I'll call and check in a few minutes. I don't have to be home until midnight anyway 'cause there's no school tomorrow."

When Kate and Cooper arrived at the ER, a trim young man was standing at the door. He and Cooper shook hands, and Cooper said simply, "This is Kate, these are the babies, where do you want us?"

His friend smiled, and walked rapidly to an examining room. "I'll have a receptionist come in after we've checked over these two to get the paperwork squared away. I'd like to have a job tomorrow, you know, and paperwork rules the roost here."

Cooper looked chagrinned. "Sorry. They've never been sick before, and, well, they're so little."

Jeff smiled. "I understand." Turning to Kate, he said, "Okay, Mama. Have you noticed any unusual behavior or any symptoms before the fever?"

"When we got home after Cooper's sister called and said she thought Wren was sick, I noticed she was fussy, of course. But she was also pulling on her ear."

"Ah." Jeff smiled and took Wren from Kate. He laid her on the exam table and looked her over once, then gently looked into both ears. "I see a very angry inner ear." He took her temperature again, listened to her heart, moved her arms and legs and looked into her eyes. As he bent down to look up her nose, she sneezed right on him. "Bless you!" he exclaimed as Cooper and Kate laughed. "She has an ear infection. I'll give you some numbing drops to put in her ear that will help with the pain. I'll also give you some oral drops for fever." He picked Wren up and handed her back to Kate. Leaning up against the exam table, he crossed his arms and frowned slightly. "I'd really like to wait about thirty six hours before I prescribe an antibiotic. If she's still fussy or running a fever, we'll re-consider."

He walked over to the sink and washed his hands vigorously. As he dried them, he smiled at Sparrow. "Let's see baby number two." He looked at Kate. "Any symptoms from her?" Kate shook her head no. "I'll warn you, she looks as though she feels fine, so she may not like me messing with her."

True enough, Sparrow put up a ruckus about being poked and prodded and over her howls, Jeff declared her healthy.

Washing his hands again, he then wrote quickly on two sheets of paper, he said, "If the fever isn't gone by Thanksgiving morning, call my house. I'll call the pharmacy and you can pick up an antibiotic. If she gets worse, of course, bring her to my office tomorrow. But I think she'll be fine by then." He stuck out his hand to shake Cooper's. "Congratulations, Coop. I didn't even know you were married."

Cooper blushed. "I'm not, Jeff."

Jeff blushed in response. "I'm sorry, man, I just assumed…"

Cooper held up his hand. "It's okay. Kate is my girlfriend who is in the process of adopting the babies." Cooper looked sly. "I'm still the sweet innocent boy you thought me to be."

Jeff threw back his head in laughter. "Good to know. I just thought they were yours because of the pink hair."

Cooper bristled. "My hair is not pink, Shrimp."

Jeff stood up as straight as his five foot five inch frame would allow. "And I am not a shrimp. I'm just very efficiently packaged."

Kate interrupted. "One of the first things I noticed about the girls was their strawberry blond hair, like Coop's. Their mother had the very same color."

Jeff turned to her. "I'm sorry about the mother. I gather she is deceased?"

"Yes. She was killed in a car wreck. No surviving family. She asked I be guardian in her will, and that I adopt them. It was quite a shock."

"I imagine so. Looks like you're doing a good job. They are healthy looking other than Wren's ear. And that's a very common illness in babies." He turned back to Cooper. "How is that cute little sister of yours?"

"Not little anymore, Jeff. She's eighteen. Still at home, in her senior year of high school."

"I bet she's a beauty now." He said thoughtfully. "As I recall, she didn't have pink hair."

Grinning, he spun quickly out of the room. "Follow me

to the desk to fill out some papers. I figure if I'm out in public Cooper won't beat me to a pulp."

"With one hand tied behind my back, buddy, one hand!" Cooper called after him.

CHAPTER THIRTY

Dr. Stiles' prediction proved true, and both babies were clear eyed and well by Thanksgiving morning. The day before had been a busy one as Cayden and Cooper cleaned the house and baby-sat, while Kate baked pies and cakes. She set the table with Cayden and Cooper's mother's fine china, counted chairs, cleaned the kitchen, and had a sense of contentment she'd never felt before.

"Am I just playing house?" she asked herself. The whole scene felt so real and so permanent. But who knew?

Thanksgiving Day was a balmy fifty-four degrees, the freezing weather gone for a while. Everyone arrived at their appointed time with covered dishes and happy faces.

As they gathered around the table, Cooper asked that they join hands. He stood, looked a little embarrassed, cleared his throat and spoke. "To me, it would be wrong to eat this feast without giving thanks. And before we can do that in a real sense, I think we should consider what we are thankful for. So, I'll start." He gazed around the table at them all. "When I look at your faces, one thing that strikes me is how we have had so much tragedy in our lives, yet God has taken care of us. I think back to the day when my parents were killed. Something I would never wish on anyone. Yet, God provided me with an aunt and an uncle who not only took care of us, but even considered how that might best be done. They asked me, what did I want to do? And I said: 'I want to stay home.' So they surrounded

Cayden and me with confidence, financial guidance, and support and most importantly, incredible love." He smiled at his aunt. "Thank you, Aunt Cynthia. I am grateful." He looked at Cayden. "I thank God He gave me a sister to grow up with, so that I would not be lonely when my parents died. I thank you, Cayden that you are a good sister and I love you." He looked at Anna and Bailey. 'You guys are such good friends. Always there to help, always there to listen. It can't get any better than that. Thank you, friends." He took a deep breath and smiled at Kate. "Kate has probably had the most difficult year. I hope she never sees another as tragic as this one has been. Yet, out of the fire God has given so much. Peace beyond all understanding. Miracles named Wren and Sparrow. A community that has come together to cheer you on and be truly happy for you. And I thank God He has allowed you in my life. I have cherished every moment we have had together. Thank you, Kate."

Cooper sat down. Each person took a turn thanking God for their lives and blessings.

But in their hearts, for that moment in time, they were most thankful for Cooper McGuire.

And then the feast began!

Anna swore she was as big as a house already. Bailey told her she would be if she kept eating the way she had been.

Aunt Cynthia warned everyone not to give Ernest any scraps from the table because it gave him gas. They ignored her, of course, and suffered for it later.

The meal itself was such a grand feast it left them all groaning and unbuttoning the top button of their slacks.

The men expressed the importance of getting right to the football game on TV, but the women prevailed in drafting them to help clean up the kitchen.

By mid-afternoon, the men were in front of the television, sleeping as the game droned on.

The women retreated to the living room, watching Wren and Sparrow sleep in their swings as Clancy and Ernest snored in tandem.

It was, indeed, a day to be thankful for.

🐾 🐾 🐾 🐾

The next morning, Kate decided to eat a small breakfast alone and let Cooper and Cayden sleep in. After feeding the babies and winding up their swings, she had actually enjoyed the quiet.

Wiping up the counter, she heard Cooper coming down the stairs.

Smiling, she turned to him. "What are you doing up on one of your few days off?"

"You know how it is. When you can, you can't." He looked around. "You already eat something?"

"Yep. Toast and oatmeal. Quick and easy. The girls actually behaved and let me eat in peace."

Cooper wrinkled his nose. "I think your peace is over." He walked over and tickled a foot on each baby. He got a return smile and kick from each one. "Somebody over here does not smell like a rose."

Clancy looked up and whined.

Kate laughed. "Well, either Clancy is the guilty party or he's begging me to intervene before he smothers to death."

She took matters into her own nose and did a little sniffing. "Ah, I do believe it's a little Wren stinker." She picked her up and Eskimo kissed her. "Congratulations! You're the winner of the next clean diaper." Wren babbled and grabbed her chin. "I'll go up and change her so you can eat without gagging. Will you keep an eye out for Sparrow, please?"

"Sounds like a fair trade." He rewound the swing. "I'm going to have some toast too, I think."

When Kate returned from upstairs, Cooper was leaned back on the sofa drinking coffee. "I've been thinking, Kate. Why don't we do something fun today? It's pretty warm. The weather guy just said it's going to get up in the sixties. Want to ride up to the state park and walk around the falls? They have a trail that's plenty wide for a stroller and it's pet friendly too."

"That actually sounds great! Want me to ask Cayden?"

"Oh, no. Cayden is doing something far more sophisticated than that. She and Mike are going to the mall."

"The after Thanksgiving sales." Kate shuddered. "Lord keep me from that mess."

"Amen, sister!"

The phone rang. Kate glanced at the clock. "Nine o'clock. Wonder who's calling this early on a holiday?" She walked over and picked up the phone. "Hello? McGuire residence."

"Yes, this is she." Kate listened for several seconds. "Of course, Monday at eleven will be fine. Did the lady who did the initial visit give you directions?" Kate nodded and smiled into the phone. "All right, see you then." She hung up and looked nervously at Cooper. "That was Roberta somebody or other. She is the social worker who will be doing the home visits until I am approved for the adoption."

"What happened to that other lady that liked dogs?"

"Apparently she does the initial approval for placement, then hands off the supervision to someone else. This new lady is coming Monday morning."

"So I heard. Do you want me to cancel my trip and be here?"

"Cooper, stop making excuses to not go. I don't want you to cancel your trip." She sighed heavily. "They only want me under the microscope, anyway."

Cooper felt a twinge of something – what? Guilt? Shame for not being available? He shrugged. "You'll do great. God will see to it. You know as well as I do you are already Wren and Sparrow's mother."

Kate nodded. "I know. This kind of thing just makes me a little anxious."

"Well, today let's just enjoy today. Let's get ready. I'm gonna take a quick shower, but I ain't shaving, ya hear? I refuse!"

Kate laughed. "You rebel. I guess I'll just have to put up with your terrible behavior."

Cooper turned to go as the phone rang.

"Again? What is this, Grand Central Station?" He groused.

When Kate finished the conversation, she turned to Cooper. "That was the guy who wants to buy my land. I'm going to have to get someone to give me a fair value appraisal, I guess. I don't know what to do."

"You don't have to do anything today, right?" He waggled his eyebrows at her.

She giggled. "You are right, Scruffy. Go shower and I'll get the girls ready. Have you bothered to wake up Cayden?"

"Nah. Let Mike learn the hard way she can't be on time."

He bounded up the stairs, and Kate heard him bang open Cayden's door. He told her it was noon. Kate shook her head as she heard Cayden squeal and leap out of bed.

🐾 🐾 🐾 🐾

The weather was beautiful. Clancy was almost giddy to be able to walk outdoors so much. The babies seemed to love it too.

They stopped at a picnic table and ate peanut butter and jelly sandwiches. Cooper poured Clancy water while Kate fed the girls some juice and baby food cereal.

"I'm so glad you thought of this, Coop. It's a perfect day." She tilted her head back and let her face feel the November sun.

"Me too. We've been stuck at the house too much lately. I guess we had to figure out these here young'uns were portable."

"Well, at three months, they're easier to get out and about than even a few weeks ago, I guess."

"So, Kate, do you know what you're going to do about your land?"

"I think I'm going to call Becca Parker Monday. She works at one of the real estate offices. She and I have been in a Bible study group together. I'm hoping she can tell me how to go about getting an appraisal. Then I have to decide if I even want to sell." She turned to Cooper. "But to be honest, I can't really see myself pouring all that energy into building when I could just buy another house when all the insurance money is settled. Plus, after the adoption is complete, I think it would be proper to use some of their money to help with a house. After all, it's going to be their home, too. With that much of a down payment, I could easily afford the house payment."

Cooper felt a strange pain in his gut. "So you've really put some thought into this house thing."

"Sure. You don't think I'm going to sponge off you forever, do you?"

"Well – with your type of woman, you never know." He dodged her elbow, jumping up and making Clancy bark.

"Just for that I ought to make you keep at least one baby!"

"Anything but that Miss Roe. Land sakes, I'd almost rather keep Clancy!"

Laughing, they started gathering up their stuff. "Did I tell you that as we were leaving the property the other day Mr. Hansard found my favorite soup spoon?"

"The real old one you eat ice cream with?"

"That's the one. I think I laid it on my dresser. I need to see if I can get it cleaned up and start using it again."

"You know, Kate, it seems like every time you go over there, sad as it is, something special happens."

"I've noticed that, too. I think it's God comforting me."

"His angels doing what He commands, I guess."

As they started back down the trail toward the car, Kate asked, "Are you looking forward to Sunday?"

"You mean church or leaving?"

"Leaving."

"No. I can't believe I'm not excited about it. Time to myself and all that. But I'm gonna miss you guys." He stopped and turned to her. Putting his hand to her cheek, he smiled. "Maybe that's the only answer from God I need. I love you so much I don't want to be away."

"That's sweet, Coop. I'll miss you too. But so much has happened, and there is so much happening every minute of every day how can you hear what He's saying to you? We've got to be sure of all this. It's not just us. It's Cayden's life. And these girls'."

"And Clancy's."

"Absolutely."

They reached the car, loaded up, and went home.

Unloading the car, Cooper helped get the babies and gear in the house, then leashed Clancy. "I'll take him for a quick walk around the block before supper."

When they were out of sight, Cooper stooped and looked at Clancy square in the face. "I got something to tell you, buddy."

Clancy sat, tongue lolling out.

"This trip I'm taking just begs for a dog to come along. I want to take you, but I can't!"

Clancy whined.

"I know, I know. But you've got to take care of all our girls, right?'

Clancy sighed heavily.

"So I'm telling you straight up front. I'm asking Aunt Cynthia if I can take Ernest. It's nothing personal, though." He lowered his voice. "In fact, I'd rather take you, okay?"

Clancy gave Cooper a big old sloppy kiss, right in the mouth.

Who knew if that was 'I understand', or ' I love you anyway', or 'Take that you idiot'.

Well, Clancy knew, of course.

CHAPTER THIRTY-ONE

Saturday was a lazy day spent in sweats. Kate cooked a big pot of homemade soup and a pone of cornbread. Cooper made a big pitcher of sweet tea and a banana pudding. Cayden set the table and invited Mike for dinner. The babies were wallowed and spoiled, Clancy fed too many scraps and the dirty dishes sat so long they crusted over, as everyone was too lazy to move.

A riveting game of Monopoly was followed by watching two movies back to back. At the end of the day, Cayden and Mike agreed to clean up the mess while Cooper and Kate walked Clancy and the babies.

The air was cool, threatening to turn cold. What was left of leaves fell, brown and brittle, skittering across the sidewalk.

"Kate, you're not a freeloader, you know."

"What brought that on?" she asked curiously.

"Yesterday I teased you after you said you couldn't live off me forever. You buy most the groceries. You paid the electric and cable bill this month, which you shouldn't have done. Sometimes I think you're too independent for your own good."

"Well, Coop, that's the cheapest rent I've ever paid. Besides, with all the baby food, formula, and diapers the grocery bill should be paid by me. We're the reason it's skyrocketed."

He put his arm around her shoulder. "You're a good

woman, my Kate."

"Thanks. You ain't so bad yourself."

"I'm looking forward to church in the morning. We've been so lazy today it'll be good to get out tomorrow."

"Do you need me to help you pack tonight?"

"Nah. All I need is an overnight bag and my Bible. I'm stopping by right after church and picking up Ernest. Aunt Cynthia said I could take him, so I won't be so lonely."

Kate laughed. "Addicted to dogs already, huh?"

Cooper glanced down at Clancy who had made a large snorting noise. "Yeah. I'd like to take Clancy but he needs to stay home and protect ya'll."

They turned and headed back for the house. Kate glanced at the sky. "It sure is getting cloudy. Have you listened to the weather?"

"No. But I don't think it's cold enough to snow."

"Winter in Georgia. One day you're sweating, the next day you're walking in snow."

"That's the truth. Hey, want some more pudding when we get in?"

"No thanks. But help yourself. I've got to get the girls ready for bed."

Dragging the stroller in, they entered the house, then went their separate ways.

Church had been the usual whirlwind and worship. Cooper had not even eaten lunch with them afterwards, instead opting to make a quick sandwich at his Aunt Cynthia's when he stopped to pick up Ernest.

Cayden had eaten lunch with Kate and the babies, helped her get them down for a nap and had gone off to the movies with Mike.

Kate heaved a sigh and flung herself sideways onto her bed.

The silence was profound. She picked up the baby monitor and listened to the twins breathing. Clancy lay on the floor, feet up in the air, snoring peacefully.

She thought about reading, and in fact, picked up the novel she'd been slowly plowing through. But three pages in, she was sound asleep.

Other than having to give Ernest a boost into the car, Cooper's trip had been uneventful. The cabin was clean, even if a bit chilly. There were two fireplaces, one gas log driven and the other wood. He started the gas logs as soon as he walked in and looked around.

The bedroom had a gas log fireplace, too, so he started it up. The bathroom had a separate wall heater. He figured he'd need to turn it on before he showered in the morning.

The kitchen was tiny, with two gas eyes, a microwave oven, and a toaster oven. A small coffee pot completed the appliances. He finally found the refrigerator under the counter. It was big enough for the few groceries he had picked up along the way.

Cabinets revealed enough plates and glasses for two folks, and there was one skillet and one pot. Plenty for him.

He unpacked his overnight bag by dumping everything into a drawer. He took his toiletries into the bathroom and laid them on the sink counter.

He then picked up his Bible, called Ernest and headed for the woods.

This is why he'd come, after all.

Cooper found a large tree to settle himself under and Ernest immediately rooted out a spot clear of leaves and went to sleep.

Cooper prayed that his mind would be cleared of outside worries and concerns, that there would be no interruptions of any kind, and that he would be able to focus solely on God's word speaking to him.

'Lean not to your own understanding...Be still and know I am God...I Am...And Jesus said, "Come"...'

He read what the characteristics were for a good wife, and knew Kate qualified. He read what love really is, and knew he felt that in his heart for her, and for Wren and Sparrow. He read how a man should treat his wife and how a wife should treat a husband. How a man should raise his children. He read until the sunlight became too dim to see the words.

"Well, Father, You confirm how I feel about Kate. I know how I should treat a wife and how she should treat me. But I still don't know, Lord. Should I ask her to marry me? Am I the man to be her husband, and am I the father Wren and Sparrow need?"

He laid his Bible on the ground, pulled his knees close to his body and rested his arms and head. He could hear Ernest breathing next to him, but then he thought he heard something else. His heart sped up and he prayed again – this time that he wasn't about to see a bear.

Raising his head slowly, his heart lurched. A doe had entered the edge of the clearing, tail flipping nervously. As she moved forward, a fawn followed her closely. And then another. The twin fawns seemed oblivious to anything other than their mother. Their mother seemed extremely nervous, and Cooper was more than surprised that she didn't sense their presence, just across the clearing, especially Ernest. 'So, is this my answer, Lord? A mother and her twins, alone, and capable?' he prayed silently.

As he sat unmoving, he saw something else out of the corner of his eye. Approaching the clearing was a large buck, eyeing the doe and fawns, nibbling at the plants. Suddenly, he raised his majestic head and sniffed the air. Turning, he looked Cooper straight in the eye. He lowered his head toward the ground, snorted and pawed the dirt. The doe looked up, alarmed. She, too, pawed the ground and she and the fawns took off, nothing but white tail showing. The buck snorted once more, shook his rack Cooper's way and took off behind the doe.

No, that was his answer!

Much later he would tell Bailey the story and say, "If that had been in a movie, I would have thought it was the corniest thing I'd ever seen in my life. But when it happened to me in real life, all I could do was praise and thank God for being so patient with one so dense He had to draw me a picture!"

From that moment on, all Cooper could do was thank God and wait impatiently to go home. He couldn't wait to propose!

He only hoped Kate would say yes.

CHAPTER THIRTY-TWO

Monday morning found Kate scrambling to get the house cleaned up before Roberta the social worker arrived. In the middle of her cleaning the phone had rung. It was her friend Becca, who promised to get an appraiser out to the property within a week. She then called and left a message on Tim Hansard's voice mail about what she was doing. She had no more than put the girls in their swings after cleaning them up from a bottle after their nap, than the doorbell rang.

She'd given up on hiding Clancy. She figured social worker number one would have written about him in detail, plus, she just didn't have the time nor energy.

She answered the bell with a smile on her face, to find a petite, dark skinned woman standing there. She was a very beautiful woman, and for a moment Kate wondered why in the world she was doing social work instead of movies.

"Come in, come in." The air was chilly and Kate closed the door quickly.

"Thank you for seeing me today." She stuck out her hand. "I'm Roberta Flint." She showed Kate her identification, smiling. "No one can be too careful these days."

They walked into the living room and had a seat. Clancy got up from his place between the swings and sat down in front of Roberta.

"This is Clancy. He's very friendly."

Roberta smiled nervously. "I'm a bit afraid of dogs, but I read the report and must say I have been impressed by your dog."

Clancy scooted a little closer and gently laid his head in her lap. It took up the whole lap.

"Oh my!" she almost squealed. "He's so – so – big!"

"Do you want me to make him move? He's trying to be gentle with you, but I think he's also trying to flirt, just a little."

Tentatively, Roberta placed a hand on Clancy's head and patted him. He raised his head, his job done, and walked back over to settle between the twins.

Kate leaned forward, carefully looking at Roberta. "I hope your own anxiety about Clancy won't change the way you feel about the twin's placement. He loves them dearly, and they are constantly entertained by him. He's a good dog, and his breed has a very long history of protecting children."

Roberta straightened her tiny frame. "I will in no way let my own prejudices color my findings. In fact, I am hoping your do- Clancy- can help change my mind a little." She reached down and started to unzip her boot. "I hope you won't find this forward, but I need to show you."

She took off the tiny boot, and slipped off the sock.

Kate groaned. Roberta's foot was mangled and old scars clearly showed a terrible injury from the past.

"I was seven. I had been playing with the children next door. Their Rottweiler had always been friendly. But on this day, when my mother called me to come to supper and I ran out of the yard, he chased me. This damage was done before the neighbors could get him off me." She sighed and put her sock and shoe back on. "I almost lost my foot. They put the dog to sleep, of course. The neighbors were inconsolable. And I was scarred as bad emotionally as I was physically."

"I don't know what to say. What a terrible thing."

"Yes. But I want you to know I've been doing intensive research. And it seems these big fellas are the kind of breed that rescue little girls from dogs like my neighbor's." She looked Kate right in the eye. "I promise you, I will not let my scars skew this in any way."

"Thanks. And I appreciate you sharing all this. It must still be painful to bring the memories back up."

"I will say I don't usually share all this with clients," Roberta said with a laugh. "But I thought this time it was vital that I do so."

They soon got down to business, and Roberta held each baby, cooing and laughing with them both. She filled out forms, asked a ton of questions and had a cup of coffee with Kate toward the end.

"There is a minimum of three home visits required by law before a court date can be set. It would be up to my findings and a committee agreement if there are more than three. If you don't mind, we can go ahead and set two more up on the calendar today."

Kate went to get her own appointment calendar and sat back down. "May I ask you something that may or may not be relevant?"

"Of course."

"And may I ask you sort of keep it off the record?" Kate blushed.

Roberta cocked her head, curious. "I'm not sure I can honor that, but I will if I can."

"You obviously know I am living here more or less as a guest due to my house fire." Roberta nodded. "Cooper McGuire lives here. He and I have been dating for some time, and before the fire and before news of babies arriving, we were probably moving toward marriage. At least at some point." Kate cleared her throat and thought for a moment. "I really had nowhere else to go, unless it was to an apartment, and he was insistent that I move in. His sister, Cayden, lives here, too, so we felt it wouldn't be improper for me to move in. We're Christians, and didn't want any appearance of behavior that goes against our belief."

"I see."

"Cooper's been gone a few days to read the Bible and pray about our situation. As you can imagine, it's been pretty chaotic the last several weeks. We've barely seen each other – I mean in a dating sense, a romantic sense - for weeks. And although this has brought us closer and there's been no conflict at all, we weren't sure if this was sort of a false set up for feelings that we should get married, or if it truly is a forever thing." Kate ran out of breath. "Does that make any sense?"

Roberta's lips twitched, then she giggled, then she laughed outright. "Not at all, I'm afraid. Your situation is completely unique, as far as I know. But what's the question?"

"Oh. I completely forgot what I was going to ask! Okay, the question is this: if Cooper proposes, and if I say yes, is that going to prolong the adoption process? Will we have to start over?"

"Ah. I see what you mean." Roberta pondered this. "He would have to be approved, just like you are being. Yes, it would prolong it a bit, and the court might ask you two to receive some sort of counseling. But, if you want my personal opinion - off the record, too, I might add - I think it would be a good thing. Children need two parents, as far as I'm concerned. You wouldn't believe the number of children I see every day that come from one parent families. It is not an ideal situation, even when the single parent is doing their very best."

"I agree with you. I've no doubt Cooper would be approved. He is a good Christian guy. He's a middle school teacher and coach. He loves these girls already. And we will receive counseling before we marry anyway. Our pastor wouldn't have it any other way."

Roberta smiled as she stood to go. "Just keep me posted on the ifs and whens." She placed a hand on Kate's arm. "I'm a Christian too. I'll be praying for the right decisions to be made by you two."

"Thanks. It's always a joy to know one more person is praying."

"Girl, in this world, the more the merrier!"

CHAPTER THIRTY-THREE

Cynthia had arrived shortly after one, carrying a huge beef roast. "I saw it on sale marked special yesterday when I ran in to get some dog food for Ernest. I just couldn't resist. I'll help you get supper on and the girls bathed and fed, but I can't stay. I've got a bridge club meeting at five."

"This is a huge roast! If you can't stay, I'll be sure to save some and one of us will bring it by tomorrow."

The women worked in contented silence and time flew by. Cayden came in just before Cynthia was leaving. They hugged, Cynthia explained why she wasn't staying, and was gone.

"How's Mike?" Kate asked. Cayden had spent most the day with him since there had been no school.

Cayden shrugged. "He's okay." She stopped setting the table and looked solemnly at Kate. "I really don't know how he is. We're trying to sort out our feelings for each other. I like him a lot, Kate. I know we're young and it will be years before we're old enough to have an education and jobs so we can get married sensibly."

Kate raised an eyebrow. "But?"

Cayden sighed and pushed some curls behind her ear. "Yeah, but. We really talked today. Should we slow down? Should we keep this pace up and drive ourselves crazy?" Cayden grinned at Kate. "Or maybe just say to heck with it and get married next weekend?"

Kate choked. "That last one? Umm, no."

Cayden laughed. "Okay. That one's out. I thought finding someone who might be 'Mr. Right' would make things so much easier! I was wrong. It's harder. Now I'm trying not to look at tomorrow as though it's just in the way and wanting to hurry up several years of my life! I've looked forward to college since I was ten years old, and now I'm wanting them to speed by." She resumed setting the table. "I don't like it one bit, either. Any advice?"

"'Fraid not. I had a boyfriend when I was sixteen. My life was very chaotic at the time and we seriously considered running away together and staying hidden until I either turned eighteen or got pregnant so we could marry and no one would stop us."

Cayden looked at her like she'd grown horns. "Are you kidding?"

"Nope. I was that crazy over him. Thank God my best friend got scared and told her mother. I was invited over the next night and her mother sat me down and we had a long talk. She convinced me to wait at least six months. Of course, I was over it in six months." Kate walked over and hugged Cayden. "I'm not saying you and Mike will be over in six months. What I'm saying is you two have years to go to school and marry. There's no rush. You can even get married after you get settled into college. But getting married right now would be a mistake."

"I know." Cayden giggled. "But it'd almost be worth it to see Cooper howl at the moon." Cayden cocked her head. "Speaking of Cooper howling, I think he must have driven up. I hear his unbelievably terrible singing voice headed our way."

They heard a small phrase of *'Hotel California'*, but

only by the words was it recognizable. Clancy whined and ran out of the room.

"He is bad, isn't he?" Kate whispered.

"The worst I've ever heard."

The door opened and a happy Cooper walked though. He grabbed Kate in a big hug and gave her a kiss, then did the same to Cayden. "Where are my little girls?"

"About ready to wake up from their nap. Go get them if you want to. Supper will be ready in about fifteen minutes."

Cooper bounded up the stairs, joined by Clancy. Both Kate and Cayden grinned as they overheard the high pitched baby talk over the monitor as Cooper cooed to the twins.

"By the time he changes them and gets them down here, we should have supper on the table. If you'll hunt up that fresh box of baby cereal, I'll feed them while we eat."

Supper was then filled with Cooper's stories of the woods and his prayer time. He shared some of the discoveries and insights he'd had, but saved the doe and her fawns. He wanted to tell that to Kate when they were alone tonight.

"Cayden, are you going to be home tonight?"

"Yeah. I've two chapters in history to read. Why? You going out?"

"I'd like to take Kate for a drive. We won't be gone long, but I'd rather leave the girls here."

"I'll be glad to watch them. If you need me to do anything specific, I'll be glad to do that too."

"You really don't want to read those two chapters, do you?" Cooper teased.

"Saw right through me." Cayden agreed.

So, as soon as the dishes were cleared from the table, Kate and Cooper donned their coats and were out the door.

Cooper stopped the car at the far end of the city park. He cut off the engine and turned to Kate. She raised an eyebrow. "Sir, what kind of girl do you think I am?"

He reached over and unfastened her seatbelt, slid her across the seat and wrapped his arms around her. "My kind." He kissed her tenderly, then pulled back to gaze into her face. "At least I hope so."

"Aren't you afraid the cops will pull in here and embarrass us?"

Cooper grinned. "I'll tell them we are only talking."

"Ah. I'm sure that's worked for thousands of teenagers around the world."

"Maybe if you scoot over a little they'll believe me. 'Cause I really do want to talk, Kate."

"About what?" Kate asked. She realized her heart was thumping loudly in her chest.

"About my trip. I hope I never neglect prayer time again. I miss too much. I spent a lot of time reading the Bible and praying. Part of the time I just sat and did nothing, trying to get my mind settled, you know?" Kate nodded. "I was praying about if the time was right for us to marry. I wanted to know if it was God's will for our lives. He answered me in more than one way, Kate."

Then Cooper told her about the doe and her twins, that just when they appeared to be alone, the buck showed up, protective, powerful and strong. "I truly felt that was God literally showing me what I was supposed to be, supposed to do. I was ready right then and there to pack up, come home, and find a preacher. But that still, small voice stopped me. I knew there was more He wanted to show me, and I had promised Him the time.

"So, with that in mind, I went to scripture about time. I found the scripture about our lives are but a vapor." He snapped his fingers. "They last no longer than that while we're here on Earth. That brought something to my mind, and it wouldn't leave me alone, so I left a little early today and went to the local library to look it up."

Cooper moved so he could look directly at Kate. "Do you remember several years ago when Voyager 1 spacecraft reached the edge of our solar system, turned around and took a picture of Earth? I think it was from almost four billion miles away. I saw the photograph today. It mostly looks like a black background with four or five streaks of color running across it. You have to look closely to see this tiny speck in one of the colors. I had to know where to look, or I wouldn't have seen it at all. That speck is Earth. It gives me chills to even think about it. Carl Sagan named the picture 'The Pale Blue Dot' and said something to the effect of: "That's here. That's home. That's us…a mote of dust suspended in a sunbeam."

Kate was nodding her head. "I do remember that photograph. It took my breath away to imagine how big God really is. How much more is there that we don't even know about? How can we be so significant to Him when we are so insignificantly small?"

Cooper agreed. "We are so tiny and insignificant except in God's eyes, Kate. To Him our lives here are so brief, and He expects us to use every minute of it for His Glory. Wren and Sparrow's lives are already unfolding before us. I don't want to miss a minute of it!"

Kate made a noise that sounded between a sob and a laugh. "It sounds like you want to marry them instead of me."

He drew her closer. "No, I want to be their father. I want to be your husband. I want to grow old with you, Kate. Maybe have more children, I don't know. I want us to be together to watch the girls grow up. I want to be yours until our lives waft up into the heavens like that vapor and we enter eternity. Be mine, Kate."

He cupped her face in his hand. "I don't want an answer now. I want you to pray this week like you've never prayed before. I assume you won't leave the girls for even a night," she shook her head, "But you can for a day or each day for a while if you need it. Cayden and I can take over when one of the ladies leaves and you can have several hours a day if you need it. Take as long as you need to until you get the answer I got."

"What did He say to you?"

"Son, what are you waiting for? The time is now." Cooper nodded. "That's what He said to me."

They sat in silence for a while, and Kate scooted next to him and rested her head on his shoulder. Finally, she spoke. "I don't know much about marriage by example, Coop. Daddy was killed when I was ten and my mother never remarried. All I have are wonderful memories of him, I guess because I was just a little girl and he was perfect to me. Mother always spoke fondly of him, and I know she had a terrible time getting over his death. But a ten year old's view of marriage and reality are vastly different, I imagine."

"I understand." Cooper said. "My parents had a good marriage. Oh, they argued some. And there was one time when I was about twelve or so, they went through a really rough time. I have no idea what was going on. I just remember trying to keep Cayden pacified some evenings when they were arguing. I was scared and she was too. But that passed. I don't know how they resolved whatever was going on, but they did. Other than that, I don't know much about their marriage. I think maybe I know more by watching Aunt Cynthia's marriage. They were so supportive of my desire to stay in our home after Mama and Daddy died. They had a very strong relationship. It was Christ centered." Cooper sighed heavily. "But I suspect the only true way to know about marriage is to be in one."

"I asked Roberta when she came over this morning for her first visit, how a marital status change would change the process of adoption." Kate filled him in on the conversation.

"You know, if you accept my proposal, Christian marriage counseling is the very first thing we have to do."

"Agreed. Lord knows, we need all the help we can get. Who in the world can give us first hand advice? 'Well, folks, this is how it happened for us when we got married right after we adopted twin infants, shortly after her house burned down.'"

Cooper laughed. "It does sound a little strange."

The mood turned solemn. "I'll pray, Coop. You know I love you. But I've sort of been holding off praying for me while I prayed for you." She looked up at him. "It may take me time. Are you willing to be patient?"

"I am. God's time, not ours. How's that?"

"His time is always perfect." She shivered. "Let's go home. I'm freezing out here!"

As soon as Kate had time alone, she was on her knees, praying.

THIRTY-FOUR

Tuesday morning dawned bright and cold. Cooper and Cayden pulled out the serious winter coats to wear to school, and Kate turned up the heat in the house.

As soon as they left and Kate got the girls down for their nap, she rushed to her Bible. She read while eyeing the clock, as Mrs. Stonefield and Genevieve were due at ten. Genevieve attended a private school, and her classes did not resume until Wednesday.

Kate settled herself on the couch, her socked feet resting on Clancy's stomach. He was snoring softly. Scripture told her to *'Wait upon the Lord'*, *'Be still and know that I am God'*, and *'Trust in the Lord with all Your Heart'*. She knew what that all meant, but what did it mean for her situation? She sat very still, waiting on the small voice inside her heart. She felt peace, but no direct answer.

"Okay, Lord, I'll wait. I'll tell Cooper that unless I hear directly from you, I'm going to put it all out of my mind until after Christmas. How's that?"

The doorbell rang and Clancy jumped up, shook himself, and trotted to the door, tongue lolling happily. Kate stretched and headed that way too.

"My, it's cold out here!" Mrs. Stonefield declared as she hurried into the house.

"Where's Genevieve?"

"She took a detour somewhere in the yard. I told her to hurry because of the cold."

The door opened and Genevieve entered, her cheeks pink from the cold.

She went straight to Kate for a hug, looking up at her. "Did you know there's a wee scoor cheetie in your yard? She's all huddled up freezing."

Kate shook her head. "I know what wee is, but scoor and cheetie? Interpret, honey."

Genevieve smiled and looked at Kate as though she thought her a rather slow child. "That would be a small brown cat, Kate."

"Oh. No, I didn't know a cat was in our yard. I'm afraid you can't bring her in. Clancy hasn't been properly introduced to cats."

"Hmmm. Perhaps I can take him out and do the introductions?"

"Clancy weighs two times more than you do, Genevieve. He's liable to pull you across the yard if he decides to take chase." Mrs. Stonefield said.

"Oh, Auntie, he's a good dog most of the time. I'm sure he'll be obedient."

Kate shrugged. "If Clancy starts to chase the cat, you let go of the leash. Call me immediately and I'll come out, okay?"

"Absolutely!" Genevieve rushed to get the leash and Clancy just as eagerly stepped into his halter.

As the girl and dog walked out the door, Kate and Mrs. Stonefield hurried to the windows to watch.

Clancy and the cat spied each other simultaneously. The cat stiffened for a moment as Clancy gave a small 'woof'. He pulled Genevieve over closer to the cat, and the two animals sniffed each other's noses. Then the cat wrapped herself around Clancy's front legs. Clancy looked a little alarmed, but allowed it. They heard Genevieve say, "Sit Clancy." And he did. The cat ambled over between Clancy's front paws and sat too, her head directly under Clancy's chin.

"Well, I guess the cat is used to dogs, anyway." Kate said, amusement lacing her tone. "I don't know if Clancy's just taken aback and doesn't know what to do, or if he's in love."

Genevieve squatted down and looked Clancy in the eye. "You're a very good boy. But it's awfully cold. Let's go back in now." She stood and Clancy followed her back into the house.

So did the cat.

Smiling triumphantly, Genevieve announced, "We shall call her 'Pluma' due to the way her tail makes a plume." The cat, although fairly short haired, had a long fluffy tail, that did, indeed stand up behind her like a feather plume.

"Genevieve, I'm not sure Cooper wants a cat. This is his house, you know."

"Ah, well, we'll take care of that shortly. If he doesn't want her, can we take her home, Auntie?"

"I don't know, dear. Your Uncle Robert is allergic to cats. She'd have to live outside, even if he says yes."

"Well, that's unsettling." Genevieve's brow furrowed. "Can we keep her in for at least now and give her something to eat?"

"Of course. We're having tuna salad for lunch, so I'll give her a bit of the tuna and some water."

As soon as Kate opened the tuna, the cat began

yowling at the top of her lungs, but she hushed as soon as the bowl was set before her, and began to eat hungrily.

Either the yowl or just the time woke both the girls up and they set up their own version of yowling.

During lunch they conversed about the cat. "If Cooper says we can keep her, I'm sure Cayden would take her to the vet for me and have her shots and a check up. I also don't want a bunch of kittens." She looked meaningfully at Mrs. Stonefield, who smiled. "And Genevieve, as soon as we finish eating, I want you to make a poster and put it out front on the light pole. She may be lost. If Mrs. Stonefield doesn't mind, I want you to go to several doors down the street, asking if anyone has lost her. Cooper knows the neighbors pretty well, I don't think there'd be a danger, especially if you have Clancy and my cell phone with you. I have some poster board and markers."

Genevieve clapped her hands together, making both babies jump. "Oh, that's a splendid idea! I'll even draw Pluma's likeness."

Just as Mrs. Stonefield and Kate finished up the dishes, Genevieve brought her poster for inspection.

"This is beautiful. It looks just like the cat! I didn't know you could draw, Genevieve." Kate was staring at the poster.

"Yes, actually I'm quite the artist. It's a natural talent."

Kate cut her eyes toward Mrs. Stonefield, who remained mute. "Go ahead and get Clancy in his harness and tape this up to the pole outside." Kate rummaged around and found the tape. "And don't forget the cell phone."

Putting the babies down for their naps, loading up the

washer and dryer again, and stripping her bed, made the afternoon zip by as usual. She heard the front door slam and thought Cayden might be home. She was right.

Cayden sat in the floor fawning over the cat. When Kate walked in, Cayden was vowing to Genevieve that she would do whatever possible to talk Cooper into keeping Pluma.

The phone rang, and it was Cooper. He wanted to know if they needed anything from the grocery store. Kate gave him a short list. "And Cooper, we have a situation here."

"Are the girls all right?"

"Yes. It seems a new critter has appeared on the scene and has stolen everyone's heart. You probably need to get home pretty quickly to nip it in the bud before she has her own bed and TV."

Cooper laughed. "What in the world are you talking about?"

Kate sighed. "Genevieve found a cat in the yard. Clancy loves her. I made the mistake of letting her come in. She has already been named, and Cayden's lying in the floor with the cat on her stomach as we speak."

"And you really think I have a decision to make? Who are you kidding?"

"But Coop, do you even like cats?"

"I liked the big tom I grew up with. He died of old age when I was fifteen. Always wanted another one, but after Mom and Dad died I just never really thought of it again. I guess I had enough to deal with trying to raise Cayden and myself."

"And now?"

"And now it sounds like we have a cat. What's his name?"

"*Her* name is Pluma because her tail is all feathery like a plume."

"Uh huh. Let me guess. Genevieve named her."

"Yep. To quote, she's a 'wee scoor cheetie'." Kate went heavy on the Scottish brogue.

"Of course she is. I suppose I need to pick up cat food."

"And litter and a big plastic box for the litter to go into."

"Where's the poop box going to go?"

"I thought the utility room."

"Good idea. Any other groceries?"

"Not that I know of. Cooper are you sure?"

"Yeah."

Kate announced the decision to clapping and cheering, at which Pluma left the room, followed quickly by Clancy.

Mrs. Stonefield and Genevieve left later than planned, Genevieve deliriously happy that no one had claimed the cat, and that Cooper had said yes to keeping it. Mrs. Stonefield said she would see Kate tomorrow as soon as she got Genevieve settled in school and a few chores taken care of.

Cayden entertained and fed the twins while Kate got supper started.

The phone rang again. It was Cooper. "Kate, I thought I'd call and tell you there's a great special on asparagus. Do you want me to buy some?"

Kate made a face and Cayden laughed. "The only asparagus I've ever met whom I liked was Junior

Asparagus from 'Veggie Tales'."

"Mother Ship to Space Cadet. We're talking food here. Hey! I just thought of something."

"What's that, Captain?"

"We can watch 'Veggie Tales' pretty soon!"

"We can watch 'Veggie Tales' now. Or do you mean without being embarrassed?"

Cooper lowered his voice. "I'm not embarrassed. I just don't watch it in front of the guys because they wouldn't understand. But now with two rug rats in front of me while you're off shopping with your friends leaving me to baby-sit when I'd rather be watching football, I can say to them-"

"Uh, Coop?"

"Yeah?"

Kate sighed heavily. "Go ahead and buy the asparagus. Sounds like a good price."

After supper (sans asparagus) Kate and Cooper cleaned up the kitchen while Cayden watched the girls. Kate told him her agreement with God, and asked Cooper to wait on an answer till after Christmas.

Cooper reluctantly agreed. Trying to cheer the mood, he reminded Kate that the next weekend was tree hunting and Christmas decorating time. They were discussing the details when Kate's cell phone rang.

It was Becca. "I think Mr. Hansard is giving you a very generous offer, Kate." She gave Kate the appraisal numbers, and Kate had to agree. She thanked Becca and hung up. Turning to Cooper, she explained the call.

"You can bank that money. Whatever you decide, it will be there."

Kate nodded. "I know you're right. It's just the thought

of saying good-bye to the first home I ever owned. I know it's gone already, but somewhere in my mind I guess I thought I could hang on to it somehow." Kate sighed. "I owe it to Mrs. Peabody to call her and give her a heads up that I'm going to accept Mr. Hansard's offer."

Cooper agreed.

Explaining to Mrs. Peabody the situation, she was in complete agreement.

"Besides," she said, "I am still almost within walking distance. You've been generous in letting me be a part of the girls' lives, and I hope you will continue to be so."

"Oh, Mrs. Peabody, you know I wouldn't have it any other way. In fact, I don't know what I'd do without you."

Satisfied, Mrs. Peabody hung up. Kate turned to Cooper. "If you don't mind helping Cayden get the babies ready for their bath, I'll go ahead and call Mr. Hansard and get it over with."

"Sure." Cooper kissed her on the cheek and bounded up the stairs. Clancy followed Cooper. Pluma followed Clancy.

Kate grinned and wondered what they would add next to the family. She dialed the number Tim Hansard had given her and he answered on the third ring. He was thrilled she was accepting his offer, and told her he'd make an appointment with his bank first thing in the morning to discuss details. He'd get back to her as soon as possible.

Kate hung up and sat down on the sofa in the semi-darkness.

Things sure were moving fast, she thought.

CHAPTER THIRTY-FIVE

The following two weeks became a flurry of activities. Kate signed the papers for the sale of the land, a check was delivered to her, and she fattened up her savings. School was wrapping up for Cooper and Cayden. Aunt Cynthia called twice a day to talk about Christmas dinner, exciting Kate so much, she got out the twins' heirloom china to just look at and anticipate the day it would be used. So much mail came that week Kate was sure the mailman would get a hernia, carrying all the sale catalogues, and "mysterious" packages she'd been warned not to open.

Roberta came to do her monthly social worker visit early because she was leaving for three weeks to vacation with family. She took one look at Pluma winding around her ankles and immediately informed Kate she was allergic to cats and proceeded to sneeze throughout the entire visit. Clancy looked at her sympathetically, gently placing his head in her lap. He only drooled on her wool skirt a little bit.

Both babies were fussy and Sparrow managed to gag and spit up the carrots that Roberta had been attempting to get her to eat. It only stained her silk blouse a little bit.

With unfortunate timing, Mrs. Stonefield and Genevieve arrived as Roberta was leaving. Genevieve was especially loud and cockney and managed to drop her Science book on Roberta's foot. It only bruised her foot a little bit.

And tore her pantyhose.

A little bit.

Kate figured social services would either come get the babies or Roberta would do a rush job on the court date so she wouldn't have to come back.

On Friday night Kate dreamed Wren and Sparrow were about five years old. Cooper, the girls, and herself were in a deep forest hunting a tree to cut for Christmas when it started to snow. Kate kept telling them they needed to hurry because the snow was getting deeper, but they ignored her, going further and further into the woods. She stood alone, and becoming afraid, called to them to wait. Cooper turned to her and said, "You are the one who needs to hurry Kate. We don't want to wait."

She awoke abruptly, heart pounding.

She looked at the clock and decided she might as well get up, as they had to take Pluma to the vet to be spayed. They would pick out a tree (at a local tree farm, not a deep forest) after grocery shopping, and then drop back by for Pluma. Maybe they could get a pizza to go or something and not worry about cooking so they could concentrate on tree decorating all afternoon. She made a note on the grocery list to pick up hot chocolate mix and popcorn.

Kate was more excited about this Christmas than she had been since she was a child. She awakened everyone, breakfast was eaten, and they were off.

Several hours later they returned, a drunken cat in her carrier, two babies asleep in theirs, and a tree strapped to the top of the car. The trunk was full of groceries.

Carefully putting the girls in their bed and turning on monitors, they went downstairs and finished unloading.

Cooper grunted as he lowered the cat carrier onto the floor. "Good thing school is out for a few weeks. After today, I think it will take me that long to recuperate." He looked around. "Where do you want me to put the cat?"

"Since we're all going to be in the living room decorating the tree, I thought I'd put her in the corner. I'll go get her litter box and food and put it near, so when she wakes up she won't have to travel far for either."

Doing so, Kate then opened the carrier's door so when Pluma woke up, she could get out without making a scene. She admonished Clancy to leave the cat alone, and after one sniff, he obeyed.

Cooper came in with the first load of groceries. "I propped the tree on the porch. I'll help with the groceries and then try to find the tree stand next."

"If you can't find yours, mine is in the basement with the stuff saved from the fire. It looked a little rough, but I think it will work."

"I may do that. At least we know where it is."

"Cooper? Are Cayden and Mike helping with the tree this evening?"

"Yeah. She's eating dinner with his folks first. They'll be here by seven."

"Good. It's gonna be fun! I'll fix popcorn and hot chocolate."

While Cooper worked on getting the tree into the stand, Kate called 'The Pizza Pig' and ordered their supper. Waiting for it to arrive, she made fresh tea and salads. Just as she finished, she heard unhappy stirrings on the monitor. Kate shook her head, grinning. She firmly believed those babies could hear the pizza truck driving toward the house.

Heading up the stairs, Cooper joined her. "I'll help you set them up and you can feed them while I set everything out when the delivery guy gets here."

The guy happened to be one of Cayden's classmates, and he talked to each baby till he got a giggle. Then he thanked them for the tip, patted Clancy on the head, and was gone. Kate had almost finished feeding the girls by the time Cooper got all the food and drinks on the table. After a quick blessing, they attacked the pizza as though they'd never eaten. Little was left to feed the begging dog, but he did get bites of crust.

"I'm going to bathe the girls and get them into their jammies." Kate said, as she checked on Pluma. "Then they can sit in their swings while we decorate the tree."

"How's the cat doing?" Cooper asked.

"I guess she's okay. She's moved around some since we brought her home. But she's not got out of the carrier yet."

Cayden and Mike arrived. While the guys toted in the decorations from parts unknown, Cayden and Kate popped popcorn and made hot chocolate. Clancy stationed himself between the two swings and Wren and Sparrow watched big eyed to the goings on.

"Are you sure kitty is all right?" Cayden asked, peeking into the cage. She put the bowl of food next to the cat. Pluma looked up sleepily, sniffed the food, and laid her head back down, closing her eyes.

"Well, I hope so. The vet said she'd be sedated for several hours, not to worry."

"Okay, I guess. You know if anything happened to this cat, Genevieve would be to bury."

"Don't I know it?" mumbled Kate.

"Here's the last of them. I don't know how all this can fit on one tree, though." Mike said.

"Some of it is for the mantle and banister. Just do what we tell you to do." Cayden patted his cheek.

Cooper shook his head. "You better run, boy, while you have the chance."

"Aw, it's not so bad." Mike blushed, making the rest of them laugh.

🐾 🐾 🐾 🐾

Four hours later, an exhausted Kate and Cooper sat, lights out, legs propped up on cardboard boxes, enjoying the twinkling lights from the tree and mantle.

Mike (they were sure) had been kissed good night, the babies too, and Cayden had said she was going to bed and sleep for twelve hours.

Kate snuggled close to Cooper, dropping her head to his shoulder. "What a day. But ain't it beautiful?"

"Sure is." Cooper tilted her head up and kissed her, long and tenderly. "I love our life, Kate. I love you."

"Oh, Cooper, I love you too." Cooper caressed her hair, her cheek and followed her jaw line down to her neck, kissing her again.

Both scooted closer, to kiss in earnest. Kate felt heat rise up, and a quiver in her belly. She pulled away. "Whoa. I'm not as tired as I thought." She giggled.

"Good thing we're so busy most the time. When the pastor asked me if we were being tempted because we were living together, I laughed in his face. But if we had more time like this, we'd be in trouble quickly." With that, he drew her back in and began kissing her.

Kate pushed him away, again. "I think we better not,

Coop. I'm tired and too easily swayed."

"I just wanna neck." He whined, trying to look as pitiful as possible.

A rather shaky 'mew' answered him, and they both looked down on the floor.

"Well, look who has awakened." Pluma looked up at her, puzzled.

Kate turned on a lamp and gently picked the cat up. She sat her in her lap and tried to see her belly. "Maybe she needs water."

Cooper fetched the water bowl, and Pluma drank daintily from it. She cocked her head at the twinkling lights reflected in the water, and stuck her paw in the bowl, removing it, surprised, when it got wet.

Cooper and Kate laughed. Sitting Pluma down to her food dish, the cat began to eat, purring happily.

"Let's leave her be for the night." Kate said. "She can sleep back in the carrier if she wants to, and I don't have to move her litter box back upstairs."

They proceeded to the kitchen, putting cups and the popcorn bowl in the dishwasher and cleaning off the counter.

Cooper pulled Kate to him once again. "Thanks for a great day. It's ended pretty good too."

Kate smiled. "Sure did. This is turning into the best Christmas of my life."

"HEY!" Cooper shouted, shoving Kate away from him.

"Well, for goodness sakes, Coop -"

He rushed past her, but it was too late. Pluma had sprung from the couch arm, landing smack in the middle of the Christmas tree. It tottered ominously back and forth, spewing decorations with each sway. Clancy started barking furiously.

Kate grabbed Clancy's collar, pulling him back, and reached up to drag the cat out of the tree as Cooper steadied the swaying.

Looking at the damage and the near wreckage, they stood in total silence.

"I guess we should take the cat upstairs after all." Kate said solemnly.

They burst into giggles.

Dodging tree ornaments scattered about on the floor, they grabbed armfuls of cat paraphernalia, and climbed the stairs for the night.

CHAPTER THIRTY-SIX

Christmas Eve brought lots of company, presents, and laughter.

Anna and Bailey invited them for brunch. They filled themselves with biscuits, jams, eggs and fruit. Afterwards they all exchanged small gifts and stayed until the babies started getting fussy.

Reminding Anna and Bailey this was soon to be their fate, they left for home and settled Wren and Sparrow in for their naps.

Aunt Cynthia called and said she'd come over late in the day and bring the turkey and get it started in the oven. Kate insisted she come for supper, to which she agreed.

A little after one o'clock, Mr. and Mrs. Stonefield arrived with an excited Genevieve in tow. "Happy Christmas!" She squealed as she flew through the door. "I've got grand presents for everyone!"

Laughing, Cooper caught her up in a hug. A surprised Genevieve blushed.

They sat around the Christmas tree, and presents were doled out. Mr. and Mrs. Stonefield loved the Christmas CD and Genevieve was thrilled with a framed picture of herself and the twins and two new DVD's she'd been pining for.

The Stonefields gave Cooper a nice pair of gloves, Kate the same, and Cayden a gift certificate at a local techno shop. The babies received beautiful handmade quilts that made Kate cry.

Genevieve could hardly wait to pass out the gifts from her. She carefully handed Cayden's to her first. It was a scarf she had knitted herself, in bright purple. Cayden hugged her and told her it was perfect.

She gave Cooper a pack of handkerchiefs with his initials cross stitched in the corners. Cooper bragged on her, insisting it was the best cross stitching he'd ever seen.

She gave Wren and Sparrow little white toboggans with their names cross stitched in pink. The names were a little crooked as she'd never tried to cross stitch that many letters. Kate told her she would keep them forever.

And, lastly, she handed a big box to Kate.

Kate opened the box and gasped. "Oh, Genevieve, it's beautiful! It looks just like him!"

Genevieve had sketched Clancy. She had captured his big smiling mug to perfection.

"Do you really like it, Auntie Kate?" Genevieve asked, wringing her hands.

"It's one of the best presents I've ever received. It looks like a professional sketch, Genevieve. I'll treasure it always."

Satisfied that her gifts had been acceptable, she asked for milk and cookies, much to Mrs. Stonefield's disapproval and everyone else's laughter.

Later that evening, as Aunt Cynthia bustled about in the kitchen, Kate lovingly set the table for Christmas dinner. She stood back and admired the finished product.

Wren and Sparrow's heirloom china glowed softly and looked perfect with goblets from Cooper and Cayden's parent's china hutch.

Kate had polished their silverware and purchased green

and red cloth napkins. She had made a centerpiece of pinecones, holly and gold Christmas balls.

Cooper walked up behind her. "This looks great. Merry Christmas, my Kate."

She turned to him, folding into his arms. "Merry Christmas, Coop."

"You think Santa will visit tonight? Those girls have been pretty naughty, you know."

Kate laughed. "I have a feeling he'll show up. Do you have the camera ready for when the tree's poised for attack in the morning?"

"Ready to go. I think all three of us have a lot of sneaking around to do tonight. But I want us to do the Santa thing together first, okay?"

"Okay. Then you stay out of my way when I put yours and Cayden's under the tree."

"Yeah, well, you better stay out of my way, little missy. I got important stuff to put under there too."

"And you both better stay out of my way." Cayden said, grinning as she walked in to find them all hugged up. "And, please, too much hugging. Let's separate a bit, shall we?"

"Ah, you're just jealous." Cooper said, hugging Kate even closer.

"Whatever," Cayden said, rolling her eyes. "The table looks great, Kate. It's so nice to have stuff like this. We've always eaten at Aunt Cynthia's before, which was nice, too. But it feels so good to be home."

Giving up, she joined them for a group hug.

It lasted a long time.

Cooper set the video camera up on a tripod to record

part of the festivities while he took snapshots of the tree with all the Santa gifts underneath. The girls had a stuffed teddy bear each, a soft dolly each, two cloth books each and new teething rings, which were about to be of imminent need. There was a doggie stocking with a new giant bone and doggie treats in it, and a kitty stocking with a new bell and a catnip mouse. Cayden's stocking was full of candy and buried deep underneath in the toe of new woolen socks was a fifty dollar bill.

Pictures were taken of each and then all under the tree. Cooper videoed Cayden opening her stocking treasures. She squealed appropriately when she discovered the money. The babies were videoed stuffing the dollies in their mouths, the teddy bears in their mouths, and then, finally, appropriately, the teething rings. Clancy was filmed gnawing on his new bone, and Pluma daintily sniffing the cat nip mouse.

Cooper and Kate insisted on a quick breakfast before the kitchen had to be used to cook dinner. Aunt Cynthia would be there shortly with her gifts and eager to begin cooking. The Christmas Story was read out of Luke, the blessing was said, and they plowed into pancakes.

At eleven Aunt Cynthia arrived, arms full of bags of gifts. "It's really cold out there. Too bad the sun is shining. I could do with a white Christmas."

Relieving her of the packages, Cooper laughed. "The south doesn't cooperate with that very often, Aunt Cynthia. I'm just glad it's cold enough for a fire." He took her gifts and placed them under the tree and she took off her coat and hung it up. "Come stand under the tree so I can get your picture. Everyone has to, it's Christmas."

"That's why I dressed half way decent." She said. Folding her hands under her belly, she smiled and waited for the flash. "Now that foolishness is over. I'll go where I'm needed." She headed straight for the kitchen.

"Kate will be back in a minute. She's putting the girls down for their mid-morning nap. I figure they'll wake up just about the time we sit down to eat."

Cynthia smiled. "Of course they will. Maybe they can have a teeny taste of mashed potatoes to go along with their gruel."

Cayden was pouring tea when Cynthia entered the kitchen. She smiled at her aunt. "Good morning and Merry Christmas! Doesn't the kitchen smell great?"

"Indeed it does! Is your young man eating with us?"

"No. He'll be with his family traveling to his grandmothers'. But he'll be over tomorrow so we can exchange gifts."

Kate entered, looking like a vision of Christmas. Dressed in a new Christmas sweater, hair pulled back with blond wisps escaping to frame her face, cheeks flushed and eyes dancing, Cynthia remarked she looked like a Christmas angel.

"Thank you! I feel so happy today, I guess it shows."

The three began a flurry of activity, bossing Cooper to do this or that every time he stuck his head around the corner. He took pictures of them cooking, those three women he loved more than anything on earth. He ducked into the bathroom for just a few minutes to thank the good Lord and wait for the mist in his eyes to clear.

Holding hands around the table laden with steaming food, each of them asked God to bless the food and thanked

Him for a particular blessing from the year. Babies, kittens, a safe home, family, friends and salvation were named. A hearty amen! And the gleaming china was filled with delicious food, goblets with drink, and chairs filled with hungry folks. Just as they raised the forks to their mouths, a wail erupted from the monitor. Each adult looked at one another, and laughter filled the house.

After dinner was done and the heirloom china carefully hand washed and draining while the dishwasher hummed with all the other things, wrapped gifts were brought out from under the tree and passed out to each one.

"Okay, how we gonna do this?" Cooper asked, hands on hips as though he was organizing his ball team for play.

"How 'bout everyone opens their gift from a particular person and then the next person does the same?" Aunt Cynthia suggested, eyeing her presents. "And I want to go first."

This made them all chuckle, and they agreed to both suggestions.

Cayden and Cooper had given Cynthia a new robe and matching slippers and Kate had chosen to give her perfume from herself and the girls. She modeled the robe, tried on the slippers and spritzed on a bit of the perfume, claiming it to be perfect, with a twinkle in her eye.

Since Cayden was squirming in anticipation, she was allowed to go next. She loved the cashmere sweater Kate presented her, and Kate was relieved she'd been so attentive when they were shopping.

She tore into the tiny wrapped box from Cooper and whooped when she saw the beautiful sapphire earrings. She leaped up from the couch and hugged him fiercely. "I'll wear these on my wedding day. For something blue!"

Cooper gave her a stern look. "They better be the something old too, by the time you marry."

Cayden giggled and put them on. "They bring out the blue in my sweatshirt." All agreed.

The gift from Cynthia was to both she and Cooper, but after groaning about it, he let Cayden open it. It was a large photo album. Cynthia explained she'd worked on it the entire year, and it showed. It was a chronological picture show of their childhood, many pictures including their parents. Birthdays, first day of school, swimming, hiking, Christmases, all was there. Even snapshots Cooper's mother had taken of his date and himself just before they left for prom that fateful night. "Last pictures my mom ever took, I guess." Cooper sighed.

"It's something we'll always treasure, Aunt Cynthia." Cayden assured her through teary sniffs.

Kate's turn was next. She opened her gift from Cynthia and laughed, which broke up the solemn moment. It was the exact same perfume Cynthia had just unwrapped from her. "Well, I know I like it!" She exclaimed.

Cayden's gift was to Kate and Cooper together, and although he whined that by the time it was his turn, there'd be no gifts for him to open, he wanted Kate to open it. It was tickets to the local theatre's new play, free desserts at their favorite restaurant, and a promise to baby-sit that night.

Lastly, Kate reached for the gift from Cooper. As she unwrapped it, she realized it was from the same jewelry store as Cayden's earrings. She hoped not at the same time she hoped…but it was tiny diamond earrings and a pendant necklace. "These are beautiful, Cooper!"

He smiled. "And maybe someday there'll be other jewelry to match."

Cooper picked up his one gift, from Kate. His eyes widened when he opened the box. "Wow, Kate, an Aviator watch."

"Yep." She replied proudly. "Nineteen time zones, a navigational slide rule, a stop watch and a day/date display."

He strapped it on his wrist to admire.

"There's one more gift from me, for the girls." Cynthia said. "Maybe we can let Cooper open it since he got shortchanged on that."

Cynthia had purchased size one sun suits for the girls. Kate thanked her, as they had nothing for the upcoming seasons.

"Nothing like planning for the future, I always say. They'll be walking by then, if you can imagine!" Cynthia said.

❈ ❈ ❈ ❈

That night, when all had settled down, Cooper knocked lightly on Cayden's door. A soft "Come in" was the reply, and he opened and closed the door quietly.

Cayden sat up in bed. "Is something wrong?" she whispered. "You're being so quiet."

"Nah, I just wanted to talk privately, that's all."

This raised Cayden's eyebrows. "Well, that's a new concept. What is it?"

He sat on the edge of her bed. Smiling, he squeezed her hand. "I've asked Kate to marry me."

He shushed her quickly before the squeal. She was able to stop it, but just barely.

"She hasn't said yes, Cayden. She's praying about it. She's going to give me her answer soon. She said after Christmas." He shrugged. "Since this is Christmas night, I figured it won't be long."

Cayden looked at him intently. "Are you afraid she's going to say no?"

"Part of me feels sure she'll say yes. But I have to admit, part of me is afraid she'll say no. I mean, she continues to make plans to build or buy a house, stuff like that. But I guess she's needed to do that in case her answer is no."

"Have you prayed about it?"

"Oh, yeah. I feel definitely God gave me the direction to ask her. I think He wants me to be Kate's husband and the girls' father."

Cayden smiled, looking relieved. "Then she'll say yes. God doesn't instruct one person one way and the other person another. Even I know that."

Cooper sighed. "Keep reminding me." He swiped his hand through his hair, leaving a trail of standing up strands. "Well, I guess I'm calling it a night." He leaned down and pecked her on the cheek. "Merry Christmas, Sis."

"Merry Christmas, Coop."

Just as he got to the door, she said his name. "Yeah?"

"This is the best Christmas gift you could give me."

He smiled. "Yeah. Good night."

"Night."

He turned off lights as he went, thinking of each person in the house, saying a little prayer. Maybe Kate would tell him tomorrow.

CHAPTER THIRTY-SEVEN

The Saturday after Christmas was spent hauling the tree out to the curb and vacuuming the mess left behind. The china was carefully put away under the dining room sideboard.

Cooper had recuperated from seeing the friendship ring Mike had given Cayden for Christmas, both Cayden and Kate reassuring him that it was a friendship ring, not an engagement ring. It was a very pretty ring, with her birthstone in the middle.

Leaving Cayden and Cooper to feed the babies, Kate cooked supper and they all ate ravenously. Cayden cleaned up the kitchen and she and Cooper cleaned up the babies.

Now sitting in front of the fireplace, feet propped up, Kate leaned her head on Cooper's chest. Just as she was about to tell him her answer, he spoke softly as he kissed the top of her head.

"I've been sitting here, looking at the fire's reflection in your hair, and looking at your profile and smelling your good woman smell. I love you so much, Kate." He tilted her chin up and they kissed. "You are so beautiful and the most fascinating woman I've ever known."

She patted his stomach. "That's just the cornbread talkin', darlin'." she drawled.

He laughed softly. "Could be. I'm a sucker for a good pone of cornbread."

Kate scooted and sat up, backing away a little, so she

could see Cooper's face. "I have been praying, and I have a real peace about saying yes-" She put a finger to his mouth before he could say anything. "But I don't know when. I mean I don't know whether to wait until the adoption process is complete, so I don't have to start over, or go ahead so they have your name at the adoption time."

"Well, you and I will just have to pray about that." He held her close. "I'm so happy, Kate. Thank you! Thank you, Lord!"

They sat for some time after that, just watching the flames consume the logs.

🐾 🐾 🐾 🐾

On the day Kate knew Roberta was to return to work at the Social Services Office, she called. Roberta seemed glad to hear from her and inquired about her holiday. Kate told her how wonderful it had been, and asked about Roberta's time with her family.

"I loved every minute of it. Especially the last one, right before I got to come back home." Her laughter filled the telephone. "I have a wonderful family, but after three weeks, I just need to be back to my regular schedule."

Kate said she understood. "I guess Dorothy was right. There's no place like home. It's hard being away, even if it's at your folks."

They chatted on a little, then Kate got to the reason she had called. "I told Cooper I would marry him. But I also told him I didn't know the best time – before or after the adoption."

"Do you want me find out what it would entail if you married before the adoption was completed?"

"Yes, please. And can you do it discreetly? If it's going to take a lot of red tape and postponement, we'll just have a long engagement."

"Of course I'll be discreet. I'll find out these facts without naming names. And may I ask what you really want? I mean, do you want a long engagement? Or if we could do something to speed it up, would you want us to put forth that effort?"

Kate sighed. "I don't know of a reason in the world to put it off otherwise. I love Cooper and I feel this is the direction God is leading us." She paused for a moment. "If we got married, I guess I would feel like the rest of my life could stop being put on hold. Sometimes I feel like I'm pretending all the time. I'm not really Wren and Sparrow's Mother yet. Although I live in Cooper's house, I'm not really his wife. Although I love Cooper's sister with all my heart, she's not really mine either. I'm in limbo."

The warmth in Roberta's voice carried over the line. "Bless your heart. I'll get back to you with the answer as quickly as I can, and that's a promise."

"Thank you. I'm not going to mention this to Cooper until I know."

By that afternoon, Roberta had called her and given her facts, as well as encouragement. Although a background check and interviewing would have to be done, the home was already approved, and that would save some time. Roberta felt she could talk to the judge and give him the situation once all the work was done, and perhaps not put off the adoption more than a month, if that. After all, a wedding had to be planned, didn't it? They weren't going to elope, were they? Roberta suggested that while they planned a wedding, the agency would proceed in approving Cooper.

Kate sat in the living room, watching the babies roll around on the floor, reaching for toys, "talking" to each other. Could, in a few months, all this really be hers? Her husband, her home, her babies. "Thank you, Lord. My heart is so full I can hardly stand it. Help me to present it in the right way to Cooper. Show us the way to proceed so that we honor You."

Cooper called before he got home. "Kate, I've asked Cayden if she'll take the babies over to Aunt Cynthia's for an hour or so this evening. I called Aunt Cynthia, and she said absolutely."

"What on earth for? You think they need to get out more?" She teased, curious as to what Cooper had up his sleeve.

"I just need to talk without babies crying, Cayden yapping, and the phone ringing. I figure we can silence the phone. Will you agree?"

"Well, sure, Coop. It's fine with me. What time do I need to have Wren and Sparrow ready?"

"If you can pack up their baby food and bottles and jammies, Aunt Cynthia said to bring them on as soon as Cayden gets home. She's fixing Cayden's favorite supper."

"They'll bathe them before they bring them home?"

"Yep."

"Wow. I'll get their things ready now."

Excitement coursed through Kate's veins. She didn't know what Cooper was planning, but she thought she could take advantage of the situation and let him know she wanted to start planning a wedding. Suddenly she stopped cold. What if he had changed his mind? What if he had decided this was all a mistake and she needed to start looking for a place to live?

"The Bible says not to fear. God is not the Father of anxiety. Go away, Satan!" she mumbled, then got herself tickled. She talked to the babies as she got their night things packed. "Mommy's not nuts. Sometimes you just have to pray out loud and confirm God's Word."

"Hey, Kate, you upstairs?" She heard Cayden slam the front door.

"Yeah. Come on up."

Cayden came into the babies' room. "What's up with Cooper?"

Kate shrugged. "I don't have a clue. He sounded pretty serious, though."

"Well, he's already proposed, so I don't know either."

Kate looked nervously at Cayden. "You don't think he's changed his mind and wants to tell me, do you?"

Cayden hooted. "Not on your life. He's nuts over you and worse over these two." She tickled both baby tummies at the same time, eliciting chuckles from both girls.

"Well, I guess we'll soon find out. I hear him pulling in the driveway."

"You'll find out, I'll be left in the dark, as usual." Cayden huffed. "At least I get pork chops and macaroni and cheese out of it."

Cooper all but pushed them out the door, then stood at the window and watched Cayden drive off. Clancy whined at him. "I'm going to walk the dog so he won't interrupt. As soon as Cayden let's us know she's there safely, we'll talk."

Kate stared at him. He was nervous, obviously. And he had this determined look in his eye that made her *more* than a little nervous.

By the time Cooper came back in, unleashed Clancy and made sure he had plenty of dog food and water, Cayden had called saying they were safely ensconced at Aunt Cynthia's.

"Cooper you're making me nervous. What in the world is going on?"

"I've just got something to say. You don't have to be nervous. Let's go sit down."

Instead of sitting on the sofa with her as he usually did, he sat in the chair opposite her. He looked her in the eye and said firmly, "Kate, we have to marry before the girls' adoption is finalized."

"Why?" Kate asked, a little indignantly. After all, he was stealing her thunder and she was feeling a little miffed.

Cooper leaned back in his chair, putting his hands behind his head. "Say Wren's full name, after you've adopted her before we marry."

Kate looked puzzled, shrugged and said, "Wren Elizabeth Roe."

"Okay, now say her name as she'll be called by, say, the teacher every morning when role is called."

Kate looked at him.

"Go ahead, just do it, Kate."

Rolling her eyes, she complied. "Wren Roe." Kate's hand flew over her mouth, her eyes wide. "Oh, my goodness!"

Cooper grinned lazily. "Now say Sparrow's name."

Without taking her hand from her mouth, she mumbled, "Sparrow Roe." A giggle escaped from between her fingers.

"See? What did I tell ya? Must have wedding before adoption."

"Oh, Cooper, this is awful! I'd never even thought of it." Another giggle escaped. "Lucky for them, I was going to tell you tonight we had a couple of months to plan a wedding. Think we can do it?"

Cooper looked at her in stunned silence. Then he began nodding his head. "Yes, I think we can do that." A huge grin split his face and he started singing 'Praise God from Whom All Blessings Flow'. Clancy gave him a horrified looked, whined, and ran from the room to escape the tone deaf noise.

As soon as they stopped kissing, Cooper dug in his jacket pocket and pulled out the engagement ring that matched her Christmas jewelry.

It was a perfect fit.

CHAPTER THIRTY-EIGHT

Pastor Matt had insisted on at least four counseling sessions before he would agree to perform the marriage ceremony. That sounded reasonable to Kate and Cooper, and Social Services gave a nod in agreement that this was sufficient to meet their criteria.

They had just arrived home from the first of these when Roberta called to schedule her next home visit. Since plans had changed to included Cooper, she had five more visits, instead of the one. Her fifth would occur the week before a tentative wedding date had been set.

That appointment made, Kate hung up the phone only for it to ring again immediately. It was Anna wanting to talk dresses for the wedding. "Since I'll be as big as a cow, I'm thinking white bridesmaid dresses with big old black spots all over them, so I'll look like a Holstein. Do you think Genevieve would mind? We could tell her she'd look like a cute little calf as a Junior Bridesmaid."

Kate laughed so hard it startled Clancy, and Cooper stuck his head around the corner with his eyebrows raised. "You, Anna, are nuts. We are getting married March twenty-eighth. You won't be all that big at seven months. And besides, only the bride is supposed to wear white."

"Oh. So what are the brown cows? Jerseys?"

"Anna, I'm thinking more along the lines of green. A very soft sage green. You can pick the style as Genevieve's will be different anyway because of her age. I just want the fabric to match."

"Shoes? My feet will be swelling."

Kate shook her head. "Let's go with ballet slippers. No problem with swelling."

"Okay. Have you planned the reception yet? What kind of food will you have? I'm already hungry all the time."

"Cynthia and Mrs. Peabody are on it. Mrs. Stonefield has agreed to do the wedding cake and the groom's cake. She's worked in a bakery before and has all the patterns for decorations. Cynthia is in charge of mints and sandwiches and Mrs. Peabody will gather all the silverware and china and such. Does that ease your mind?"

Anna sighed. "I suppose." Kate could hear Anna tapping her nail on the phone. "So, how did your session with Matt go?"

"Fine. We filled out questionnaires. We have homework. Some of it seems kinda silly since we have been in the circumstances we've been in. But Matt says once we're married, the shift will change a lot of the way we view things and want to handle things. I know people come into marriage with all sorts of expectations. He says we've got to look at some of this and make decisions before they happen so we don't hit roadblocks as unexpectedly as we might."

"Bailey and I had pre-marital counseling. It was really helpful. We thought we knew everything about each other because we dated for five years. Ha! We didn't know squat. It's true you don't really know someone till you live with them."

"And even though Coop and I are living together, we're not living together, you know?"

"Yeah. I guess that will take some getting used to!" Anna giggled.

"Cute. I was talking about feeling like it's my home, and helping make financial decisions together instead of separately. Parenting the girls together instead of Cooper just making suggestions, feeling like Cayden's my sister too." Kate sighed. "I can hardly wait."

"I'm so happy for you, Kate." Kate heard a sniff on the other end. "Gosh, I'm so emotional now. I cry at the drop of a hat!"

"Friendship tears are good." Kate said.

As she hung up, Cooper wanted to know what the laughing was about. He just shook his head when she told him.

"Poor Bailey. Ain't no telling what he's living in."

"Cooper!"

"Well, Anna has always been a little flighty. This must be something else."

"What will you do if I ever get pregnant?"

"Hire a financial advisor? Buy a van? With two young'uns already and a giant dog, I'll just have to pray a lot and depend on the good Lord."

"Can you imagine those who used to have ten or more children? How in the world did they ever manage?"

"Beats me. I may want more kids later, Kate, but I can assure you that number has never crossed my mind."

"Thank goodness!" She looked at him thoughtfully. "We've not really discussed other children."

"Do you want more?" He scooped her up in his arms. "We've been so busy with the twins, I guess it's been hard to think about more."

"I think so." She laughed a little. "Not anytime soon, though. But I'd like to give Wren and Sparrow a sibling or two. I'm surprised at how much I like being a mother."

"Do you want to continue to be a stay at home mom?" He kissed her on the nose.

"With the girls' inheritance and insurance money from the house, I can easily do that for a few more years. But I don't know about future babies. Could we even afford it?" She chewed on her lower lip a little.

"We can't live extravagantly, but yeah. The house is paid for. I guess we could decide that when the time comes."

Kate nodded. "It's good to know there are options." She tilted her head. "I have daydreamed about names. Not in a serious way, but still…"

"Okay, shoot. Like what?"

"Well, if we had girls, I like Larke and Raven."

"Ah, a continuation of the birdie theme. I like it. But what if we had a boy?"

"The only one I can come up with is Robin. He could be named in honor of Wren and Sparrow's biological mother."

"Nope. That's a girl's name."

"Not necessarily. What about Robin Hood?"

"I thought it was Robbing Hood and besides, he was fictional."

"No, it was Robin Hood. Okay, how about Robin Williams, he's real."

"Our son would have ADHD."

"Christopher Robin."

"Also fictional and that was probably his last name."

"A. A. Milne had a son really named Christopher Robin."

"Did they call him Robin?"

"No." She grinned at him. "And even though he is fictional too, what about Robin, Batman's sidekick – you know, a superhero?"

Cooper looked at her incredulously. "You think Batman's scrawny sidekick is a superhero?"

"He's not scrawny! Well, how about Robin Gibb and Robin Thicke? That way, he might be musically talented."

"What about ROBIN LEACH?" Cooper roared, a smirk on his face. "He could tell us about the rich and famous." Cooper poured on the thick cockney accent, mimicking the famous announcer.

Kate frowned. "That's not fair. Okay, we could name him Robert and call him Robin till he was old enough to change over. That's how Robin got started in the first place."

Cooper took a deep breath. "ROBIN LEACH." He yelled.

Kate covered her ears and started laughing. "Okay, okay, you win. No boy Robins. You sure are hard to please."

"Yes I am, Miss Roe. That's why I'm marrying you."

"Oh, did I agree to that already?" she asked innocently.

Cooper shook his head. "Don't make me holler his name again."

Before she could reply, he kissed her soundly. Which led to another kiss, which led to another kiss…

CHAPTER THIRTY-NINE

The last counseling session with Matt had been a very emotional one. Tears had been shed as they promised one another to have a marriage like the Bible instructed, a covenant made before God. Matt had challenged them to look long and hard at personal quirks, expectations, selfishness and differences. Some of it made them both very uncomfortable, some of it made them burst into uncontrollable laughter, some of it into uncontrollable tears. They grieved for loved ones and how their lives might have been different. They talked seriously about parenting beliefs and how they would handle differences.

And at the end of the last hour, Matt had prayed with them and asked when dress rehearsal for the wedding would take place.

Roberta's last visit was equally emotional. She had become attached to Wren and Sparrow over the past several months, watching them grow and change. She even gave Clancy a hug as she left, with a promise to come to the wedding.

And suddenly, Kate and Cooper found themselves only days away from their marriage vows.

March twenty-eighth dawned cold and snowy. Kate was awake before the twins, gazing out the window, wondering about the weather. She thought if it snowed too much there wouldn't be many guests, but that was all right as long as the preacher could make it. She looked down at the Bible in her lap, reading from Proverbs: 31: 10-31 and sighed. *'A wife of noble character – worth more than rubies, bringing good to her husband, caring for her family. She provides for the poor and needy. She does business, making and selling garments, supplying merchants, considering a field to buy, planting a vineyard from her earnings. She is industrious, never idle, full of dignity, respected and praised by her husband and children. She speaks wisdom and instruction, she is to be given the reward she has earned'* ...She had big shoes to fill.

She bowed her head. "Lord," she whispered softly, "I love Cooper so much. Thank you for showing me what kind of man he really is. I can see the daddy in him every day. But more importantly, I can see You in him. I know the road will be busy you've put us on. Help me to be the kind of mate you expect me to be, as well as the kind of mama." She raised her head at the first whimper coming over the intercom. Glancing out the window, she put her Bible on the nightstand, stood and headed for the door.

Cooper was in bed, arms raised with his hands tucked under his head. He, too, had been watching the snow. For some reason he saw it as a true blessing on this day. Such thanksgiving filled his heart he felt tears in his eyes. "Thank you, Lord." It would certainly take God's help to be the kind of father and husband he intended on being. He heard footsteps in the hall and knew Kate was up. The footsteps sounded heavy, he figured she had both girls in her arms, headed for the kitchen. He heard Clancy trotting right behind her.

His wedding day had started and he didn't want to miss a thing.

🐾 🐾 🐾 🐾

The phone rang off the hook all morning. Well wishers, weather reports from every source who had an opinion, the florist re-assuring them there would be no problem getting everything to the church, the pianist who called to tell them he had a four-wheel drive and not to panic. The soloist who called to say she was riding with the pianist, so not to worry. The caterer who was double checking to make sure the fellowship hall door would be unlocked as scheduled, Aunt Cynthia warning them somebody better get her, she wasn't driving in any snow of any kind! Mr. and Mrs. Stonefield assuring them their truck could make it and would they like them to pick up Cynthia? They were sure they could squeeze her in beside Genevieve. Roberta Flint called to tell them the court date was May fourteenth. "I knew you'd be busy this morning – and by the way I plan on coming, I'm used to snow – but I thought this would ease your mind. I'm just sorry it's such a long wait. The dockets are full, and this is the best we could do." Anna and Bailey called with bawdy remarks, and finally the pastor asking if they were nervous.

Nervous? Who the heck had time to be nervous?

The snow kept coming down in great soft flakes, piling up like downy clouds on the ground. Cayden came in around eleven from the yard, brushing snow off her coat. "Four inches!" she whooped. "And it hasn't slowed a bit."

Cooper glanced at Kate, who was getting the babies' outfits packed carefully in plastic bags to change into at the church.

"You okay with this? I mean, if it's only us few

chickens, you won't be disappointed?"

Kate smiled up at him. "Not at all. The only thing that will be a downside is so much food. But I suppose everyone can divide it up and maybe most of it won't go to waste."

Lunch was a quick affair of sandwiches and chips. They put the girls down for a nap and Kate got in the tub with promises from Cooper and Cayden they would listen out for the babies so she could "primp" uninterrupted.

She sank into the tub, a rare treat for her. Usually it was a fast shower, with one eye on the clock. Although today she was very aware of the time passing, she'd given herself plenty of it for this luxury. Forty-five minutes later, rosy from the bath, she stood in her bedroom eyeing her wedding dress. Instead of wearing it to the church, as planned, they had all decided it was better to dress at the church because of the snow. She had wrapped her dress in extra plastic at the bottom so if it drug on the ground accidentally it would still be dry.

She, Cayden, and Anna had shopped for dresses and had been extremely fortunate to find what she was looking for at the second bridal boutique. Her dress was a soft ivory, fitted at the waist. It was heavy wool, tea length. Tiny pearl buttons lined up like little soldiers all the way down the back and there was a smattering of pearls across the bodice and cuffs. Anna would put her hair up for her at the church, and they had strands of pearls to run through it. She made sure the pumps were snug in their box. She'd never paid that much for shoes! She had purchased some tiny pearl earrings, too.

Making sure they were in her jewelry pouch, she

fingered her mother's wedding ring. She had convinced Cooper she'd rather wear her mother's ring than a new one, and it did look lovely with her new engagement ring. She would hand Cayden the ring at the church for it to be given to Cooper during the ceremony.

Her underclothes were laid out on the bed, and she was going to put them on under her sweats, so her outer clothing could be quickly changed at the church. She fingered all the lacey lingerie and giggled. If that didn't knock Cooper's socks off, she didn't know what would.

She checked her makeup bag and it was brimming with magic.

Kate looked at herself in the mirror and smiled. She would be one beautiful bride, if she did say so herself.

When she came out of her room, she could hear Cooper talking. She went down to the kitchen and found he was conversing with Clancy, who was looking pretty spiffy too, after his trip to the groomer yesterday.

"Am I interrupting anything important?" she asked.

Cooper grinned. "Nope, just reminding him how to behave. I know Jeff Burgess personally. You know, the guy who owns the catering business?" Kate nodded her head. "He says he'll make sure Clancy is okay during the wedding. He's going to keep him in one of the Sunday School rooms next to the fellowship hall. He'll give him water and has purchased a big bone for Clancy to chew on to keep him occupied."

At the word bone, Clancy's ears perked up. He was to be there for pictures directly after the ceremony. Then Mr. Stonefield was going to take him back to the house, walk him, and see him safely back in. They had graciously agreed to move in with Cayden and the babies for the three days Cooper and Kate would be gone on their honeymoon, so Mr. Stonefield and Clancy had been busy making friends the last few days.

"Thanks for taking care of all that, Coop. I hope we don't forget something. I feel like we're moving the entire house."

"I've got my stuff packed. I shaved and showered while you were in the tub. Cayden is now doing her beauty routine. I've got my stuff loaded. Bailey has our tuxes and I'll kill him if he doesn't bring them, so that takes care of that." He glanced at the clock. "We need to be there in an hour. Can you think of anything that needs to be done besides loading up stuff?"

"I guess not. The wedding party should be there the same time we arrive. Pastor Matt should be there about now to let the caterer and florist in. I guess he is, since no one's called screaming. Have you heard any more about the weather?" She glanced out the window. Snow was still falling.

"They are predicting up to eight inches by tonight."

"Wow! Think we'll be able to get to the cabin?"

Cooper lowered his eyelids in an attempt to appear sultry. "Oh, yeah, baby. Wild horses can't keep us from it."

Kate shook her head and laughed. "But eight inches of snow might. Seriously, Coop."

He shrugged. "We've borrowed the best four wheel drive with great tires. If it looks like it won't make it, I guess it's the 'Dew Drop Inn' for us."

"I'll keep my fingers crossed." Kate replied dryly.

The girls woke shortly after that, Cooper made a

hundred trips to the car, they made Clancy wear plastic "booties" from the front door to the car, loaded everyone else up, and they were off to the church.

It was still snowing.

After a drive that took twice as long, and unloading the car which took three times as long, Kate felt like she'd been in a foot race when she sat down for Anna to do her hair. Anna's belly kept bumping into her back, which would make them both laugh every time. Anna had stopped once to let Kate feel the baby move.

Anna had already done her own hair, and her face was flushed with excitement. The soft green gown that fell in folds down her growing body looked lovely. Cayden stood next to them, finishing her make-up. Her dress, the same shade of green, was fitted and showed off her slender figure. Genevieve's hung on the door awaiting their arrival. Her dress was simple in lines, but Kate had made sure it had a grown up flair to it so that Genevieve would feel she was dressed appropriately for a Junior Bridesmaid.

Genevieve and Mrs. Stonefield arrived just as Anna finished Kate's hair. They all complimented the curls cascading around Genevieve's face. Ribbons, the exact shade of her dress, laced in and out of the curls.

"I'm as excited as I can be!" Genevieve exclaimed. "I look nearly grown, don't I?"

All the women agreed she certainly did.

Kate slipped into her own dress, and Cayden did the honors of buttoning the many pearl buttons up the back. Kate finished the look with the pearl earrings and touched up her make-up with fresh lipstick. She stepped back from the mirror to take a critical look at herself.

All the females had a dreamy look on their faces, which confirmed what Kate had predicted: She was, indeed, a beautiful bride.

"The only thing that concerns me is walking down the aisle alone."

Mrs. Stonefield clutched her hand. "Sweetie, you won't be alone. Your Heavenly Father will be right there with you."

Genevieve came back to report that the church was beginning to fill up, despite the snowy day. "There are even some little old ladies out there. Reckon how they managed to get here?" she mused, making them laugh.

There was a knock on the door. Mr. Stonefield and Bailey stood there with Wren and Sparrow. The babies were matching beauties in soft green and pink, and much to Kate's surprise looked no worse for wear since she'd dressed them. Leaving them in the hands of the men had made her doubt that possibility, and she felt a little ashamed at the assumption. She still had a sneaking suspicion that Mrs. Peabody had been supervising.

They all cooed at them, and Kate checked for dry diapers.

"We're all about ready out there. I must say you are gorgeous, Kate." Mr. Stonefield said, admiration in his eyes.

"I'll say." Bailey grinned. "All you ladies are ravishing. Amazing what a little war paint will do."

"Very funny, Bailey." Anna said, looking at her husband menacingly. "That tie cutting off the circulation to your brain?"

"Aww, Anna, you know it's hard for me to be serious."

He blushed and everyone laughed.

The music began to play, and Kate listened to the beautiful words of the soloist as she brought the message of God's love for a man and woman.

Bailey had somehow disappeared during this, handing Sparrow off to Mrs. Stonefield.

Kate peeked out the doors as the music changed and watched her dear Cooper follow Pastor Matt out, with Bailey at his side.

Two of Cooper's coaching buddies, Sam Renford and Robert Baker had been acting as ushers for the event, as well as Mike, Cayden's boyfriend. Sam and Robert now came and seated Aunt Cynthia, then Mr. and Mrs. Stonefield, who were holding Wren and Sparrow.

Kate waited nervously behind Cayden, Anna and Genevieve. She watched them get in line to go out and her eyes widened in horror. "Genevieve! Stop! The back of your dress!"

They all looked back. Genevieve had made a last minute trip to the bathroom, and somehow toilet paper had gotten tucked inside her panty hose, bunching her dress up under the hose and trailing the paper.

Genevieve looked at her backside. "Ach, I'm not used to these daft stockings. Too much ado." She turned her back to the mirror and began to giggle. "I'm a wee eedjit, I am."

Kate held the bouquets as Anna and Cayden hurriedly repaired the mess.

The two ushers were waiting outside the door, quizzical looks on their faces. Finally, Anna stepped out for Sam to take her arm, then Cayden took Mike's, and lastly

Robert escorted Genevieve down the aisle, who helplessly continued to giggle all the way, eliciting puzzled smiles from pews in her wake.

As Kate stood there, a moment alone, she felt the Holy Spirit's presence as surely as if she did have her daddy with her. Then a distant noise had her tilting her head, listening. Was that thunder?

The music changed, Mrs. Peabody opened the doors, and Kate began her march toward Cooper. The smile that he offered her threatened to do her in, and she blinked rapidly to keep the tears at bay.

Reaching the altar, she took his arm, smiled deeply into his eyes, turned toward the preacher, and heard a strange click as the electricity went off. Kate heard a deep, muffled bark from Clancy, way down below them.

There was a murmured surprised among the congregation.

"Well!" Pastor Matt exclaimed. "Good thing ya'll have candles lit everywhere."

This brought forth chuckles from everyone, especially when one child proclaimed loudly, "I ain't afraid of the dark no more, am I Mommy?"

In the quiet of the twilight glow, the church still as warm as the mood that encased them, Cooper turned to Kate and vowed to her an ancient Scottish covenant:

"You're blood of my blood,
And bone of my bone.
I give you my body that we two might be one.
I give you my spirit till one life shall be done.
You're blood of my blood,
And bone of my bone."

Kate became Mrs. Cooper McGuire. And Cooper became the happiest man on earth.

CHAPTER FORTY

The wedding party pictures had gone smoothly. Even Wren and Sparrow had cooperated beautifully. On cue, as soon as their part was done, they began to fuss and then full out cry from being held too much and needing food. Mrs. Peabody and Mrs. Stonefield took the twins to the church nursery to feed them and put them down for naps. Clancy had been the perfect model, posing as though it was an everyday thing for him. The photographer had fallen in love with him and found out from Kate where a puppy of his breed might be purchased. Soon it was all done but Kate and Cooper's portraits, then Kate alone for a few.

By the time the newlyweds arrived downstairs, the reception was in full swing. Anna came up to them as they entered the room. "You've got about a hundred people here wanting to wish you well and see you cut the cake so they can get home while the roads are still passable. Someone went out and measured the snow and said we were up to five inches already."

"Let's get this show on the road then." Cooper began milling about one end of the room and Kate took the other. They had decided ahead of time they didn't want a receiving line.

Within twenty minutes they were posing with the knife behind the cake. Kate heard Cooper's stomach rumble when she gave him the posed bite of cake. Raising her eyebrows, she asked, "Hungry, are we?"

"Starving," Cooper answered around a mouthful of cake.

As soon as they both grabbed a bit of the enormous amount of food they were paying for, they rallied around for the next thing the guests were anticipating.

The single women gathered and Kate threw her bouquet. It went straight over Genevieve's head, grazed Cayden's fingers, and landed right in Mrs. Peabody's open palm. Everyone cheered. She blushed and did a quick curtsey.

Cooper's turn involved sliding Kate's skirt up to reveal a lacy garter. Guys whistled and clapped. Cooper couldn't resist snapping her thigh with it before he pulled it down her leg. She yelped and smacked him upside the head, causing the guys to roar with laugher and catcall: "That's the way it'll be from now on!" and "We see who the boss is gonna be!"

She threw the garter and it landed on the caterer's head. He looked surprised, as he was bent over the food at the time. He took it off his head, grabbed the girl working next to him, kissed her soundly, and proposed. She said, "Sure," shrugged, and went back to work.

The caterer grinned. "Romance is in the air!" and sailed back into the kitchen, causing more laughter from the guests.

Shortly afterwards, folks began to leave. Kate and Cooper left the room to change clothes.

As Cooper came out of the bathroom, Bailey sidled up to him. In sotto voice he said, "I checked with Uncle Ben. You remember he works for the road department?"

"Yeah." Cooper waited.

"It's bad. Real bad. They have ten inches up there already. He said the road crews have worked all day and can't keep up. I told him why you needed to get to the cabin."

"Yeah?" This was getting interesting.

"Yeah. He said he believed the crew might need to detour 'round what they were doing and clear those last five miles if you'll leave now. He said he couldn't promise when they could get back to clear that road again. Since it's still snowing so hard, he said you could get snowed in five, six days, maybe more."

"What a shame." Cooper deadpanned.

"I know!" Bailey was almost giddy with excitement.

Poking out his chest, Bailey informed Cooper proudly of what he'd been doing. "So, I just went to the Piggly Wiggly and bought you some extra groceries." He took a deep breath and listed the food, "T-bone steaks, chicken, a loaf of bread, peanut butter, baking potatoes, eggs, a coke, and beanie weenies."

"Beanie weenies?"

"I was in a hurry. I was thinking protein for energy."

"Ah, well, thanks, man. I'll hurry Kate up and get outta here."

They high fived one another and hustled to get this thing wrapped up.

Cooper found Kate going back into the reception area. "Bailey called his Uncle Ben with the road department up at the cabin and he said we need to get there while we can. So we need to hurry, Kate."

"Let's say good-bye to everyone and get gone, then."

Kate's idea and Cooper's idea of 'getting gone' were

slightly different, especially when it came to Wren and Sparrow. She'd thanked Mrs. Peabody for keeping the reception moving smoothly, she'd thanked Aunt Cynthia for keeping the brides book, she'd thanked Anna, Cayden ('my new sister'), and Genevieve for being her bridesmaids, she'd thanked Pastor Matt for performing the ceremony. As she started toward the florist and caterer, Cooper reminded her they had to go or it was the 'Dew Drop Inn'. So, instead, she'd detoured into the nursery, hugging Clancy furiously, and telling Mr. and Mrs. Stonefield how much she appreciated them disrupting their lives to be with the girls, and proceeded to go over lists (again) of where, what, when and how, much to Mr. Stonefield's obvious amusement.

Then she turned to the sleeping babies and watched them carefully for a few moments. When she raised her head, there were tears in her eyes. "I'm ready." She nodded to Cooper.

He stepped past her and gazed at his daughters and sighed. "Me too."

Walking out, he found Bailey had already made sure their stuff was packed. Anna had stored all the wedding paraphernalia and promised to get the tuxes back on time.

Giving one last hug to everyone, Cooper helped Kate in the SUV, walked carefully to the driver's side and climbed in. With one last wave, they eased out of the parking lot, skidding into the street.

Bailey winced. "And they're off," he muttered. "Like a herd of turtles."

CHAPTER FORTY-ONE

The trip to Lake August was harrowing. The roads became more treacherous the further into the mountain area they drove. Twice Cooper pulled over, wiping his palms on the wheel, easing his shoulder muscles. Once, they considered turning around. Then quite suddenly the roads improved.

"Now, why is that?" Kate wondered. They were about five miles from Lake August.

Then realization dawned and they said in unison, "Uncle Ben!"

The forty-five minute drive had turned into almost three hours by the time they pulled into the cabin's yard. "I feel like kissing the ground." Cooper said, stretching his legs.

"You mean the snow. I can't see the ground. I'm just glad I have on boots." The snow was above her ankles.

"Let's unlock and turn on lights then walk out to the lake before it's too dark."

They could see it just a short distance away, so Kate agreed.

Inside the cabin felt fairly warm, and there was a bottle with a note on the kitchen counter. Kate started toward it, but Cooper said, "Leave it. We'll be right back. Daylight will start to fade in a few minutes and I want to be inside for the night before then. I bet the temperature will drop even more."

Signs From God

They grabbed their coats and gloves out of the SUV and trekked to the shore of the lake. The beauty was almost overwhelming. The lake had frozen around the edges; the trees were laden with snow. The ground was untouched except for the occasional print of an animal. "Look at this one, Cooper."

Kate had squatted down to look at a large print. Cooper's eyes widened. "That's a cat paw. And it's big. Has to be a mountain lion. All the more reason to get in before dark."

"Are you serious? Here, in Georgia?"

"Sure. They aren't the big ones like in California, but I don't really want one watching me from the trees, do you?"

"Uh, no." Taking one more look at the pristine scene, she was ready to go.

"Let's get the food in first," Cooper said. "I think Bailey sent some perishable stuff. I hope it's still good."

Opening the back of the SUV they began unloading the food. "He bought a cooler and put stuff in it!" Cooper exclaimed. "That boy thought of everything."

Two trips later, finding a few sandwiches, nuts and chips as well as wedding cake wrapped up from the reception, they had emptied the car of all the food as well as luggage.

"Whew! I'm beat!" Kate exclaimed, pulling off her coat and gloves. "And we've still got to put the food away."

"Don't get too tired." Cooper waggled his eyebrows at her, and she swatted him, blushing.

Turning to the counter, she said, "This is sparkling grape juice, compliments of Lake August. She read the note. "Congratulations newlyweds! We hope your stay is delightful in every way. You will find the fridge and pantry well stocked for your three day stay. Please read carefully the instructions regarding the generator and supplies in case of a power outage. There's plenty of wood under the porch for fires in the bedroom fireplace. WARNING: The living room fireplace is, in reality, a gas log heater, DO NOT use wood! You will also find sealed matches, two oil lamps and two battery operated lanterns for use during any power outage that might occur during your visit. We hope none of the supplies will be necessary, but being prepared is our motto! Enjoy your stay! It's signed Management." Kate turned to Cooper. "Boy, they do like to be prepared."

Cooper pointed to the other paper. "Is that the generator instructions?" He picked it up. "It tells where the gas cans are and how to crank the thing. There's a switch in the fuse box you throw before you crank it." He walked over to the wall and opened up the door to the box. "I see it." He closed the door back. "It will run the refrigerator and water pump plus two power outlets. We can plug in a lamp and use other stuff one at a time, like the toaster or the coffee maker. Says the hot water heater and cook top are gas." He turned to Kate. "Looks like we're set, no matter what."

"Makes me feel safe." She snuggled up to Cooper. "This is gonna be a perfect honeymoon. Snowed in on a mountain by a lakeside with the best man in the world." She looked up and they kissed, long and hard. "I'm a little nervous about tonight." she confessed.

"Excuse me, but this is Cooper you're talkin' to. We'll muddle through this thing, then be fabulous lovers at the end of our stay."

Kate giggled. "We may have to practice."

Cooper looked at her seriously. "I have no doubt about it." He kissed her again.

"Cooper?"

"Yeah?"

"I'm hungry. Embarrassed, but hungry."

He sighed. "Me too. Why don't we eat the leftover reception sandwiches and chips. We can even have wedding cake for desert."

"Sounds good. Wanna eat in front of the fireplace?"

"The real one or the easy one?"

"Let's go easy first. You can build a fire while I'm getting ready for bed in the bathroom."

He gulped. "Okay-dokey."

Cooper fiddled with the gas logs and got them working while Kate put food on their plates. They sat cross legged on the floor and ate, sharing the bottle of grape juice. "Silly question time." Kate said.

"Shoot."

"Should we inventory our food? All this talk of power outage has me a little nervous."

"Probably not a bad idea. We'll do that in the morning after breakfast, okay?"

Kate nodded. "Do our cell phones work here?"

Cooper smiled and tucked a stray strand of hair behind Kate's ear. "Missing the girls?"

She ducked her head. "I guess I am, a little."

"Me too. The cell phones work outside close to where the SUV is parked. I figure I can check for messages two or three times a day. Want to check in before we go to bed?"

"No, but will you check for messages? I'm sure if anything was wrong, they'd call us. No need for us to call them, right?"

"Are you sure?"

"I think so."

"I'll do that now, if you'll clean up our mess. Then while you, um, uh – get ready for bed, I'll build a real fire in the bedroom. How does that sound?"

"Perfect." she gave him a quick smooch. "Go check."

When Cooper came back in to report there were no messages, Kate was coming out of the bedroom. "I've got my stuff in the bathroom."

"I'll build the fire." They stood there looking at one another for a moment. "It's still snowing." He said absently.

"Oh."

A span of silence.

"I love you Cooper McGuire."

"I love you so much, Kate McGuire."

She gave a nod of her head. In a moment, he heard the bathroom door click shut.

Cooper found the fire easy to start as kindling was laid and there was a gas starter that helped it burn smartly. His kind of fire, he thought. He saw that Kate had turned down the bed, and his palms started sweating. Why was he so nervous? How difficult could this be? "I just want to be good to her, Lord." He muttered.

"This is my gift to you, my son. It is a wonderful pleasure to be used between a man and a wife. A union to bring you closer and dearer to one another."

Heaving a reassured and thankful sigh, Cooper walked

into the kitchen, washed his hands, turned off the lights and turned down the heat. He went back into the bedroom and slipped off his shoes and socks, his jeans and shirt and got into bed. He wondered if Kate would be all right with this being his side of the bed.

The bathroom door opened. For a moment Kate was illuminated from the bathroom light. Turning it off, she walked over to the fireplace. She was in a heavy robe, but looked at Cooper and smiled. She slid the robe off and he almost choked. How could so much pink and lace cover up so little?

There she stood; backlit by the fire, so beautiful, so feminine, all lace and pink fluff. His eyes traveled down her long legs to her slender ankles… to find wool socks.

She giggled. "You can't have everything, Coop."

He grinned, then laughing out loud, motioned for her. "Come here, you."

And then they practiced.

CHAPTER FORTY-TWO

When Kate awoke, she was spooned by Cooper under a pile of bed covers. The fire was out and the room was bathed in that dreamy light that only snow could provide. She eased out from his arms and looked out the window. Still snowing! She shivered and quickly reached for the robe draped across the bottom of the bed.

She wrapped her arms around her knees and watched her husband sleep. He looked like a little boy, except for the fact he needed a shave.

"I know you're lookin' at me."

"How can you, your eyes aren't open."

"I feel you. And I feel snow still coming down, too."

"You sure are feeling a lot this morning."

"Come here and I'll feel some more, woman." He growled.

"Cooper! That's ugly." she said primly, but scooted just a tad closer. She squealed when he grabbed her under the covers and started tickling her. "Stop! Stop!" she giggled.

He did stop, and kissed her. "Married life is great." he said.

"I agree. We've had so long to determine that; we've become experts."

"Ummm hmmm. You smell good." He said, nuzzling her neck.

"Thank you. But from the sounds of your stomach you

need something that smells more like bacon."

"Yeah. In a minute." He pulled closer, kissing her again.

Later (after practice), Kate surprised Cooper with biscuits. "Aunt Cynthia packed six of her homemade biscuits and a jar of her homemade blackberry jelly for us to have for our first married breakfast."

"She's a good woman. What else do we fix?"

Kate looked in the fridge. "There's bacon or sausage and also a ham, but the ham would have to be in the oven a while. We have eggs, thanks to the management and extra thanks to Bailey. Butter and apple jelly, coffee's making, there's o.j. and a gallon of milk, whatever you want to drink."

"We'll feast like royalty!" Cooper was washing his hands. "I'll set the table and we'll cook together." He turned and looked at her thoughtfully. "You know, this all seems so natural for us. We've been sharing the kitchen for a while now, and we work well in tandem. It's nice to finally have the rest of the relationship, isn't it?"

She stopped setting stuff out from the fridge and hugged him. "Yeah. Yeah, it is."

Cooper said an unusually long blessing. They ate as though starved. Right in the middle of breakfast, the electricity went off. Cooper stopped chewing, listened, then shrugged. "We seem to have already developed a tradition in our marriage. Wherever we go, the power goes out."

Kate sighed. "Well, I don't much like that one. Now what?"

"I guess as soon as we finish eating, we start planning out when to run the generator and inventory the food, like you said to do. First, I'll go outside and check messages and get a fire going in the bedroom before a chill sets in." He scooted his chair out, turned on the gas logs and sat back down to finish his meal. "Don't run the water till the generator is running. Then we can do the dishes, flush the toilet and bathe. I guess catch some water up in pans for us to drink and wash our hands, and we'll leave the generator off for several hours. I'll read about how long for us to space it out and still keep stuff in the refrigerator good."

"Pioneer days, I reckon. Okay, well, we need to charge our phones while it runs, too. We sure don't need to be stranded with no phones."

"Good idea." He rose. "Is there a broom or something I can measure the snow?"

Kate opened some kitchen drawers and found a ruler. "How's this?"

"Not long enough. I'll vouch there's more than a foot out there. I'll take the broom and mark off the depth on the handle, then we'll measure that."

He bundled up and while he was outside, Kate cleared the dishes, stacking them so they could be washed quickly. She glanced out the window and could see Cooper talking on the phone. She frowned. He was only going to check messages. Surely something hadn't happened?

He snapped the phone closed, reached for the broom he'd propped up on the SUV, and stuck the handle into the snow. He held the placed carefully and headed back inside.

She met him at the door with the ruler. "I can't believe it! Seventeen inches. Are you sure you held the place?"

"Yep. And I called Bailey, he says they have nearly a foot of snow at home. They all lost power last night. He's envious we stayed toasty all night. I asked him to check on our family and he said he already had. For some reason, our house still has electricity. I guess it's off in spots. He said the Stonefields invited them to come on over. I told him to go. He said they might if the power wasn't back on by late afternoon."

"Sneaky way to check on the twins, while you were at it."

"Thanks. I thought it was pretty smooth. Bailey said they were fine. He could hear Clancy barking and Mr. Stonefield said Pluma was teasing him about a toy."

"That's reassuring and good to hear everyone is going along as usual. I feel like we're a million miles away."

"Looks that way outside, too." He thought for a moment. "This is what I'm going to do. I'll go in the cellar and check for anything there that might be helpful. I'll go to the outbuilding and check on gasoline supplies for the generator and gas for the grill. I'm going to check the gas tank out here and make sure we have plenty for the logs and cook top and hot water heater. I know there's plenty of wood to burn, but we'd get mighty cold if that's all we had." He kissed her sweetly. "Not what I'd envisioned for after breakfast activity, but it'll have to do."

She smiled. "Me either, but we'll work hard and deserve a reward. I'll inventory the food. Then do you think we can walk out to the lake again?"

"Sure. It's beautiful. Take the camera."

*****

Some time later, Cooper was back in, cold, but satisfied. The tank was eighty percent full, there were three gasoline cans full for the generator, and there were two tanks for the gas grill. In the cellar he'd found two extra bottles of oil for the lamps, half a dozen batteries for the lanterns, lots of matches in a sealed jar and discovered where to prime the water pump if necessary.

Kate had inventoried the food: four t-bone steaks, four large chicken breasts, four baking potatoes, two sweet potatoes, one pound of butter, the rest of the bacon, a small pack of sausage, the small ham, a small container of potato salad, a bag of salad greens, one cucumber, two tomatoes, a small bottle of salad dressing, a bottle of ketchup, a bottle of mayonnaise, a jar of mustard, a can of black eye peas, one can of cream corn, eight eggs plus the dozen Bailey sent, one small bakery's loaf of sour dough bread as well as the loaf of wheat from Bailey, a can of spaghetti sauce and noodles, two small French bread loaves, one pound of sugar, one pound of coffee, a small box of tea bags, a small carton of half n half as well as the rest of the milk, orange juice, grape juice and three bottles of soft drinks, a four pack of Jell-O vanilla pudding, two bags of microwave popcorn and a pack of microwave rice. One can of beef and vegetable soup. The jar of peanut butter. Oh, and the beanie weenies. They still had a big piece of wedding cake and some chips left from yesterday.

"Sounds like we could stay here for several days and not go hungry." Cooper said as she rattled off her list.

Kate agreed. "If we have a heavy mid-day meal, then a light supper, we have six days, thanks to Bailey. That doesn't even count the breakfast food. We could survive on eggs and toast if we had to for a few days."

"Don't forget the beanie weenies."

"Who could?"

"Talking about all this is making me hungry and we ate a couple of hours ago." He grabbed her around the waist. "I figure I need to wait at least another hour to crank the generator. Can you think of anything to keep me entertained until then?"

"Cards?"

"Nope."

"A board game? There's a few in the living room."

"Nope."

"Me?"

"Oh, yeah."

The hour passed quickly.

Afterwards, Cooper cranked the generator while Kate straightened up the bed, picked up dirty laundry and stuffed it in a pillow case, and waited for the pump and refrigerator to cut off so she could cook.

At long last they stopped their humming, and Kate heated up the ham and half a loaf of French bread. She opened the can of black eye peas, made tea, and set out the potato salad. When the ice maker finished, she spread out the ice on a big pan and laid the chicken and steak on top of it, clearing a shelf in the fridge to set them on, thinking that would keep them colder while the refrigerator wasn't running as much.

She ran extra pans of water for their use between generator runs and made sure the commode was flushed.

Running hot sudsy water to let this morning's dishes soak, she decided that keeping a house with intermittent electricity was a pain.

Setting the table, she glanced outside to check on Cooper. He was working on the gas grill, clearing the top of snow, checking the lines, and reading instructions on how to attach the canister. Grilled sounded pretty good to her right now, one less thing to clutter up the kitchen.

She cocked her head. Something was strange about the outdoor scene, but she couldn't put her finger on it right away. Then it struck her. It had stopped snowing!

She opened the back door to the porch area where Cooper was studying the gas grill manual to check the temperature. Fifteen degrees. "How much snow?"

"It stopped snowing at nineteen and a half inches. Looks like the sun is trying to come out, too."

"Yay! Maybe we'll get power back on."

"Don't hold your breath. I just talked to Bailey. The whole town, as well as the next town up the mountain, is out of electricity. Snow plows haven't been able to keep up and a lot of people are stranded without heat. He's helping transport some elderly people out of their homes into the civic center where they have a generator running to provide heat and a soup kitchen."

"Oh." Kate said in a small voice. Then she felt a thrill of panic. "What about Wren and Sparrow?"

"He said Mike had taken a small generator over and got a heater going. He also started a fire for them. We're on city water, so they have no worries there. And the stove top is gas, so they can cook. They'll have to bed down in the den for heat, but that won't be a problem. They can put the girls in their Pac n Play to sleep. The Stonefields have a couch each and Mike brought his big sleeping bag for Cayden."

Kate grinned. "Watch out, Coop. Mike's a hero, now."

"Tell me about it." He muttered. "When's grub ready,

woman?"

"Touchy, are we? I'm about to set the table. Give me ten minutes."

🐾 🐾 🐾 🐾

After lunch, clean up, and shutting off the generator, they bundled up and walked to the lake.

Kate snapped pictures, and they took turns posing for each other. "It's so quiet. Snow muffles everything. I don't hear birds, or noise of any kind." She took another picture of a stump covered with so much snow; it looked as though it had a giant white top hat perched on it. "You know, I forgot to ask how Genevieve is fairing at her cousin's house."

"They are pretty far out in the country. They are either well prepared or miserable. I don't know the folks. But I bet it's not quiet."

Kate laughed. "Hardly. Genevieve is a lot of things, but quiet isn't one of them." Finding more prints, this time startling in their likeness of a baby's hand, Kate made sure she got close up photos of the impressions the raccoon had left in the snow.

Straightening up and arching her back, stiff from bending so much, Kate said, "Maybe we can come back in late summer or early fall and bring everyone. Wouldn't this be a fun vacation?"

"Aren't you having fun now?"

"I am, actually. Granted it might be more fun if I could laze in front of the fire and challenge you to a humiliating game of rummy instead of feeling like I'm on the set of 'Little House on the Prairie', but considering it's my honeymoon, it's all right."

"That so?" He hugged her up, hard as that was to do

with all their clothing. "Let's go back to the house and I'll try to make it more than 'all right', all right?"

She smiled demurely. "All right."

It was better than all right.

CHAPTER FORTY-THREE

Day five arrived with no electricity. Bailey reported that power had been restored to almost everyone, and word from his Uncle Ben was at least two more days before they could get near Lake August. Being reassured that they were fine, they still had food, and were not tired of each other yet, made Bailey heave a great sigh of relief. He couldn't help but tell folks about the extra groceries he'd supplied at the last minute, which, at least according to himself, had saved their lives. In reality, it really was keeping them from getting hungry.

Thanks to Kate rationing breakfast meats and egg portions for breakfast, (in spite of Cooper's whining), and cutting chicken pieces in half to serve, today would be their first meatless lunch. She'd served the last of the sausage this morning, but they still had eight eggs.

She looked at her supplies: half the salad greens, one sweet potato, one can cream corn, one pack microwavable rice, one can spaghetti sauce and noodles, the can of beef and vegetable soup, one liter of Sprite, a bag of microwave popcorn. A few tea bags and a little bit of coffee. And, thanks to Bailey, a loaf of bread and a jar of peanut butter. And, of course, the can of beanie weenies.

Kate thought those were looking better by the day.

Lunch today, she thought, would be the spaghetti and a very small salad each with toasted bread and Sprite to drink. Of all the choices, that sounded the least desperate.

They could have the popcorn tonight for supper and dream of eggs and toast for breakfast, because she knew they – especially Cooper – would go to bed a little hungry.

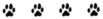

At the end of day eight, food left: one egg, a little less than half a loaf of bread and half the jar of peanut butter.

And the can of beanie weenies.

A veritable delicacy.

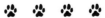

They awoke to day nine very hungry. She cooked the last egg with reverence, toasted them one piece of bread each and spread peanut butter on it. She made the coffee weak, but that was okay, because they had no cream. Cooper's blessing sounded like he really meant it, and she knew she did.

They were even more fervent in their thankfulness by lunchtime when they ate the beanie weenies with a peanut butter and mayonnaise sandwich on half a piece of bread.

Late that afternoon when Cooper went out to check for messages, there was one from a happy Bailey who was reporting Uncle Ben's crew was headed out first thing in the morning to scrape the road, and they would be at the cabin personally as early in the afternoon as they could.

Cooper and Kate would be home before nightfall.

They danced around the living room as giddy as children on Christmas morning; and in celebration halved a heavy laden peanut butter and mayonnaise sandwich and drank very sweet weak tea. It was delicious, as the taste of victory always is.

They spent the next morning packing and cleaning up the cabin. Kate cleaned the refrigerator, finding a lost cucumber in the back of the vegetable bin. She hollered for Cooper and they halved it and ate it like greedy children at chocolate.

By noon they were completely ready to go. They'd eaten the last of the bread, and felt like they never wanted peanut butter or mayonnaise for the rest of their lives.

Cooper ran the generator one last time so they could clean the bathroom and kitchen sink. He called the management of Lake August and they told him to leave the grill and generator as is and they'd come by and service everything. They were relieved Cooper and Kate had fared well, and they hoped to get to their offices at Lake August by the next day.

Uncle Ben was the most beautiful human being they'd ever seen in their lives when he drove up about three thirty that afternoon.

Calling the house as soon as they got under way, begging for food, had rewards. After hugging babies, Clancy, and all adults, they feasted on fried chicken, mashed potatoes, green beans and corn bread with chocolate cake for desert. They moaned in tandem after the meal.

It was true that there was no place like home.

CHAPTER FORTY-FOUR

Less than a week after arriving home, temperatures were in the high fifties and spring, albeit belatedly, was in the air. Kate had spent the day after their homecoming washing clothes and loving on Wren and Sparrow, with Clancy taking every step she took. While the girls were napping, she began moving her things into the master bedroom with Cooper. It was a bit further from the nursery, which made her uncomfortable, although the monitor was what she relied on anyway. The girls had grown in the ten days they had been gone, and were sitting up now, mostly on their own. Sparrow had even said "Dada" last evening. When they called Aunt Cynthia to tell her the news, they could practically hear her eyes rolling over the phone, even though she didn't say they were imagining things.

For three days, Cayden giggled every time she walked by Cooper's bedroom, embarrassing Kate to no end and pleasing Cooper the same.

Late April arrived and Cooper made reservations at an exclusive restaurant to celebrate Kate's birthday. They were almost asleep in their expensive soup by the time it arrived because Wren and Sparrow had cried most the night before, each cutting their first tooth.

Cooper kept the window down all the way home, with music blaring, just to make sure he stayed awake.

The next morning while Kate made breakfast, the twins cracked everyone up by panting like Clancy. When the adults laughed, the babies laughed.

The first of May, both girls were saying Mama as well as Dada and had added Cayden to their verbal skills, although it sounded more like "Kahdee!" (which she was to be to the girls for the rest of her life.)

And the morning of the court date, May fourteenth, Wren and Sparrow took turns pulling up in their baby beds for the very first time.

CHAPTER FORTY-FIVE

Checking diaper bags one last time, Kate stacked all paraphernalia by the front door and leashed Clancy for a quick last minute walk so he could be comfortable while they were gone. Cooper was checking the locks on all other doors, and Cayden was 'almost ready'. The Stonefields, Bailey and Anna, Aunt Cynthia, Mrs. Peabody, Pastor Matt, and Mike were all going to be in the courtroom for moral support or any kind of personal testimony that might be needed.

She was thinking about how nice it had been working with Roberta, and hoping she would stay in touch when someone knocked on the door. Clancy began barking furiously, and being thankful that he was already on the leash, Kate opened the door.

A uniformed man stood there. Behind him, in the driveway, Kate could see a van with 'Jonah's Exterminating – We do a whale of a job!!' painted on the side. It was blocking their vehicle. Trying to hide her irritation, she smiled and said, "Yes?"

"Good morning! Mrs. McGuire?"

"That's right. Can I help you?"

He looked a little puzzled, but bulldozed right on. "Well, ma'am, I'm actually here to help you! I'm here for the yearly examination and spraying of the foundation."

"Oh, dear, we can't possibly do it now! We're on our way out the door to a very important meeting."

"That's fine! I'd rather you not be here. Place needs to be vacated, in fact."

Kate felt herself practically go limp with relief. "Wonderful! Well, just go about your business, then. We'll be gone within five minutes."

"Yes ma'am. As long as everyone is out of the house by the time I start spraying. Man, woman and child I always say! Not to mention pets."

"Yes, of course." Then she really heard what he said. "Pets? You mean like dogs and cats?" She asked wildly.

His smile faltered a little. "Well, yes ma'am. And any other little creature you might have."

Kate dropped her head. "Cooper!" she hollered.

As she turned around she saw Cayden standing there with a stricken look on her face. "It's my fault, Kate. As usual, I forgot! I'm so sorry! What can we do?"

Cooper walked into the foyer. "We'll just have to take them with us. We don't have time to board them. Everyone we know will be at court with us." Cooper shook his head. "I'd be furious with you Cayden, if I had the time." He looked at his watch. "Call the Stonefields. See if Genevieve is with them and if she can pet sit in the parking lot."

Lip quivering, Cayden nodded her head.

"Ya'll are going to court?" the exterminator asked hesitatingly.

Ignoring him, Kate said, "I'll walk Clancy while you get the carrier out of the garage for Pluma. We have to hurry."

Cooper turned to the exterminator. "Some days living with that female is worse than a prison sentence." He muttered something about sisters.

"You all going to court?" he asked again, this time taking one step backward.

Cooper heard a baby start to whimper. "What? Oh, yes. We'll all be out of your way."

Cayden came back in tearful, but relieved. "They said that would be perfectly fine. Genevieve said she'd rather be outside with the pets than inside a stuffy old courtroom."

Cooper nodded and went to check on the babies.

"You all going to court?" the exterminator asked meekly.

Cayden shook her head. "Yes, and if we're late, I'm gonna get killed, or at least put under house arrest."

Kate came back in at the same time Cooper came out with the carrier. "The girls are getting restless, Kate. If you'll tend to them, I'll get the pets in the back of the SUV. I don't know how we're all going to fit with Clancy going too."

"I called Mike. He's coming by to get me. I explained what happened. I'm really sorry, ya'll. I didn't do it on purpose." A tear trickled down Cayden's cheek.

Cooper glared at her, but Kate gave her a quick hug. "If we can leave right now, everything will be all right. We won't get in trouble."

The exterminator stood quietly, his eyes getting a little bigger – if possible - when the twins were brought out, dressed to the nines. "What pretty babies!" he exclaimed.

"Thank you," Kate said. "This is Sparrow and this is Wren."

He waved at them, and they giggled. "Will you need to get in the house?" Cooper asked him.

"No, sir. I'll just get started on the inspection now that

ya'll are leaving, for, uh, court. If there's a problem, I'll give you a call tomorrow." He hesitated. "You will be available tomorrow, won't you?"

"Who knows? But you're welcome to try." Cooper answered as they all stepped out onto the porch and he locked the door behind them.

"Cooper! The diaper bags." Kate called.

He dropped his head for a moment, unlocked the door, got both diaper bags, set them down, re-locked the door, and picked them back up, muttering something under his breath the whole time.

The exterminator wasn't sure what he was muttering, but it worried him just the same. He could have sworn Mr. McGuire had said something about 'a warden'. He shook his head sadly. He sure hoped everything turned out all right. He'd hate to know that poor woman had to raise them babies by herself.

🐾 🐾 🐾 🐾

They pulled into the courthouse parking lot. The Stonefields were waiting on them, and as soon as Genevieve saw them, she got out and started jumping up and down.

The parking lot was generous, with a lot of shade trees and plants. Cooper backed the SUV into a spot, keeping the back in the shade. He got out and opened up the back window so Pluma could have fresh air. He hoped no one would get on to him for back-in parking.

"This is so nice." Kate commented as she walked around, joining him. "Look at the rose bushes! They are really beautiful. Someone must spend a lot of time working here. There's even a water fountain thingie over there." She pointed to the end of the row where they had parked.

"Hello everyone!" Genevieve exclaimed, still hopping around a bit. "This is a most exciting day!"

Kate hugged her. "It certainly is, Genevieve. I'll be so glad when all this is over and there's no more legal stuff to worry over."

Genevieve tiptoed, looking at Pluma and sticking her fingers between the wire to pet her.

"You know not to let the cat out of her carrier, right?" Cooper asked.

Genevieve looked offended. "Of course I do, Cooper. I'm not a child."

"No, you're a pogo stick." Cooper muttered under his breath.

Kate hid her smile. "Well, I know Clancy is certainly looking forward to being with you. This is a great place to be while you wait on us." She turned to Cooper. "Don't we have a folding chair in the back here somewhere? We could get it out and Genevieve could sit part of the time."

Cooper nodded wearily and drug out the chair, almost tipping over Pluma's carrier; which would have probably opened and sent him over the edge. He sat the chair close to the largest tree. He then went over and opened the tailgate the rest of the way, leashing Clancy and letting him jump down. Clancy wiggled all over when he saw Genevieve. "You are a glutton for punishment, aren't you?" Cooper muttered to the dog, as he watched his eager response.

"Come here, ye great beastie." Genevieve said, stooping down and giving the big dog a hug. "We'll have a grand time."

Cooper looked alarmed, but before he could say anything, Kate shot him a dark look and Mrs. Stonefield intervened.

"Now, Genevieve, you know not to leave this spot, correct?"

"Yes, Auntie, I know."

"You have my cell phone?" Genevieve nodded in the affirmative. "We'll sit in the very back of the courtroom. Your uncle's cell phone will be on vibrate. If the least little thing occurs, you are to call immediately."

"And don't let Clancy step off the grass. The asphalt will burn his paws." Cooper interjected.

"And if anyone suspicious approaches you, call immediately." Kate added.

"Please! One at a time!" Genevieve held her hand out dramatically. "Aren't you people going to be late?"

With that, they retrieved the sleeping Wren and Sparrow from their car seats, hauled the giant diaper bags out, and headed toward the courthouse.

Hearing a horn honking, Cooper turned around. It was Cayden and Mike. "Wait for us!" Cayden called as Mike whipped the car into a slot. "There's construction going on above Mike's house and I thought we were going to be late!"

As they approached the courthouse, they saw Cynthia and Mrs. Peabody waiting just inside the doors, both of them beaming.

As the group grew, Cooper led the way, spotting Roberta Flint just outside the courtroom doors. She smiled when she saw them, and hurried over. Grasping Kate's hand and looking at both of them, she said, "What a great day for you! We'll get you as close to the front as we can. The judge likes for the little ones to go first, so they don't get fussy and disrupt courtroom proceedings."

They went straightway into the courtroom, dropping people off as they went by benches. Mr. and Mrs. Stonefield to the very back, Cynthia and Mrs. Peabody in the middle on the end of a bench, Cayden and Mike only a few rows later. Roberta led them forward, pointed to the bench and waved bye. There was one other couple sitting on the second bench, the woman hold a tiny, sleeping baby. The couple grinned broadly when they spotted Kate and Cooper, each toting a sleeping twin. The man leaned over and whispered, "Congratulations! I bet ya'll will be as glad as we will be when this mess is over."

"You got that right," Cooper whispered back as the bailiff walked in and asked for an "all rise".

The bailiff continued. "This court is now in session. The Honorable Randolph O'Reilly presiding."

A rather disheveled judge rushed into the court room, scowling and motioning the bailiff over with an impatient wave of the hand. If possible, the courtroom got even quieter, all straining to hear their conversation.

After seating the courtroom, the elderly bailiff hobbled over to the bench, a curious look on his face. "You all right, Yer Honor?" he asked, cocking his head to one side. This was obviously not a routine thing.

The judge was trying to straighten his robes, which seemed to have been put on rather hastily. "I was fine until I got out of my car. There's some child in the parking lot with this monster of a dog and she had him out in the middle of my prize roses!" Judge O'Reilly's face began to redden. "Gunther, you know I brought those roses straight out of my garden at home! And you know what a mutt does to flowers – he either digs 'em up, tramples 'em down or raises a leg in salute." The bailiff's eyes began to widen as the judge continued. "Now, I tried to reason with the girl, but she was adamant the dog," and here the judge poorly mimicked a heavy English accent, "was *only smelling the roses'* ". Judge O'Reilly ran a hand through his bright red hair, making it stand straight up in the middle. "I oughta bring 'em in for contempt of court!"

Gunther raised a surprised eyebrow. "Can you do that?"

"Well, of course not. But somebody needs to make sure my roses are not being destroyed!"

Gunther nodded and walked over to a deputy and began speaking in a low voice. Kate and Cooper strained to hear, but with their hearts beating in their ears so loudly, they found it near impossible. They made out the bailiff saying, "Hiz honor is flippin' his lid! Can you go out and make sure them durn flowers of his is all right?"

The deputy shrugged and walked out.

The judge began to shuffle papers in a rather haphazard way. Kate leaned over to Cooper and whispered, "Coop," but before she could say more he jabbed her painfully in the ribs. He looked at her sideways and shook his head once, a wild look in his eye. No way did he want this associated with them.

A few tense moments later, the deputy returned, approached the bench, and assured the judge the giant dog was doing nothing but delicately smelling each blossom. Judge O'Reilly muttered under his breath, "It's not natural! The dog should be doing something dog like." He looked up at the deputy and growled, "Keep an eye on 'em. If one bloom is damaged, I hold you directly responsible!" The deputy gulped and positioned himself near a window, straining to see outside. "And if I get my hands on that child's parents, I'm going to have my say."

He then looked down at the papers in front of him and barked, "McGuires! Approach the bench."

Kate felt like she might faint, but kept saying to herself, *'If you faint, you'll drop the baby. Don't faint, don't faint.'*

They stood before Judge O'Reilly as he kept his head down reading the contents of the folder in front of him.

He looked up suddenly and glared at Kate. "Are you Katherine Coleen Roe McGuire?" he asked accusingly.

She swallowed hard. "Yes, Your Honor."

He swung his gaze to Cooper. "And are you Cooper Sean McGuire the Third?"

"Yes, Your Honor." No, he thought wildly, I'm just some bozo she picked up off the street to help carry babies.

"Which one are you holding?" he asked Kate.

Startled, she forgot for a moment. "Uh, Wren, Your Honor."

Judge O'Reilly nodded his head. He stood suddenly. "I'll see you in my chambers in five minutes." And he hurried out.

Kate and Cooper just stared at one another. Kate began to tremble. This was nothing like she had imagined it would be. Where was the kindly judge who would bless this adoption and send them on their way?

"It'll be okay," Cooper whispered, desperately hoping that was a true statement.

Roberta appeared out of thin air it seemed, and touched

Kate's elbow. "Kate, Cooper, just come this way. I'll show you where Judge O'Reilly's chambers are located."

She hurried them out of the courtroom and stood with them in the hallway. "Let's make sure we give him the full five minutes," she said, glancing at her watch.

"What the heck is going on?" Cooper asked, voice low and tinged with anger.

Roberta smiled faintly. "I'm not sure, but the Judge is upset, and I think it's more than Clancy and Genevieve around his rose bushes." Her smile turned into a huge grin. "I bet ya'll 'bout spazzed when he came in talking about that."

Kate looked at Roberta as though she'd grown an extra head. "To say the least! Don't you dare tell him they belong to us!"

Roberta laughed. "Don't worry, I won't." She glanced at her watch again, arched her eyebrows, gave them the thumbs up sign and knocked on the door.

"Come in!"

"Oh, lord," Kate whimpered.

"It's okay, Kate." Roberta assured them both, gave a short wave and walked off.

They entered Judge O'Reilly's chambers slowly. Cooper felt Sparrow stir a little and he said a fervent prayer that if she woke up now, she'd be in a good mood and not roaring like the lion that brings in March.

Judge O'Reilly stood. "Have a seat, here in front of the desk."

They sat, and both babies began to move about, obviously awakening from their morning nap.

Kate could have sworn she saw the judge's mouth

twitch a little bit, but he scowled extra hard to make up for it. "Do you need to tend to the infants before we talk? Perhaps get a bottle ready?"

"Yes, thank you, Your Honor." Kate looked desperately at Cooper and together they wrestled a diaper bag open and produced two bottles at the ready.

Judge O'Reilly sat back in his chair. "Now first of all, I want to say," he nodded his head and steepled his fingers together. "I've read this file with great interest. It is an unusual case, to say the least. All family deceased, from the looks of it, a mother who desired someone whom she thought decent to raise her children if necessary, but failing to notify you at all. Is that right, Mrs. McGuire?"

"Yes sir. I was completely taken aback when I was told about it."

"And I understand you were still single at that point?"

"Yes, Your Honor. Cooper and I had been dating for some time, though."

The judge's eyes strayed to Cooper. "And you, young man, how did you decide not to run as fast as you could away from this sudden, very complicated situation?"

"I never considered running. But I had to think about how involved I wanted to be. It was a struggle that I prayed about and talked to my pastor about."

"I see. And obviously you decided marriage, and becoming an instant father to boot, was the right thing to do."

"I realized it was the only thing to do."

Both babies stretched, opened their eyes, struggling to sit up. They gazed around the room, uncertain. Bottom lips trembled, both looked toward the parent who was holding them and started to wail. The judge was silent as he watched them comfort the girls and then offer them each a bottle. Each baby looked at the bottle and decided it was safe enough wherever they were and began to greedily drink.

Suddenly Judge O'Reilly leaned forward, his arms on the desk. "I don't usually share personal things about myself with clients. But I feel as though I must today. I was orphaned at a young age and adopted by distant relatives who took me in and never looked back. My parents had only been married a few years, and my brother and I were the only children." He looked up. "My twin brother." He sighed heavily. "Charles was killed in the same accident that took my parents. I barely remember any of them, but of the three, Charles is the one I remember – and miss – the most. There's always been something missing in my life and I know it is Charles." He cleared his throat. "This particular adoption warms my heart. It has affected me a great deal." He smiled. "And then you walk in with redheads!"

There was silence for a few minutes, neither Cooper nor Kate knowing how to respond.

Judge O'Reilly continued. "You have done a great honor to God with this, and I know you will continue to do so. I'd love to see you all again sometime, just to hear how you are doing."

"Absolutely, Your Honor!" Cooper said enthusiastically. "It would be a pleasure."

For a moment the judge looked shy, as though he was afraid to ask something. Kate resisted the urge to look out the window to see if pigs were flying.

Clearing his throat again, the judge asked, "Do you think I could hold one of the babies?"

Kate smiled. "Of course. You may hold them both." Seeing the panic in his eyes, she added, "One at a time."

They all stood and Judge O'Reilly came around the desk and held out his arms. Kate handed Wren to him, staying close and smiling at Wren when she drooled milk down her chin. Kate reached for a cloth and wiped the baby's mouth, which kept her occupied for a moment. Then Wren began to look around to see what was holding her up. Her eyes widened and she puckered up when she saw the judge's unknown face. "Let me take her before she cries," Kate said. "That way she won't get Sparrow all riled up and you can hold her a minute."

Cooper handed over Sparrow, who looked up and grinned at the judge, delighting him. "Why, hello there! You aren't afraid of me, are you?" They all stood around, smiling at babies. And when it was over, Wren and Sparrow were legally theirs.

It was a day none of the adults in that room would ever forget.

🐾 🐾 🐾 🐾

Circling back to the front door of the courtroom, they found Cayden and Mike waiting. When Cayden and Mike saw them come around the corner, Mike stepped back in and motioned to the Stonefields. Mr. Stonefield walked quickly up the aisle and motioned for Mrs. Peabody and Cynthia to leave.

Cayden hugged Cooper. "From the looks on your faces, brother, I'm guessing everything is good."

About that time they all stepped out, and Cooper grinned broadly. "Have you guys met Wren and Sparrow

McGuire yet?"

There were hugs, kisses, handshakes, and pats on the back as everyone celebrated with giddy relief. "Let's get out of here before the judge leaves and sees us with Genevieve and Clancy." Kate said.

Spilling out into the parking lot, they spied Genevieve sitting, quietly reading to Clancy. They were propped up under the tree, and Clancy had his head in Genevieve's lap. She smiled when they walked toward her. "Are we ready to go, then?" she asked calmly.

Cooper raised an eyebrow. "Aren't you even gonna ask how it went?"

Genevieve looked puzzled. "How could it go any other way than finished? These are your daughters, Cooper. You know the Lord had this planned."

Cooper shook his head. "Genevieve, even you make sense sometimes."

Since they had planned a little party in celebration back at Cynthia's, everyone said quick good-byes before Kate and Cooper could get animals and babies situated. Genevieve begged to ride with them, promising she wouldn't mind being smushed in the middle between the girls.

Since it was a short ride, they agreed.

Huffing and puffing, Cooper got Wren situated first, instructing Genevieve to get in the middle and fasten a seatbelt. It was a fairly warm day, and by the time he started buckling Sparrow in, he was sweating.

Kate handed him the diaper bags and he stuffed them in the floorboard, behind his seat. Then he walked to the back, lowered the tailgate and returned the folding lawn chair, making sure it was secured before scooting Pluma's carrier back so Clancy could jump in. But when he turned to let Clancy by, he was nowhere in sight.

Cooper's heart almost jumped out of his chest. "Kate!" he hollered louder than was necessary.

"Over here." she called. Clancy was relieving himself on the trunk of a large tree. Then he daintily sniffed a rose one more time before trotting beside Kate to the vehicle.

"Man, you like to live dangerously, don't you?" he asked.

"He had to go. And it never hurts to stop and smell the roses." Kate handed the leash to Cooper.

"Ha. Very funny. Get in." He said, rather sharply to Clancy.

Clancy glared at him and sat down.

"Oh, come on Clancy. It's hot. The judge scared us. The babies are hungry."

"And I'm being mashed beyond recognition." Genevieve called.

Clancy just sat.

Cooper blew out air between puffed cheeks. "Okay, okay. I'm sorry. None of this is your fault."

Clancy hopped into the back of the SUV, tail wagging. Cooper shook his head. He looked at Kate and mouthed, "Your dog."

She grinned and headed for her side of the car.

Cooper bent down to fasten the tailgate, and Clancy bumped him right in the face with his big old butt.

Cooper glared. "You did that on purpose, mutt!"

Clancy kept his back turned and sat down.

As Cooper opened the driver's side door to get in, he

heard giggling from Kate and Genevieve.

"Oh, you think that's funny?"

They nodded their heads. Yes, they did.

Cooper smiled. "Of course a giant dog's butt in my face after I apologize to him is hysterically funny. Hey! I may not agree, but we have so much to celebrate, who cares? The girls are ours, lock, stock and barrel. No more worries." He started the car. "I say that calls for a celebration. Right?"

"Right!" Genevieve cried from the back seat.

"Absolutely." Kate agreed.

Putting down the windows as he drove out of the parking lot, Cooper began to sing at the top of his lungs. *"I'll Fly Away"* was the song choice, and a painful rendition it was.

"Oh, Cooper, no!" Kate exclaimed.

Clancy had thrown his head back and started howling, frantic because he couldn't escape.

"For pity's sake! Stop it before we are all deafened!" Genevieve cried.

The security guard had watched the whole thing through the courtroom's partially opened window. He waited until they were out of sight before he so much as blinked. He finally had to fully turn his back on the courtroom because he was sure the amusement showed on his face. His bird's eye view of it all had been trained on the girl and the dog, per the judge's orders. So that dog was theirs! Wait till the judge found that out! And from what he could tell, the dog ran the show. A grin split his face as he heard the yowling rendition of *"I'll Fly Away"*. He guessed the mister got revenge after all. Shaking his head, he turned back to the courtroom.

He reckoned those babies would have an interesting life, if nothing else. One thing he knew for sure by watching all this, there was a lot of genuine love underneath the shenanigans. He could always tell, and he prided himself on the fact.

Yep, a lot of love.

EPILOGUE

Two years later:

The smell of grilling steak and chicken filled the backyard air, making stomachs growl.

Almost three, Wren and Sparrow were showing David, Anna and Bailey's son, how to make 'cupcakes' in the sandbox. The kiddies' pool had been their first stop, but when Clancy joined them, they abandoned water for sand. They were now coated in wet sand and oblivious to the adults around them.

Cayden and Mike were in the kitchen fixing salads and baking potatoes, while Bailey and Cooper cooked at the grill. They were in a deep discussion about vacation plans for late fall. They were going back to Lake August, as they had every year since Cooper and Kate's honeymoon. They were renting the biggest cabin this year because Mike was going with them. Even at that, Mike was going to have to sleep in the same room as the twins and David. Mike was paying the extra rent and bringing along some of the groceries, so the expenses wouldn't be any more than they were every year.

Cooper and Kate were thrilled about his engagement to Cayden, especially since they'd promised it would be a two year engagement. They planned on getting married the month after Cayden graduated college.

Anna and Kate were in lounge chairs, eyeing their children as they chatted. "How much longer, Coop?" Kate hollered.

"You've got about fifteen minutes before everyone needs to be at the table."

"I guess that's our cue to rinse off the crew," Anna sighed, trying to sit up without much success. She groaned. "I hate it when I start getting this big. It's like hauling a watermelon around."

Kate laughed. "That's a perfect comparison. The beached whale one is worn out."

"My only consolation is you are bigger than me." Anna giggled.

"Not fair!" Kate said. "I'm further along than you."

"Not by much." Anna said, observing Kate's daily growing belly.

"At this point, five minutes is a lot." They both laughed. Then Kate tried to wiggle out of the lounge chair, and finally giving up, yelled for Cooper to lend a hand.

He trotted over and heaved both very pregnant women out of their chairs. "May I suggest you ladies sit in a straighter chair for the next six weeks or so? You could hurt a man's back." As Kate raised a fist in mock threat, he backed off, grinning. "I'm kidding. Neither of you weigh more than a leaf or a feather." He wiggled his fingers at them and trotted off.

"That's why I married him," Kate muttered, "Prince Charming in the flesh."

Clapping her hands, Anna got the little ones' attention, and at the mention of 'maybe ice cream after supper' they came out of the sandbox willingly. Squealing as they got rinsed off with the water hose, teeth chattering as they were quickly dried and dressed, the three ran happily to the small table set up just for them.

Cayden and Mike came out, Cayden already having prepared pint sized bites of potato and bread and a little bit of greens on the side, Sippy cups of milk, and celery sticks stuffed with peanut butter as a special treat.

"You're going to be a great mama someday, Cayden," Anna remarked, observing the work. "You already know how to do it all."

Cayden agreed. "When Wren and Sparrow arrived it was all hands on deck. I was glad to learn. It's habit now. This next baby will be a breeze, lots of experience and only one this time."

The guys brought the steaks and chicken to the table, tea was poured, and heads bowed.

As the meal was eaten, names were tossed around for the unborn babies. Anna and Bailey knew theirs was another boy, and were considering naming him after her father.

Cooper and Kate had chosen not to know the sex because the boy's name was still an issue after all these years. They had decided if the baby was a boy they'd have to make a decision quickly and perhaps there wouldn't be so much bickering about it.

As for the girl's name, it was still a tossup between Larke Abigail and Raven Victoria. They figured they'd know it when they saw her.

Plus, they simply felt safer, doing this pregnancy the 'old fashioned way' and having no procedures done that weren't absolutely necessary. They hadn't even done some that the doctors assured them were safe. This baby would be what it would be. Period.

As they lingered over the supper table in the yard, the sun began to drop lower in the sky making Venus visible. Crickets, tree frogs, and the occasional whippoorwill, filled the air as a slight breeze lowered the summer temperature. Clancy had abandoned the pool and had his head in what was left of Kate's lap, hoping she'd eventually notice and give him a leftover bite of whatever.

Too soon, it seemed, the toddlers began to fuss as their bedtimes approached and pregnant women began to tire out. Kate's back started that now familiar ache.

Company said their good-nights after a quick clean up. Even Mike left early; as he had an early assignment the next morning.

Two sleepy girls were carried in by Cooper. Kate scanned the yard to make sure everything had been brought in. Calling Clancy, she opened the screen door for him and turned the porch lights off.

A few hours later, everyone slept, and the McGuire household was at peace.

For about four hours.

At ten the next morning, Larke Abigail McGuire entered the world.

And ten minutes later, Raven Victoria McGuire entered the world too, much to everyone's surprise and the doctor's embarrassment.

Tiny but perfect.

With strawberry blonde hair, the same shade as their sisters' and their daddy's.

Who, by the way, still says he does *not* have pink hair.

Four years later, they found Clancy lifelessly still between Wren and Sparrow's beds, where he had gone to sleep with the girls. Having spent the last night of his twelve years on old Earth right where he belonged, the loss was at least bearable.

That same year they got an exact look alike in puppy form, who they named Mac.

And that same year, their son was born. He arrived big and healthy with a full head of nice, medium blond hair, much like his mother's, with nary a pink streak to be seen.

He was not gifted a name for three days. After much pouting, (Cooper), and much sulking, (Kate), his first name was chosen.

His middle name they agreed on instantly and tearfully.

Cooper called their son Robbie, Kate stubbornly called him Robin, and by the age of eight he settled it himself and demanded everyone call him Rob.

And that's what Robert Clancy McGuire was called for the rest of his years.

The family had their ups and downs, as all families do, but mostly they lived happily ever after.

Or, as Genevieve would say, "Per ardua!"*

THE END

---

*A Scottish Gaelic Creed which translates: "Through difficulties to heights!"

Matthew 6:25-26 *Therefore, I tell you, do not worry about your life, what you will eat or drink or about your body, what it will wear. Is life not more than food, and the body more than clothes? Look at the birds of the air; they do not sow or reap or store away in barns, and yet your Heavenly Father feeds them. Are you not much more valuable than they?*

About the Author

Kathi Harper Hill has lived in the North Georgia Mountains all her life. She has been writing since the age of ten. After taking early retirement as a professional in the mental health field, she began devoting more time to her craft. Her stories focus mainly on relationships between people, and how relationships force growth in the characters.

Besides loving to write (and read), her other interests include teaching Bible classes, interior design, and music. Kathi has been a soloist since the age of fourteen.

Hill is the author of five books. Her first, "Falling", was published in 2009. Her children's book, "The Crow and The Wind" a little book about a Big God, was first runner up in the mid child division at the 2011 Georgia Author of the Year Awards. Hill has been the recipient of numerous awards for her short stories over the years. One of these winning stories appears in "The Christmas Closet and Other Works".

She and her husband, David, (who illustrates all her books), live in a Victorian cottage with their daughter, Anna Kate, and current menagerie of pets: American Bulldog, Molly, The Great White Cats: Lily, Frost, and Eli. Anna Kate's cat, Mimi, joins the fray.

WHAT OTHERS ARE SAYING ABOUT KATHI'S BOOKS:

ON Falling:

I really enjoyed Falling. It kept me interested in what was going to happen next and it had a lot of substance and meaning about morals and God. It had a happy ending but had a few turns here and there, like real life. I hope she writes more books like this, our society is lacking in morals and this book appeals to all ages. J. Rogers

The book was a well written respectful romance book that anyone would be proud to read. M. Pierce

The book "Falling" told an interesting, beautiful love story without using any vulgarity - what a refreshing concept! I enjoyed reading it from start to finish and have given this book as gifts to friends. They gave it a thumbs up as well! Kathi Hill is a gifted writer who uses her talent to uplift others while telling stories that are relevant to today. Jeanne Addy

"This book should be read by every girl - and boy - for that matter - before they begin to date to find out how to have a Christian relationship. James Holt, Pastor

I thought: It must be a great book since James never reads anything unless it pertains to his sermon. He came to bed at one a.m. and said he'd read "Falling" in one sitting! So I thought I should read it too! (I did and enjoyed it!) Betty Jo Holt, pastor's wife and retired teacher.

"Falling" is an enticing book which asks and answers many questions that face young adults today. From the chance meeting of the famous and the wounded through the delicate plan of God, the author weaves a story that is fast paced and delightful for audiences of all ages. Marsha Benson

I couldn't wait for the book signing, so I ordered the book off Amazon. From knowing Kathi I wasn't surprised that it was a great book! A. W.

My wife purchased the book but I picked it up to read first. I cried in the middle of the story. What a book! I really enjoyed it. Morris M.

Falling is an excellent, well written book. With humor, Christian values, and a great story-line, it is a book that girls -and guys- will love. Would recommend it to all, especially young adults, for an all-around enjoyable story! David Lawrence

I just happened by the bookstore on the day of Mrs. Hill's book signing for "Falling". Since I work with young people, I purchased a copy and went home to begin reading it over lunch. I sat for one and a half hours without moving until I finished it! What a great book! I rushed back to the bookstore and purchased two more copies, and have been passing those around to "my kids" ever since. Bravo! P. Miller

A copy of "Falling" was donated to the high school library where I attend school. There has been a constant waiting list to read this book. When I finally got a turn, I could see why! I could picture the characters and scenes just like they were real. I hope she writes another book like this. Amanda W.

ON: The Crow and The Wind:

This book is a great book for little kids because of the simple story line and wonderful illustrations. But it has a deeper meaning that my 11 year old classroom really discussed, as we are studying symbolism. I recommend this to any parent or teacher who wants to get across the idea that there is someone bigger than us! Mary Sawyer

This book is a must read for both young and old! A beautiful creation and the author has a great idea of how to get through to people and share the beauty of God. The drawings alone are worth the purchase to see! Awesome book. Fos B.

The Crow and The Wind is a wonderful book for the child who hears it and the adult who reads it aloud! Both will be blessed by the content of the message and the detail of the illustrations. It's a book that belongs on every bedside table to be shared at bedtime. It will ease the troubles of the day by reminding readers that there is Someone bigger than us who is in charge! Jan B.

The Crow and the Wind is a children's book. Or is it? This book can be enjoyable and meaningful to Children of all ages. For anyone who still has an imagination and a belief in things not-seen. Actually it is love story about a crow and the wind. They find each other and ultimately God the Creator. The illustrations by David Hill only add to its charm. Nancy Vaught

The Crow and The Wind is a wonderful little children's book with a great big message! Kathi Harper Hill captures the reader and any little listener within earshot as she takes the crow on a journey of discovery. The beautiful illustrations provide the reader with colorful imagery as the story of God's presence, love and power are told. Hill's words are teaching and the lessons learned are indeed blessings of affirmation! Tony Smith

I enjoyed reading this story even though I don't have small ones. The story reminds us that we can stray from out creator. Then circumstances lead us back to the fold. Well written and beautifully illustrated. I loved the book. I recommend the book for middle schoolers. A great edition to a child's Christian library. Sue H.

This book takes a child back to an earlier and more rural time. It can be enjoyed by a child for its' visual appeal and its' very positive message. The group of children to whom I read were all attentive and were stimulated to ask many questions. David Lawrence

One Old Crow's Journey to the Truth: In an enchanting mix of old-time Appalachian religion, George MacDonald, and C. S. Lewis, Kathi and David Hill tell a smart and engaging tale of one old crow's journey to the Truth. You couldn't own a better bedtime story. Tina T.

This is a lovely book, with a gentle humor and beautiful illustrations. I was enchanted and have shared it with my friends. Lynnie O.

The Crow and The Wind is such a wonderful book. The story is great. I love the illustrations. I have already recommended this book to several people. This is a "must have" book! Connie G.

I bought this book for my grandson. We have thoroughly enjoyed reading it together. He loved the story and the illustrations. I'm sure that it will be one book that we will read over and over again. Would highly recommend this book. Cathy R.

Kathi would like to hear from readers. Contact her at cherokeeirishtemper@yahoo.com.